STRIVERS
ROW

During the 1920s and 1930s, around the time of the Harlem Renaissance, more than a quarter of a million African-Americans settled in Harlem, creating what was described at the time as "a cosmopolitan Negro capital which exert[ed] an influence over Negroes everywhere."

Nowhere was this more evident than on West 138th and 139th Streets between what are now Adam Clayton Powell, Jr., and Frederick Douglass Boulevards, two blocks that came to be known as Strivers Row. These blocks attracted many of Harlem's African-American doctors, lawyers, and entertainers, among them Eubie Blake, Noble Sissle, and W. C. Handy, who were themselves striving to achieve America's middle-class dream.

With its mission of publishing quality African-American literature, Strivers Row emulates those "strivers," capturing that same spirit of hope, creativity, and promise.

Bliss

Bliss

A NOVEL

GABRIELLE PINA

STRIVERS
ROW

VILLARD

NEW YORK

LIBRARY OF CONGRESS CATALOGING-IN-PUBLICATION DATA

Pina, Gabrielle.
Bliss : a novel / Gabrielle Pina.
p. cm.
ISBN 0-375-76103-9
1. Women musicians—Fiction. 2. Overweight women—Fiction. 3. Violinists—
Fiction. I. Title
PS3616.I53 B55 2002
813'.6--dc21   2002020673

Villard Books website address: www.villard.com
Printed in the United States of America
24689753

First Edition

Book design by JoAnne Metsch

For

Gracian
Lillian
Marjorie
Denise
Diane
Delores
Darlene
and
Maia

"Sometimes a lie is the best thing."

PROLOGUE

*T*he obituary was succinct, vague. There was no photo, on the off chance that someone somewhere would recognize her. She'd changed drastically over the years, altered her appearance, refined herself, often even slipping into an endearing accent that wasn't native to her tongue. She'd told people that she was from France when they inquired, and that she became Francesca's guardian after her parents were killed in a terrible fire. "Raised that child like she was my own," she'd once declared to a journalist from *Time* magazine. She exuded such wisdom, such confidence that no one ever questioned her or wondered aloud why she and the famous violinist looked so much alike.

Lillian SaintClair (November 1, 1925, to May 1, 2002), longtime companion and devoted friend to noted violinist Francesca Valentine, passed away on May 1 after a long illness. Ms. SaintClair had no children.

Francesca stood in the cemetery with the others and repeated Hail Marys in her head. That was the only prayer she knew. She'd heard it so many times in Italy that it had become etched in her mind. Many important and influential people had come to pay their respects to Lillian. She would have appreciated that. She would have appreciated the flowers flown in from Hawaii.

"She's taking it pretty hard," she'd heard Jon, her son, say earlier. She gazed at the coffin one last time before they placed it in the crypt. She was a believer in restraint, normally so efficient and reserved during a time of crisis. She'd taught her children to avoid public displays of affection. "The whole world needn't know what you're feeling inside," she'd said on more than one occasion. How ironic that she couldn't seem to stop crying and carrying on now, making a spectacle of herself. She knew they were watching her.

Her heart ached and she wanted to throw herself on the coffin and beg Lillian to get up, come home, and stop being so dramatic. But that would cause too much attention, and the children might get suspicious. Lillian had been in their lives for as long as they remembered—lived with them, traveled with them, was a part of their family. They called her MyLil, short for "my Lillian." Lillian had liked that. She had been the only person Francesca could trust completely. Lillian knew every mistake, every triumph, every life-altering experience and never betrayed her or allowed her to feel sorry for herself. Lillian was the safety net when life got too rough for Francesca to handle, and now she was gone.

A part of Francesca thought she'd feel relief when Lillian passed, but the only thing she felt was alone—utterly, completely alone. No one understood, and she couldn't explain, why this woman was such an integral part of her existence. Why she was allowed free rein in her life to do and say what she pleased. Samuel, her fiancé, often asked, "Just who does she think she is?"—annoyed that she was always around, interjecting her opinion. "Doesn't she have any family to help take care of her?"

"We are her family," Francesca would respond quietly. "Leave it alone, Samuel. You know how important she is to me and the children." But he didn't know. He could never know how profound an effect Lillian SaintClair had had on her life. Francesca looked up and saw him speaking to Jon and Jessica, consoling them. He nodded in her direction. She turned away, suddenly ashamed of herself. The lies were so thick now, she didn't know if she could ever navigate her way to the truth. She desperately wanted to tell Sam, Jon, and Jessica, but Lillian wouldn't allow it, even in the end.

"Leave it be, child," Lillian had said the week before she died. "Promise me you'll leave it be."

They were coming to take Francesca home now. She felt them guiding her toward the car. Her legs folded beneath her and she cried out for Lillian, startling onlookers. "Is that Francesca Valentine losing control?"

She started to crawl toward the casket, ignoring the gasps and the "Oh my God's." They held on tightly. Sam and Jon struggled to lift her up. Jessica stroked her hair, called her Mama. They didn't know what she'd lost, and she didn't know how she was going to survive the night knowing Lillian wasn't down the hall, a few steps away. She wept for the hell Lillian had had to go through to get here. She wept because her only link to the past, to herself, was gone forever, but mostly she wept because she'd just buried her mama and couldn't tell a soul.

Part 1

CHAPTER 1

MAY 2002

Prominent violinist's life exposed. Noted violinist Francesca Valentine's past is revealed. Can you guess which classically trained musician used to weigh 300 pounds . . . see page 8 for details. Ms. Valentine, who just appeared on *60 Minutes* last week and has received numerous awards for achievement in the field of classical music, finds herself in the middle of a scandal of sorts. It appears that she is not who she has claimed to be . . . story at eleven. Francesca Valentine, born Claudine Jenkins, could not be reached for comment. . . .

This is unbelievable, Mother. What is going on? Did you know there were reporters outside? Mother? What in heaven's name are they talking about? Who in the hell is Claudine Jenkins? Oh my God, Mother, is this you?"

Francesca couldn't bear to answer her daughter. Jess was waving some clipping in front of her face, ranting like it was the end of the world. Perhaps it was; only time would tell. She bolted to her favorite place—a refuge where she wouldn't have to see the stricken look on Jess's face, glimpse the questions burning in her eyes. What would she say? Where would she begin? How would they ever be able to look at her the same way again? She didn't think there was anyone else alive who really knew her, the girl she used to be, the pathetic creature plastered across the front page of every major newspaper and sleazy tabloid. She'd been wrong. Francesca stared at the framed magazine covers that were hung along the walls of her expansive dressing room. She smiled; she was beautiful. Sometimes it was almost impossible to believe that she looked like that, so captivating that people wanted to take her photograph and so alluring that men would want to be seen with her in public. Didn't they understand that the woman on these walls was the only woman who mattered? That other woman, the one in the clipping and on the news, didn't exist anymore. Why was that so hard for everyone to accept? People change. She began to weep. She believed she had taken care of everything, wrapped up every loose end, severed all ties that connected her to Claudine. Claudine. It felt like a lifetime since that name had rolled across her tongue. She hadn't planned on ever uttering it again or remembering anything about that woman. Now partial truths were everywhere, and ignoring the countless inquiries wouldn't make them disappear. Samuel, her fiancé, and her children, Jessica and Jon, would discover that she was a liar, a perpetrator, a common hypocrite. She'd succeeded in reinventing herself. They'd had no idea until now that she used to be someone else.

"HAVE YOU SEEN her?" Jon asked Jessica.

"Yes."

"Is she talking? Has she said anything? There's got to be some reasonable explanation for this. We're going to sue the bastards for slander, that's what we'll do."

"No. She's not talking to me, anyway. She locked herself in the dressing room when I asked her about this . . . this . . . ridiculous photograph."

"Does Sam know? Mother. Mother, come on, Mother, open the door." He pounded, hoping she would say more to him than she would to his sister.

They were discussing her like she was some criminal. She heard the agitation and anxiety in their voices, especially Jessica's. The girl damn near thought she was royalty. Francesca worked hard to make sure her baby girl never felt less than, beneath, anyone else. Perhaps she overdid it just a little. She said a silent prayer that this wouldn't destroy Jessica. Jon was resilient, he'd be all right, of that she was certain. She laughed at the irony of it all. After all of this time, fate would force her to reveal everything. She'd been discovered, found out. She wasn't necessarily concerned about Samuel's reaction or the backlash from her adoring fans. She had to make her children understand that she had done what she had to do for their survival and her own. They were grown now. They would forgive her eventually. She could handle this. Claudine Jenkins could handle anything.

Francesca straightened her floor-length gown and opened the door. They were waiting for her. Judgment cometh.

"Yes, Jessica," she said as she reached for the newspaper clipping. "This was me."

"I think I'd better sit down," Jon said, motioning for his sister to join him. "Was that really your name, Mother? Claudine Jenkins?"

"If I'd been born with a hillbilly name like that I would have changed it, too," Jessica added.

"You were, and I did," Francesca answered.

"Mama, what are you saying?"

Jon interjected, "Why don't you stop asking so many questions, Jess, and let her explain before you get hysterical."

"Explain what, Jon—that she's lied to us all these years, every day of our lives, Ms. Perfect, Ms. I've Never Made a Mistake? Don't sit there and act like this revelation isn't affecting your pristine image of her—I know it is. I know—"

"You don't know anything yet, Jess, so sit down and shut up. Can't you see how difficult this is for her? Try thinking of someone other than yourself for a change."

"Go straight to hell, Jon."

"Enough of this bickering. Do you want to hear this or not, Jessica?" Francesca said softly.

"Look, it doesn't matter what's disclosed in this room today or any other day, Mother—my name is Jessica Marie Valentine, and I was born and raised right here in San Francisco."

"No," Francesca answered quietly. "Your name is Lula Mae Jenkins, and you weren't born anywhere near here."

"Good Lord, Mama." Jon spoke nervously. "What have you done?"

"Get comfortable, both of you. This won't be easy for any of us. Yes, it will be difficult for you to hear, and even more painful for me to confess, but I'll start from the beginning, the very beginning. A long time ago, before either of you were born, someone gave me a violin."

CHAPTER 2

JANUARY 1968

"*D*eeny! Claudine! Get yo bacon-eating ass in here and clean up this kitchen. Um, um, um, big, fat, and lazy, just like yo triflin' mama. You ain't gone be that way round me though, 'cause I ain't havin' it. Claudine, do you hear me talkin' to you? This shit better be cleaned up by the time I get home from church."

Claudine heard him. She always heard him, and she knew better than to acknowledge him, respond, or give the slightest impression she was participating in his biweekly tirade. She tried that once, attempted to explain that it wasn't her mess. She had heard ringing in her left ear for three days behind the backhand he had given her for having the nerve to speak to him at all. She could still hear him mumbling under his breath as he walked around, inspecting every room. He liked to do that. He thought he was the black Sherlock Holmes. She guessed it made him feel in control.

"Walkin' round here suckin' up everythang in sight. Gone fall through the floor into China one of these days. Ass so wide, gone have to grease the door frame with Crisco so you can slide through. Messin' round with you gone make me late for my solo."

She lingered in the small bathroom until she felt the walls

vibrate. It seemed as if the whole house shook when he slammed the front door. He was her daddy all right, and he hated her just as much as she despised him. It had always been that way. She couldn't remember a time when it was any different.

Claudine made her way through the house until she reached the kitchen. It smelled odd. Her house usually had a peculiar smell. She couldn't put her finger on it, but she knew it wasn't normal for a clean house to have such an odor. It reminded her of funk, pee and her brother's farts, all mixed up. She lived in a duplex, the Tilbos on one side and Hattie Mae, her mother's sister, on the other. Hattie Mae wasn't home much, though; always had something to do, somebody to see, some place to go. She didn't have an official job to speak of, but she did have some official money. She owned a sky blue Chevrolet, the Press & Curl around the corner, and the entire house they lived in. Claudine noticed very early on that her daddy, "the Deacon," might talk crazy to most people, her mama included, but he never raised his voice to Hattie Mae; nobody did.

Claudine wiped the last piece of egg from the counter, dried the heavy cast skillet, and scrubbed away bits of raw egg that had congealed on the side of the stove. She wrinkled her nose in disgust. Bone made this mess. He never cleaned up after himself. Her brother was so vile that she didn't see how those fast girls could stand to be around him. No one ever made him clear the table or change his own sheets, and he had nothing else to do but breathe. She, on the other hand, continuously had rooms to clean, crusty sheets to change, and an early violin lesson to get to before class.

It was a blessing that she was still allowed to play. The Deacon despised it, said only uppity white folk wasted time on such foolishness. Told her that she was too fat to sit on one of those itty-bitty stools to play it anyway; her ass would probably swallow it whole, he said. He came up with everything he could to dissuade her from pursuing the one passion that propelled her into a state of bliss. When she practiced, she became someone else, and her everyday reality melted away until she transformed into that gorgeous, svelte girl who lived in a regular house with normal, loving parents. No matter what he did, the Deacon couldn't compete with the extraordinary world she'd created for herself. He would bang on the walls when she practiced at Hattie Mae's, or play the Temptations real loud to confuse and disorient her. But working that bow was addictive, and she was oblivious to everything else. He didn't care to understand what that violin did for Claudine, but he was forced to accept it. And as much as he tried to intimidate her, he couldn't destroy the finely crafted instrument because Hattie Mae Jones had given it to her when she was five and paid for the lessons. She could still see the Deacon's face when Hattie Mae had marched through the front door with that case wedged under her arm. He'd looked like he was ready to snort fire out of his rather queerly shaped nose, which reminded Claudine of a hammer without the handle. Willamina, her mother, had just hung by his side like an extra appendage, twirling what was left of her hair. The entire house had become still, always silent as soon as Hattie Mae's long legs strode into their duplex. Hattie Mae didn't speak to anyone else in the house that morning. It had been as if they didn't exist at all. Claudine was the only person she saw. That day was by far Claudine's favorite day. It had been the first time that she felt important, like she mattered. Claudine closed her eyes. She could still see Hattie Mae kneeling in front of her, feel the brim of her wide hat touching her small forehead.

"C'mere, Claudine, and put that raggedy doll down. I bought something for you to learn."

"What is it? Did you bring one for Bone, too?"

"No. This is for you and for you only." Hattie Mae had opened the case and gingerly handed her the instrument. For a moment, Claudine could have sworn that she saw Hattie Mae smile, but that would be impossible. She'd heard her mama say once that no one but Jesus had ever even seen a laugh pass the lips of Hattie Mae Jones.

"It's called a violin. Now go on, touch it, feel it, get to know it, 'cause from now on you're going to be spending a lot of time with it. Go on, name it if you want to."

"Looks like a guitar. You gone teach me how to play it, Aint Hattie Mae?"

"No, but somebody is. Now go slip that new green dress on that I bought you last week and hurry up so I can do something decent with that hair of yours. Your mama obviously thinks that hair combs itself, and we don't have all day, hear? You have an appointment to keep."

They had left minutes later, still talking only to each other, Hattie Mae daring the Deacon to say one word. The two of them had been a sight to see, Hattie Mae prancing out of the living room, with a hat on the size of Texas, and Claudine right on her heels, with her new best friend, Betty, clutched tightly next to her heart.

Claudine didn't remember her mama ever saying much. She was usually in a daze, always sipping on a little taste of vodka to calm her nerves. Willamina kept to herself mostly. Only really initiating conversation when it was absolutely necessary. When she was ready to talk, she talked to Bone. They were close, those two, always had their heads together about something or other. It was as if they were the twins in the family.

Claudine and Bone didn't look alike, but their mama had said that they came from the same egg. No one would ever guess, though, because they behaved like they had no connection to each other at all. They never referred to one another as twins. She was Fat Deeny to anyone who cared to know, and he was simply Bone. The Deacon had started calling him that when he was four because he gnawed on a bone just like a dog. Bone didn't discriminate, either. He loved them all—ham bones, steak bones, rib bones, chicken bones—and he'd pay you a whole dollar to let him suck a pork-chop bone off your plate. He didn't like Claudine much, either; always had something contemptuous to say and, like the Deacon, insulted her violin every chance he got. He called her stupid, told her she might as well chop Betty up and use it as toothpicks to pick Vienna sausages out of her teeth. Nobody wanted to hear a fat girl punish an innocent fiddle. Wasn't she tired of boring the whole block with that god-awful noise? he asked each time she ventured to practice. No one had ever expected anything would become of her dedication, no one except Hattie Mae.

Claudine was twelve when the letter arrived at the door by special delivery. She had been accepted by the Atlanta Youth Symphony Orchestra. That was five years ago. Now she was first chair and the only black in the Colborne Academy of Music, where she currently performed in the orchestra. The music director said she was exceptional, unlike any young violinist he'd ever heard. Soon she would audition for the New England Conservatory of Music. People were traveling from all over Georgia to hear her play. The confused masses had a difficult time believing a fat black girl from Marietta could play the violin like she was born with a bow in her hand.

CHAPTER 3

"Claudine."

"Yes, Mama."

"You seen your brother?"

"No, Mama."

"Did the Deacon go to work?"

"I don't know, Mama."

"Make sure you back here on time. Frying chicken livers. Know how much you like 'em and rice and gravy."

"Okay, Mama."

Claudine hurried out of the house, still hugging Betty to her chest like it was a child in need of extra-special attention. She was seventeen and eager to audition a complicated concerto for an orchestra that was forming at Emory University. The headmaster of the Colborne had tried to dissuade her, told her she shouldn't bite off more than she could chew. She ignored his pessimism and continued to practice. The music director worked her three times as hard as everybody else. She loved it, expected it, but most of all depended on it to get her through the week.

By the time she made it to the bus stop around the corner and down the street, she was breathing hard and sweating profusely. People were staring, and stains were beginning to show on her clothes. She wiped her forehead with the back of her hand and boarded the bus.

Claudine noticed the familiar face gazing at her intently but assumed it was because she looked crazy and unkempt. She closed her eyes and tried in vain to ignore him. She was in the middle of performing a Tchaikovsky concerto when she felt the hard poke on the side of her right thigh.

"Hey, ain't you Bone's lil' sister?"

"What?"

"Fat Deeny. Right?"

Claudine couldn't believe that Willy "The Earl" was sitting next to her, let alone attempting a conversation. Everybody called him that because he walked around with a royal strut like he had a cape attached to his back and red velvet underneath his shoes. It was a good thing that he was built long and lean like a pole bean, because there wasn't much room left on the seat. She held her arms tightly against her body and hoped he couldn't see the moistness seeping through her starched white blouse.

"My *name* is Claudine."

"I hang out with your brother sometime."

"I know who you are."

"Is that right." He leaned closer. "You kinda cute for a big girl. Anybody ever tell you that, Claudine?"

"No."

"I see the pretty girl inside, waiting to bust out of those big-ass clothes."

Claudine scooted closer to the window. What did he want with her? Wasn't there someone thinner he could sit next to and aggravate? Why couldn't he just go away? She wasn't in the mood to hear any fat jokes this morning.

"Awl, baby, don't be scared. I been watching you for a long time. You know you oughta lose some of that weight. I bet people tell you that all the time, huh?"

"Why don't you go and sit somewhere else?" Claudine murmured and stared straight ahead. She was accustomed to Bone's ignorant hillbilly friends commenting about her size, but this was different. Bone wasn't around instigating, egging everyone on. Why was Willy Earl messing with her, anyway? He could be talking to anybody, good-looking boy like that. She'd heard other girls whispering about his tight behind, on the afternoon bus and at the Press & Curl on Saturdays. She knew wiry was supposed to be a good thing, and she guessed being bowlegged didn't hurt him either.

"You do kind of have a cute face though. See, most people can't see it hiding under all dem layers of fat. But I'm special. Willy 'The Earl' notices everythang."

"Is that so? What makes you so different from everybody else, Willy 'The Earl'?"

"How 'bout I pick you up later, and you can find out for yourself?"

"I don't think so. I know what you do, Willy Earl Jenkins. Besides, my daddy would kill me for sure, showing up with the likes of you."

"I ain't worried 'bout all that. You'll come around. Hey, why you always gotta carry that case? Bone say you think you can play that thang or something."

"Bone is a jackass, and this 'thang' is called a violin. Excuse me, my stop." Claudine prayed that he would move into the aisle and allow her to pass. If she waited any longer for him to become a gentleman, she would miss her stop. Arriving late was not tolerated. She would have to endure squeezing by him. He grinned. She inhaled, tried desperately to hold her stomach in and focus on the rear door of the bus. She could feel his legs against her legs, her elbows brushing his chest, and his hand felt the complete curve of her ass as she bolted out of the narrow door. She was angry, humiliated, and strangely flattered at the same time. No one had ever wanted to touch her before. Super-smooth Willy "The Earl" Jenkins felt her booty. Today was a good day.

CHAPTER 4

*T*here were thirty-six applicants and only one opening
for violin. She'd been instructed to have the concerto memorized. Her performance needed to be flawless, ex-
ceedingly better than the thirty-five others. Claudine wasn't
nervous. She was accustomed to this tense, charged atmo-
sphere. Being the only brown face in a concerto competition
was all she'd ever known. She waited her turn and disregarded
the piercing stares, the whispers meant to destroy her concen-
tration. She'd rehearsed with a pianist countless times, until
playing the recently written Barber Violin Concerto felt as
natural as peeing. She'd replayed the music in her head while
she ate, when she bathed, and had listened to recordings of
Jascha Heifitz for hours. Her aunt Hattie Mae spared no expense in obtaining what Claudine needed to be the best. Nothing would stop her from sweeping this competition, not even a
judge's skepticism. She heard them. They wanted her to.

"I just don't think a colored has the talent to pull this off."

She was next. She could see their faces, the five people she
intended to dazzle, astound with her mastery. She recognized
them all: two instructors from the Colborne, the concert-
master from the Atlanta Youth Symphony Orchestra, the business manager from the Atlanta Youth Symphony Orchestra,

the chair of Emory University's music department. They'd all come not only to judge the competition but to witness the anomaly she had become. She smoothed her pleated, navy blue skirt and announced her selection, causing gasps of disbelief. The audience and the judges smirked at her bold choice of repertoire. They didn't know her. Winning the first round was easy. In that afternoon, she became the inspiration for their gossip, a novelty, an exception, a credit to her race.

"How in the world did that colored gal learn to play like that?"

No one wanted to select Claudine as the winner, but there was no alternative. During her second performance, she played more magnificently than before, immersing herself completely in the material, moving the chair of Emory's music department to tears.

CLAUDINE ASKED AGAIN. She was dying to know if Hattie Mae thought she was improving, still believed she was exceptional.

"Gran-T, how was that?"

"Girl, do I look like somebody's old aunt to you?"

"No ma'am."

"Well then call me Hattie Mae like everybody else and go tell that illiterate daddy of yours I'm home now, so he can stop banging on my damn walls. Gone cause me to get a headache, makin' all that racket, and nobody round here wants me to start achin'."

Hattie Mae sucked her teeth and eyed Claudine up and down. She'd known the girl was unique from the day she was born. She couldn't make that dummyseed Willamina understand that Claudine was blessed with a gift from the good Lord Almighty. And the Deacon, he was simply too backward to explain anything to at all. He understood only two things, fear and money.

"You make sure you tell your dim-witted daddy exactly what

I said, you hear? And don't forget the part about being illiterate. Tell him I think he looks like a possum in the face, too."

"Yes, Gran-T. I mean Hattie Mae."

"And Claudine. Leave Betty here from now on. We wouldn't want anything to happen to her. Lord, then I'd have to kill somebody. You know how much that thing cost me?"

"No ma'am."

"Well, never you mind. It ain't none of your business no how. Now go on. I need some peace. And Claudine!"

"Yes ma'am."

"That was beautiful. You did good at that competition today. I want to hear a different one, comberto, whatever y'all call them, next week."

She watched a jubilant Claudine exit through the back door. Everything was going exactly the way Hattie Mae had planned. Her patience was paying off, and Claudine was tough; she'd made sure of that. Now she'd have to start paying Claudine a little more attention than usual. Spend more time teaching Claudine how to take care of herself. The girl couldn't go off to Boston weighing over two hundred pounds. That just wouldn't be right. That fancy audition was about six months away. If she placed Claudine on a special diet and put the fear of God into Willamina to stop dipping everything in corn meal and slapping it in some grease, Claudine could go to that conservatory seventy pounds lighter. And there was no doubt in Hattie Mae's mind that they would accept Claudine. The girl had made her proud, keeping up in school and staying away from those swayback sluts Hattie Mae saw hanging out in the Press & Curl every Saturday morning. And Claudine never needed to be reminded about practicing that violin. In the beginning, Hattie Mae had worried secretly about boys chasing after her, but she'd relaxed when she realized that Claudine craved banana pudding more than some knucklehead's attention. Now she was seventeen, almost on her way out of Marietta. Hattie Mae would instruct her to stop eating so damn much and prepare to leave this place. She had to make Claudine understand that there was no coming back here, ever. Hattie Mae exhaled deeply and reached for a cigarette. Once Claudine was on that plane to Boston, life would change, and they would both be free.

Hattie Mae walked around for the fifth time and inspected her furnishings for dust and fingerprints that didn't exist. No one was allowed in Hattie Mae's house for any reason, not even people she halfway liked. No one except Claudine. Everybody else spoke to her through the screen door, even Willamina, Bone, and especially the Deacon. She usually made him yell from the sidewalk, like a bum. She was a stunning woman, Hattie Mae. Somewhere around forty, no one knew for sure. Smooth skin the color of a roasted walnut, waves of shiny black hair that cascaded toward the middle of her back, and an hourglass figure that moved grown men to start speaking in tongues at the mere mention of her name. A woman whom other women hated with a passion but knew better than to disrespect.

Hattie Mae ran a warm bath. She had to leave soon. He was expecting her, and arriving late was not an option.

CHAPTER 5

*E*xhausted, Claudine walked out of the Colborne building to discover Willy "The Earl" standing next to a brand-new, canary yellow Camaro. He was there waiting for her like a real boyfriend. She tried to mask her delight and appear indifferent. Hell, she couldn't even fool herself, let alone him. There was something about him that made her heart flutter. He was brash and conceited, long and lean, and he cocked his head to the side when he thought he was sharing something especially valuable. He motioned for her to come closer. He was smoking something. She knew she wasn't supposed to get in the car, but she was caught off guard, and today everything seemed heavier than usual.

Faculty and students alike used to say obscene things to Claudine when she left through the front door of the prestigious academy. She'd rushed home to Hattie Mae once, sobbing because another student had called her a fat nigger bitch and hissed that she should be eating watermelon and scrubbing his toilet instead of trying to learn white folk's music. Claudine spied Hattie Mae coming out of the headmaster's office the next day—seemed like the offensive comments ceased overnight. Most times, they all still looked at her like she was some kind of subnormal freak on display. It didn't bother her, though. She was almost famous. Her picture had been in the *Atlanta Daily World* twice. She had even posed with the governor once, at a special assembly.

"Well, you gone get in or keep pretending like you ain't happy to see me?"

"I'll get in if you take that stocking cap off your head."

"Look, Claudine . . . I don't see anybody else here waiting to pick you up. C'mon, girl, I ain't got all day."

Claudine smiled and opened the door. She was almost eighteen now, and she could accept a ride if she wanted to.

"You're going to have to drop me off at the corner, Willy Earl."

"Can't we spend a little time together first, get something to eat?"

"My mama made dinner."

"Girl, you a woman now. You need to learn how to relax and quit worrying about yo mama and them."

He drove her to the Dairy Queen on the other side of town, their side. She didn't know if this was considered a real date, but she was certainly going to assume it was. He must really like her, driving all the way downtown. She scanned the area for Bone, making sure this wasn't one of his cruel jokes. Oddly enough, she didn't feel like the punch line.

"Is Bone around here?"

"I didn't drive all the way over here to talk about Bone. Okay?"

"Okay," she replied, relieved and thankful.

"So how long you been playing this violin?"

"My ainty gave it to me when I was four or five."

"And you been playing it regular all this time, going to this peckerwood music place?"

"Yes."

Claudine watched Willy Earl nod his head like he was impressed. She wanted him to like her. She knew he was a numbers runner, but who wasn't? The Deacon did that and much more, and he didn't think she knew about his little side jobs. Why would he mind her being with Willy Earl, anyway? They were both probably cut from the same cloth. And Bone. Bone didn't care about her one way or another.

Claudine was too nervous to enjoy the burger and fries in her lap, so she sipped on a cream soda, hoping her stomach would settle. There were other girls outside drinking malts— skinny girls without elastic waistbands, pointing at them, whispering, laughing. "Is that Willy 'The Earl' Jenkins with Fat Deeny? That ass gone make a permanent dent in his new interior. Hope he brought all his money for that appetite. Hey, Willy Earl, bet you can't drive past thirty-five!"

Claudine heard them taunting her, goading him to respond. For the first time, her weight was an embarrassment. She had developed a delicate relationship with the rolls that decorated her body. There was a certain comfort in being heavy. Fat kept her safe, insulated her from the pain of her everyday existence, protected her from emotions she didn't wish to feel. Being rotund had never bothered her before. She had her music, and there had never been any boy to impress. Now the roundness had become her enemy.

"What, you not hungry? C'mon now, I know you likes to eat," Willy Earl coaxed.

"Can you take me home now? I'm not feeling too well."

"Oh, they bothering you? They not bothering me. I gots me a sweet slice of heaven in the car; they just don't know it yet."

"Please, Willy Earl, I just want to go home," Claudine pleaded, close to tears.

Willy Earl took the scenic route to Claudine's house. He didn't know why he was bothering with her, exactly. There was just something about her that intrigued him, piqued his curiosity until he couldn't stand it anymore. He couldn't confide in anyone, either. The crew would clown him for days if they knew he was trying to rap to Fat Deeny. She was definitely way too much girl for him, would probably break his narrow ass in two. But he wanted her, and he couldn't help it. He knew those fine girls at the Dairy Queen upset her, hurt her feelings. He wanted her to feel bad, bad enough to lose the weight. Then he could prove to everybody, show all the gang, what he had seen all along. He knew she didn't realize what she had underneath all that blubber, and he intended to use that information to his advantage. He would make her want him. Be her first cherry popper. It would be easy to get her juices flowing. There had been no one else. Everybody knew it. She was fresh, untouched virgin meat. He liked that. Then, depending on her attitude afterward, maybe he would keep her around. She'd have to maintain the curves, though, and stay away from those hot-link sandwiches. He laughed aloud, causing her to look.

He placed his hand on her knee when he reached the corner. He turned off the ignition and licked his lips for effect. She allowed his fingers to inch toward her inner thigh, just like he knew she would. Willy Earl could see her pert nipples straining against her blouse, begging his tongue to make an introduction. He reached for them and licked slowly until he felt her body arch. He gently tried to guide her hand down there, toward his third leg. She blushed and found a spot instead on the middle of his back.

"Let it out, baby, let it all out," he whispered in his best Lou Rawls imitation, when he sensed her indecision.

She hesitated at first, then began to caress him slowly, working her way toward his hips, causing his Levi's to tighten in anticipation. She was ripe and ready, moist and sweaty. He'd felt it all along. The familiar low-throated moan was all the incentive he needed to go for the gold.

"Willy Earl, ooh, Willy Earl," she murmured.

"That's right, baby, say my name."

He felt her warm breath on the back of his neck, brushed her soft hair from his eyes. He slid one hand under her shirt, cupping her large breast, and shoved the other snugly inside the elastic waist of her polyester skirt. He heard the glass shatter. He never saw the bat.

CHAPTER 6

*C*laudine sat stiffly in front of Willamina and tried again to close her blouse. Despite repeated attempts, she couldn't concentrate on the tiny holes that were supposed to secure the buttons. Threading a needle with a piece of grass would have been easier. She focused on a spot on the wall, Willamina's lime green slippers, anything to keep her mind off the blood that decorated her bra, now polka-dotted with pea-size splotches. No matter where Claudine looked, Willamina kept staring at her like she was seeing her for the first time. Her mother couldn't protect her. They'd both been here countless times, waiting for the inevitable.

The last few hours were a blur. Claudine had heard Willy Earl screaming, but someone pulled her from the car before she could see what was going on. It had all happened so fast. It was dark then. She remembered floating heads peering at her from the sidewalk and how she'd been unable to distinguish one angry voice from another. She'd hid her face in shame and called out for Willy Earl. Maybe it was another numbers runner or some hustler he'd crossed. She wanted to ask her mama if he was still alive, but Willamina had a bizarre look on her face. Claudine had never seen it before. And the

Deacon just kept pacing behind her, striving to rupture her eardrums.

"Look at her, Mina, trying to fasten up her clothes now, like she's shy. You shy, girl? What? Answer me when I'm talking to you!"

"I—"

"Shut up! Messin' round with that boy on the corner like some . . . some backwoods hussy."

"Be careful, Luther Mack," Willamina interjected quietly, her eyes never leaving Claudine's face. Claudine braced herself. If Mama was calling him by his Christian name, all hell was about to break loose.

"Be careful of what? Her?" he said, pointing next door. "Puhleeze. Claudine better be careful. Now everybody at Bethel AME gone know I got a fat tramp of a daughter."

"Luther Mack, keep your voice down. Don't want to rile anybody up for nothing," Willamina warned again. Claudine began to cry. If she could just get up, make it to her room. It was only fifteen steps away. She'd counted them in her head.

"Sit yo elephant ass down. I ain't done with you yet."

The Deacon pushed her. He stank of pickled pigs' feet and sweet cologne. He'd also been drinking, and despite repeated warnings from Willamina, he was getting louder, as if he wasn't afraid of Hattie Mae.

"Mama," she whispered.

"Oh, now you want your mama. Why didn't you call for your mama when that boy had his hand between your legs? Didn't hear you calling for your mama then. Did you hear your name, Willamina? Naw, ain't nobody heard shit except the sounds of you and that pop-eyed boy getting yo asses kicked by God knows who. You dead from the neck up if you really think that boy wants you."

"He likes me," Claudine countered. "He picked me up today."

"That boy couldn't pick you up with the help of Jesus. He'd break his own back. He just wants to get between your colossal thighs, and you too dumb to see that. What you think, just 'cause you play that damn violin, you lucked up on some common sense, too? What would a boy like that want with a girl like you? I swear, these here niggas don't care what a girl looks like as long as they can get that tail."

"Stop it!" Claudine screamed, standing. "I can have a boyfriend if I want to. I'm almost eighteen years old. I might be fat, but I'm not dumb, Daddy, and you can't tell me what to do anymore."

The Deacon and Willamina looked at her like she had another head protruding from the side of her neck. In one fluid motion, Willamina reached for the Deacon and the Deacon lunged at Claudine. He shook her until she thought her eyeballs were going to roll out of the back of her head.

"Ain't nobody gone take you into no sidity music school, heffa. Hattie Mae got you believing you leaving here. You think them white folks gone accept somebody like you? You must think you pink underneath all that blubber. You ain't going nowhere but to somebody's kitchen to fry chicken. You hear me?"

"I have a gift," Claudine managed to say before he grabbed her fingers and began to squeeze.

"Not anymore."

"Enough!" hissed a familiar voice. "I said *enough*. Luther Mack Tilbo, if you ruin that girl's hands, I'll split your head clean in two."

Everyone turned to face Hattie Mae, who stood in the doorway. She looked beautiful, like she had just strolled right off the pages of one of those glossy fashion magazines. The Deacon thought she looked better than any white woman he'd ever seen, what with her hair swept up off her face like that and those scarlet lips. She carried a little purse in one hand that looked like it was made of real diamonds. But Claudine didn't notice any of that. She didn't admire the matching red finger-nail polish or the imported, black, Italian patent leather pumps. The only thing that caught and held her attention was the blood-stained bat resting comfortably in Hattie Mae's other hand.

$\mathcal{H}$attie Mae had watched the commotion unfold in front of her from the darkness of the hallway. For once she'd wanted Luther to scare the living shit out of Claudine. The girl was about to throw her life away, messing around with that peel-head boy. She should have killed him. She was sure, though, that he wouldn't be sniffing around Claudine anymore, like some mangy dog in heat. Showing up at the Colborne like that, up to no damn good, probably looking like a hoodlum. And Miss Claudine had surprised her. Hattie Mae should have seen it coming. She'd expected the girl would get the tingle sooner or later. She'd just fooled herself into thinking Claudine didn't think about such things. Hattie Mae shook her head in disgust. The boy was absolutely revolting. She would not allow anyone or anything to interfere with her plans for herself or Claudine, including Claudine. The girl had no idea what was at stake here. Hattie Mae had to become more involved. Willamina obviously couldn't handle the situation anymore. The woman looked like hell, anyway. Hattie Mae regretted she ever let her live next door. Hell, she regretted many things in her life, but she didn't believe in backsliding or moaning and groaning about situations you couldn't change. She was moving forward, and she planned to take Claudine with her. He wouldn't be able to follow Hattie Mae six states away, not when Claudine made a name for herself. He wouldn't be able to do anything without destroying everything he'd built for himself.

He was waiting for her now, probably eyeing his watch, tapping his fingers on the table, and telling somebody what to do. She couldn't go to him tonight, with Claudine like this. He would be angry, and there would be consequences for her absence.

"Claudine, go pack all your things now. You're moving next door with me."

"Now, Hattie Mae, let's not—"

"Shut up, Willamina. You were going to let him hurt her hands, ruin her chances to go to Boston."

"No I wasn't. I told Deacon not to—"

"Not to yell, Willamina. You told this fool not to yell when you should have done something before he tried to maim the child. You're supposed to protect her, or have you forgotten?"

"Awl, Hattie Mae, I—"

Hattie Mae raised the bat and pointed it at the Deacon.

"Luther Mack, if I were you, I'd shut the hell up, 'cause I still might split your head open sometime tonight."

"Now, Hattie Mae, I didn't mean—"

"Don't go to sleep, Luther Mack."

Claudine listened to them go back and forth while she threw years' worth of stuff in suitcases, paper bags, anything she could find. It would be easier if she could carry her belongings next door a few items at a time, but Hattie Mae said pack everything, and that's what she was doing.

It was evident that Hattie Mae was the one she should be asking about Willy Earl. Claudine was strangely relieved. If the Deacon had whacked Willy Earl with that bat, he'd be dead, but Hattie Mae . . . Hattie Mae couldn't kill anybody. Beat them till they were almost dead, maybe, but not dead. Claudine knew Hattie Mae was a force to be reckoned with, but she was still the same woman who bought Claudine's clothes from Sears, and styled her hair when Willamina wasn't interested in remembering her name.

Claudine needed to find out about Willy Earl. Where the hell was Bone, anyway? He could find out for her, get a message to Willy Earl. This whole mess had turned ugly fast, and she didn't know why. She'd never seen such calm fury. And the Deacon and Willamina, her own parents, hadn't even protested when Hattie Mae ordered her to pack her things. Sometimes it was like they weren't her parents at all. Her aunt had always called the shots, made the important decisions. Deep down, she'd always felt like she didn't belong in their house anyway. If it weren't for Hattie Mae, her parents wouldn't notice her at all. Every time she tried to approach Willamina about feeling invisible, the words became lodged in her throat, and Willamina would yell, "What! What!" By the time Claudine could muster the words to ask her mother why she disliked her so, Willamina would be passed out on the bathroom floor.

Claudine hurriedly changed her clothes. She wanted this night to be over with. She needed to soak in a hot bath, sleep, and try to forget she ever saw Hattie Mae leaning on that bat.

CHAPTER 8

"How long you staying over here? I heard you was the reason Willy 'The Earl' walking around dazed and confused. What the hell was you doing with him anyway?"

Claudine eyed her brother suspiciously. He actually seemed concerned about her. He kind of looked like a frog in the face. She wondered if any of his girlfriends ever told him that. They were twins; thank God they didn't look alike. She wanted information about Willy Earl, but she had to be careful. Ever since that awful batting incident a month ago, Hattie Mae watched her like a hawk and picked her up religiously from the Colborne, every day. If she could only get Willy Earl's phone number, arrange to meet him somewhere, find out what happened that night.

"Be careful, Bone! Don't drop any of that on the floor. You know you aren't even supposed to be in here," Claudine answered, rolling her eyes, ignoring his questions.

"So, have you seen Willy Earl? How's he doing anyway?" Claudine asked innocently.

"He talks with a stutter now, that's how he's doing. Like you don't know. He ain't gone be called Willy 'The Earl' no more. He been demoted to just plain old Willy Earl."

"I don't know what you're taking about, Bone. He can't be doing that badly. I heard he was working at Snookie's Garage."

"Yeah, they keep him in the back, though, 'cause he talk funny, spittin' on people. Heard he can't help it, though. Hattie Mae must've cracked his head good. Wish I coulda been there to see that. Did you try to sit on his lap? Didn't know old Willy was into heavyweights."

Claudine watched him laugh hysterically and tried to appear nonchalant. She wished he'd choke to death. Sitting there, making fun of her while he ate a neck-bone sandwich. She'd never seen anybody do that but Bone.

"Want a bite?"

"No. That looks nasty, and anyway, I'm on a special diet. I'm going to lose this weight before my audition."

Bone laughed even harder. Claudine became more determined.

"Sheeet, you gone be holding up the Chicken Shack tomorrow. C'mon, Fat Deeny, there's a whole box of fritters just sitting on the kitchen table, all alone, all flaky with pounds and pounds of butter."

"Get outta here, Bone, or I'm gonna tell Hattie Mae you dripped neck-bone juice on her sofa, then *you* gone be talkin' funny."

CLAUDINE GAZED AT herself in Hattie Mae's full-length mirror. She must be really fat. Stupid Bone hadn't even noticed she'd already lost one dress size. Sixty-five pounds to go. She could do that in four months, re-create herself into someone Willy Earl could love forever. She opened Hattie Mae's closet and stroked the black velvet dress. There were real pearls sewn onto the hem. She felt them every day, careful to wash her hands first. Hattie Mae had brought it home the day after she'd beaned Willy Earl upside the head.

"I want you to wear this dress for your audition," she'd said matter-of-factly. "Get over that trifling-ass boy. Nobody needs to be that scrawny anyway. It ain't natural. Everything will be better for you once you squeeze into this dress, you hear me? Just stop eating so damn much."

Surprisingly, it had been easy for Claudine to stop eating. When she wasn't practicing, she felt his hands on her body. Just the memory of him, when his name had passed her lips, excited her need. That horrendous night, she'd experienced something she hadn't thought could ever be possible. Someone wanted her. A man desired her. He saw who she was and wanted her anyway. And at that moment, when she'd felt her body quiver underneath his hands, those two hundred pounds had disappeared along with her constant cravings for peach cobbler. Now she constantly craved Willy Earl, wondered what he was doing every day, if he was thinking about her. She could take him with her. Maybe they could get married. Nothing could keep him from her if he saw the way her behind swayed in that dress.

Whatever Hattie Mae had said to her parents worked, because Willamina and the Deacon barely spoke to Claudine anymore. It was a blessing, living next door. She discovered that she didn't miss them, either. She still heard them fussing through the walls sometimes, but they sounded so far away.

CLAUDINE PULLED THE scarf closer to her face. Willy Earl had promised to meet her here. He'd sounded nervous on the phone. She could barely understand what he was saying. And she'd thought Bone was just messing with her head. It wouldn't have mattered if Willy Earl were missing one eye; she couldn't stay away any longer. She needed to know if there was a chance. She wanted him to see her, recognize that she was shrinking by the day, becoming everything he wanted.

"Cl-Cl-Claudine, baby, I-I-I-I'm here."

She turned and prepared to kiss the man of her dreams.

CHAPTER 9

"*Y*ou sure been spending a lot time at home, Hat-tie Mae. If I didn't know any better, I'd think you had yourself another fella. But then I say to myself, 'Har-lan, she wouldn't do that 'cause she knows you'd kill her and any nigger she was with.'"

She could hear the edge in his voice, sense his agitation with her. Hattie Mae rang for someone to clear the breakfast dishes. She used to do it herself, but he'd put a stop to that. Said it made her look too common. He'd been asking a lot of questions lately, and yesterday she spotted Jimmy, one of his longtime drivers, following her home. He hadn't put a tail on her in a long time. So now she was back to being spied on. She placed her hand on his shoulder and chose her words carefully.

"I told you my niece been in some trouble lately, Harlan. I been spending more time with her, making sure she's practic-ing and not fooling around with this no-account hooligan."

"This is your sister's child, right? The one who thinks she can play the violin like a white gal. You know the only reason she gets all that attention is because there's never been a col-ored anything around here that can play the violin at all. You do know that, don't you, Hattie Mae? I hope you're not still putting false notions in that girl's head. Phew, that's a big girl, too. Tell me something, Hattie Mae, was your mama a great, big, old, fat woman?"

How long would it take to separate his head from his body? Would he holler her name when he took his last miserable breath? How quickly could she pluck his eyeballs out of his head and feed them to BoBo, the gardener's three-legged dog? If she cracked him hard upside his left temple, would he wobble slightly before he hit the floor? Hattie Mae wrapped her hand around the base of an impressive brass lamp on the dining room table and squeezed. She wanted him dead. She imagined him sprawled out on the impeccably polished hardwood floor, his legs jutting up in the air like a roach. Seventeen odd years she had had to listen to him eat, talk, laugh, breathe. If she could just hold on, she wouldn't have to see his pasty face much longer. She would have to be careful, though. She couldn't play her hand before it was time, or slip up and make a careless mistake. The devil didn't give any second chances.

"What exactly is going on with this niece of yours? Hell, Hattie Mae, you ought to be grateful somebody's chasing her. I can send Jimbo to talk to the boy. Hell, Jimmy knows who he is, knows where he works. These days Jimmy knows everybody you and Claudine talk to, been giving me regular updates on you. Say the word, Hattie Mae, and we can have her married off by the end of the week. And then I can have you all to myself again." He grabbed her around the waist and held on tightly, looking up into her round face.

"You belong to me. I don't like sharing you with other people. I admit it. I don't care if she's your niece, either. You're supposed to be available for me whenever I want you. Wasn't that part of the deal?"

"Harlan, please. I can handle this. I have to watch out for Claudine. Willamina is no kind of mother to that girl, never has been. She needs someone to look after her. You understand, don't you, Harlan?"

"I understand that that simpleminded sister of yours has

been a pain in the ass ever since you allowed her to move into that house with those pickaninnies. What the hell is wrong with her anyway? Is she retarded or something? She's the one who's supposed to be worrying about that girl. Get this under control, Hattie Mae, or I will. I expect you to be here when I need you. Understand?"

"Yes," she said. It was barely a whisper.

"Now don't look at me like that, Hattie Mae. My goodness, you've spoiled Claudine her whole life, buying that violin, having her clothes made, and all that nonsense. I tell you, though, I wouldn't admit this to anyone else but you, but she does play almost as well as my Lavender, and that's high praise."

Hattie Mae nodded her head in agreement, forcing a smile to spread across her face. His pinch-faced daughter couldn't play spoons, let alone get into the Colborne without a well-placed phone call and a sizeable donation. She removed his hand from hers. He was a short man, only coming to her breasts, standing. If you heard him speaking or saw him on the television, you'd think he was ten feet tall. It was often said that he had the voice of a giant; but truth be told, he was just a peanut of a man. She wanted to bend him over her knee, break his body in half. Although, most men were petite to Hattie Mae. She stood nearly six feet three in flat shoes. He was still rambling on, but she couldn't hear him anymore. In all this time she hadn't figured out which was worse—giving herself to him over and over again or being in jail, staring at the walls and imagining what life was like on the other side.

At one point she had thought he would tire of her, search for someone younger, prettier, shorter, but she was all he wanted year after year. He'd said, "You can leave when I get bored." And like a fool she'd held on to those words, thinking he would become uninterested eventually. Right around year five or so, she knew he would die first before he released her from their agreement. He had everything, and he still wanted her. Over time she became cold and aloof, unresponsive to his touch, but he craved her nevertheless. Her adjustable attitudes were irrelevant. His desire to possess her was the only thing that mattered. In his mind, he owned her, and for Hattie Mae that was no different than living behind those bars.

"I can take care of you and her at the same time. It won't be this way for long. I can handle it."

"You better," he said, and straightened his tie.

How many times had she heard those words? He used them to frighten and intimidate her. In the beginning she had thought she had everything under control. He was just a man, and men could be dealt with. She had had no idea how powerful he was or how formidable he would become. Hattie Mae had never been scared of anything or anyone in her whole life. She was a fighter. Her mama had raised her that way. Taught her that she was worth defending, protecting. She had been young and stupid when Harlan Tillford got her paroled, but that was then. Too much had changed. Too much was at stake. She would escape, leave without his permission, and he would come after her. When he did, she would be ready. It would only take a moment to rip his heart out. His annihilation was just a breath away.

"Hattie Mae. Hattie Mae. Are you daydreaming again? I have a speaking engagement to get to, and I expect you here when I return this evening."

"Harlan, I need to pick up Claudine. I'll—"

"Why don't you make one of your famous sweet potato pies, darlin'. Haven't had one in a while. Prepare it in the kitchen downstairs, and use the good brandy."

"Harlan, please."

"I can hear Jimmy shuffling around the corner. You mind your manners, now, you hear?"

Any more protest would annoy him, so she closed her mouth. Pleading would be useless. He'd made his decision.

She would have to arrange to have someone else pick up Claudine. Surviving here had been much easier when Harlan's wife was alive. He grasped her hand under the table.

"I'll be looking forward to that pie, Hattie Mae. Jimmy, you want a sweet potato pie? Make one for old Jimbo here, too."

Hattie Mae nodded at Jimmy. He refused eye contact and spoke directly to Harlan.

"Thank you, Governor. My missus loves pie."

CHAPTER 10

*C*laudine was euphoric. She was playing better than she'd ever played, mastering a French violin sonata, and losing weight at a rapid pace. The audition was approaching, and she would be prepared mentally and physically. People were starting to look at her differently, acknowledging her on the street and nodding like she was someone important. She felt visible for the first time in her life. And Willy Earl was right there, hiding on the sidelines. He was absolutely terrified of Hattie Mae, so they were careful never to be spotted together in public. Lately, though, they'd been able to see each other more because Hattie Mae wasn't home as much. Bone was supposed to pick Claudine up from the Colborne. He was usually late. She was usually gone. Neither made a fuss about it. They had a silent understanding. She gave him gas money on Mondays. He kept his mouth shut the rest of the week. She didn't know how Bone found out about her and Willy Earl, but he did.

Willy Earl was picking her up today in the alley behind the cafeteria. Claudine pulled out a tube of lipstick, Plum, and a small bottle of perfume that she'd swiped from Hattie Mae's dresser. It was only a matter of time before she would be in that dress—hallelujah. She had a boyfriend, a real boyfriend. She wished she could shout it to the world.

Willy Earl adjusted his hat and eased the antique gold Impala down the narrow alley. He'd had to get rid of his sweet yellow Camaro after Claudine's demented aunt busted out all of the windows. He still couldn't believe that that had happened to him, Willy "The Earl" Jenkins. Folks would be talking about his ass kicking for years, telling their kids, adding on shit as they went along. He just knew it. He'd been deeply humiliated by the whole incident. Getting his skull damn near cracked open by a woman. Seemed like everybody knew what had happened but him, and no one wanted to talk about it. They'd just nod their heads and laugh like hell, pointing at times like he was some kind of freak on display. Even the boys wouldn't cut him a break, mocking him every time he turned around. "Wil-Wil-Willy Earl," they'd say. "How-how-how's yo head?"

The whole town knew he'd been caught in his car trying to get into Fat Deeny's panties. Enraged, he'd been ready to go hunt somebody down, shoot their kneecaps off—until he found out from Adell the humpback, who smelled of pickles, that Hattie Mae was the one who had tried to pop his head like a watermelon. He would have sworn in front of Jehovah on a stack of Bibles that it was Monkey Man from the liquor store who had yanked him out of the car like that, with such force. Willy Earl never saw or heard the calm fury. All he remembered was the feel of that bat on the side of his head and the sound of bones breaking. He woke up in the colored hospital outside of Valdosta, fifty miles from home, talking crazy. Afflicted. Head bandaged, cheeks all swollen, and no familiar faces to answer any of his questions. He didn't have to be clocked over the head again to get the message. Come to think of it, though, he'd never heard a word when Hattie Mae had been slamming his face against the concrete. He just knew after that that Claudine was off limits. And he'd had every intention of leaving her alone, forgetting about her completely, until she called him, tracked him down in the back of Snookie's Garage like he was her man. He'd hung up on her the first five times. Told her she wasn't worth getting dead over. But she'd persisted, and he finally gave in and agreed to meet her on the other side of the tracks, under the bridge on Sycamore Street.

Claudine didn't laugh at his stutter or, like his mama, tell him that he was a waste of skin. She didn't even mind that he sprayed her cheek with little droplets of saliva whenever he struggled to speak. She acted like she didn't notice it at all. Claudine made him feel like a man again, and by the time she'd wrapped her big arms around him that day, he wouldn't have cared who was looking. His baby was going places, and he was going to be right there with her. Make a fresh start somewhere else. By the time evil-ass Hattie Mae figured out what was happening, Claudine would be Mrs. Willy Earl Jenkins, and there wouldn't be a damn thing Hattie Mae could do about it.

Willy Earl looked up from his imaginary wedding in his uncle Marvell's backyard and caught Claudine watching him. She looked so pretty standing there, smiling. He'd never even had to mention those extra pounds. She was handling it herself, staying away from the Rib Shack and walking by the Cobbler King like it wasn't even there. Willy Earl was impressed. He leaned over and opened the passenger door.

"Wha-wha-what you waiting for, baby?"

"Oh, Willy Earl, my audition is in three weeks. Three weeks! And guess what? The Juilliard people want me to audition, too."

"Where's that?"

"In New York! The director's sure I'll be offered a full scholarship from either Juilliard or the New England Conservatory, maybe even both. I know I'm ready. I'm just so nervous. Oh, I can't stay out too long tonight, though. Hattie Mae is supposed to call me at seven o'clock."

"Well, we g-g-g-got a lil' time," he said, reaching for her ever-shrinking thigh.

"Willy Earl Jenkins. Not back here, behind the school!"

Moments later at their secret place, Claudine panted in the backseat while Willy Earl wasted no time unzipping his pants. He'd lifted her skirt and unbuttoned her blouse already. She was too shy to ask him to put his mouth to her breast. She was cautious but unable to stop herself from wanting more.

"C'mon, baby. Just t-t-touch him. He-he won't bite ya."

She reached for Willy Earl and heard him moan. Claudine liked that she could make him moan.

"My-my turn," he whispered, and explored her with his tongue until she called his name and promised him the world. They pressed themselves against each other, entwined in the moment, oblivious to the person who was only a few feet away, watching.

CLAUDINE STRAIGHTENED HER skirt one more time. It was dark in the house, and she was relieved she would be alone. She'd almost let Willy Earl do it to her and probably would have if he hadn't noticed the time. She was glad, though. She wanted to wait until their wedding night. Make it special. She opened the door, humming Mendelssohn, and her hand found its way to her nipple as she remembered Willy Earl's lips there. It took her only a second to smell the cigarette.

"You must think you smarter than me," Hattie Mae said calmly, advancing toward her.

The backhand caught Claudine by surprise. Hattie Mae yanked the violin from her hand and, though it was still dark, refused to turn on the light. Hattie Mae never raised her voice; just every time she had to fix her face to say Willy Earl's name, she slapped Claudine hard. She claimed his name left a bad taste in her mouth.

"So you would rather be chasing after that island heathen Willy Earl than practicing for your audition?"

Claudine cupped her stinging cheek with her right hand and felt around for the wall with her left. She prepared herself for the next strike and prayed that Hattie Mae wouldn't have to utter his name again.

"Hattie Mae, please, let me explain."

"Explain what, that you been lying to me all this time, sneaking around behind my back? Allowing that reptile Willy Earl to put his filthy hands on you?"

Falling backward, Claudine licked blood from the inside of her lower lip, slipped to the floor, and yelled into the darkness.

"I don't understand you! I practice every day! Every day! My grades are perfect. Look at me! I'm thinner, just like you wanted. I've done everything you wanted me to do."

"Not everything," Hattie Mae hissed.

"Why? Why can't I have this one thing? Why can't I be with Will . . . him?"

There was an uncomfortable silence, the kind that makes you deathly afraid of what is about to happen next, and gradually Claudine became aware of how hard she was breathing, how hard Hattie Mae was breathing. Their exhalations sounded exactly the same. When the lights finally came on, the violin was in the middle of the floor, and Hattie Mae was standing over it with an axe.

"Which is it going to be, Claudine, him or Betty? You can't have both. You can't do both."

"Why, Hattie Mae? I've never asked you for anything."

"Why? Because you've worked most of your life to master this violin, play the way you do. Your feelings for Willy Earl will fade; your need to belong with this instrument won't. It has become a part of you, a part of me. Trust me on this, girl. Is he worth it? Is he worth me chopping Betty up into little pieces, destroying thirteen years of hard work just so you can move over into that two-room shack? Is that the life you want for yourself, Claudine? Because getting up in the morning and fighting the rats for breakfast is how your every day will begin." Hattie Mae raised the axe when Claudine didn't respond.

"No! . . . No, you know that's not what I want."

"Prove it."

Claudine began to cry. "Please . . . please don't," she pleaded, inching toward the violin. Why did this have to be an all-or-nothing decision? Hattie Mae was right about one thing—she couldn't bear to part with it. Who would she be without Betty? And, God help her, she couldn't imagine not loving Willy Earl Jenkins. Why couldn't Hattie Mae understand that her feelings wouldn't just disappear because she wanted them to? Hadn't her aunt ever loved anyone?

"Well?"

"I'll come straight home from the Colborne from now on."

"And . . ."

"And I'm sorry I've been lying to you."

"Promise me, Claudine. Promise me you'll never see him again."

"I promise."

"Now go on, clean yourself up. There's some red beans and rice on the stove."

Claudine reached for the violin, wiping her nose with the back of her hand. She hugged Betty close, like she was five all over again, and continued to weep quietly because she knew she'd just made a promise she would never be able to keep.

CHAPTER 11

"Heard tell Hattie Mae whipped your tail good. I knew it was coming sooner or later. You'd think after the last beating she gave stick boy, you'd know better than to be messin' round with him anymore."

Claudine rolled her eyes and listened to the Deacon. He had returned to laughing at her. He sat on the porch, picking his teeth, blocking her entrance.

"Excuse me, Daddy, I need to go practice."

"Your mama wants to see you, made you some Frito pie."

"Willamina? Willamina wants to see me?"

"That's your mama, ain't it? Lord have mercy, this girl done lost some fat and gone deaf," the Deacon responded, irritated at having to continue the conversation. "Just 'cause you livin' next door don't mean she ain't your kin no more. Ought to be ashamed of yourself, ignoring your own mama. It's a sin. That's what it is."

"I didn't think she wanted to talk to me."

"Go on," the Deacon said, sliding over. "And brang me some of that Frito pie."

"Mama," Claudine whispered, standing in the doorway of the kitchen, "you wanted to see me?"

Willamina didn't answer at first, just motioned for Claudine to sit down. Claudine tried to stare a hole through her back and wondered if she could feel it. She imagined her mama must have been pretty once, like Hattie Mae, before the Deacon, before the alcohol. She would never know. There weren't any photographs of Willamina before she and Bone were born, and Willamina was not one for discussing her past. Claudine wondered if her mother had ever been happy at all. She wondered if her mother had ever really loved her.

Willamina seemed comfortable with the distance. Claudine couldn't remember if they'd ever had a conversation that lasted more than ten minutes. She couldn't recall a time when Willamina's hand wasn't wrapped around a fancy liquor bottle. There was an ocean between them, and after Hattie Mae gifted her with the violin, Claudine lost any interest in crossing it. Her mother was so ineffective, always giving her power over to the Deacon or Hattie Mae. Claudine didn't respect her, and she knew Willamina sensed it. Picked up on her silent disapproval. Claudine had been accused her whole life of thinking she was smarter than everyone else in this house. She'd always assumed Willamina merely tolerated her. She treated her and Bone so differently, doting on him, ignoring her. Claudine resented Bone for eliciting emotion, any kind of loving response, from their mother. The only thing she ever felt from Willamina was contempt.

Claudine scanned the room. For a woman who didn't work, she owned plenty—clothes, furnishings, wigs—and Claudine couldn't imagine the Deacon buying them for her. He always had money, but he wasn't known for sharing it. She didn't comprehend how their relationship worked. She just knew she never wanted one like it.

"Where's Bone?" Claudine ventured.

"I didn't call you in here to talk about Bone. Aren't you going to audition soon for that fancy music school in Boston?"

"Next week."

"Well, you look good. I know you'll show them white folks a thang or two."

Claudine carefully searched Willamina's face for signs of dementia. It was the first time in years that Willamina had paid her a compliment, acknowledged her ability. She'd yearned for this moment for a long time, and now that it was here, she felt uneasy, uncomfortable.

"I didn't think Hattie Mae shoulda beat on you like that. You grown now. It's natural for a girl to want some attention. You can tell her you don't want to play that thing anymore. Stand up for yourself!"

"But I love playing it, Mama. I really do."

"Un huh, you do whatever Miss High and Mighty wants you to do, just like the rest of us. If she gave you a damn soupspoon to slap up against your knee, you'd be playing hambone in the middle of the street right now, thinking that was special."

Willamina took a drink from her highball. She'd had five neat in the past two hours. She'd sworn eighteen years ago, on Bone's life, that she'd take this to her grave, but she didn't want to hold it in any longer, protect that controlling, cold-hearted witch. Hattie Mae would kill her for sure, but she was dead already, her insides cold and numb from the lies. Her whole life had been a blur, whizzing by, leaving her behind. She used to be something else, once, and now she was worthless, unnecessary, and damn near bald. Most times she couldn't remember her own name. Years of drinking had dulled her mind and extinguished whatever fire she had left simply to continue. The only person who kept her going was Bone, and now he didn't need her anymore. And after everything she'd sacrificed for him, the ungrateful little bastard. He didn't have two words to say to her unless she was handing him a plate of neck bones. She steadied herself on the kitchen sink and turned to face Claudine.

"You turning eighteen in one week, and it's high time you

knew the truth, walking around here like you on top of the world, looking down your nose at the rest of us, at me." Willamina smiled and took another drink. "I'm gone put you in your place once and for all, you hear me? Damn that bitch, Hattie Mae, and her midnight promises. Damn everybody."

Claudine heard a door slam. Hattie Mae was home, and she was supposed to be practicing. "Mama, I've got to go now."

"Sit down!" Willamina yelled. Claudine flinched at the harshness in her voice. She'd begun to slur her words.

"You think you know every goddamn thing, doncha? You think I've liked being your mama? You think I wanted to be your mama? You think you somebody special 'cause you lost all that weight and play that stupid violin. You ain't no different from me, you know. You think I've been a bad mama to you; well, I ain't—"

The closed fist seemed to come from nowhere, catching Willamina on her right side, knocking her to the ground.

"Hattie Mae wants you next door," the Deacon said, avoiding Claudine's eyes. Confused, she stood up, grabbed her case, and watched as he stepped over a broken Willamina and refilled his bowl with Frito pie.

CHAPTER 12

Hattie Mae was waiting for her. There was only one week until the audition, and she wanted nothing to deter Claudine from performing like an angel. Hattie Mae knew she had scared her the other day, but the girl had to learn what was important, and what you relinquish when you're trying to better yourself. She'd slapped her good, tried to shake some sense into her. Hattie Mae was about ready to put Willy Earl Jenkins six feet under, but she'd promised herself long ago that she would never abuse Harlan's power like that. Then she'd be no different from him, disposing of people like they were trash. She had enough to answer for when she met the Maker; she didn't need to add anything else.

Hattie Mae prayed she'd gotten through to Claudine. She'd hoped threatening to chop her precious violin into firewood would shock some sense into the girl. She cringed at the memory and became amused at her own theatrics. Only she knew she'd never intended to do a damn thing to that violin, let alone cut it in half. That instrument was their salvation.

"Hattie Mae, I'm home. I know I'm late but Mama wanted to see me and—"

"I know where you were. It's all right. I don't want you going over there anymore, you hear? You need to stay focused on this audition."

"I think she was trying to tell me something. Maybe I should wait till things calm down, go over later."

"No. Willamina was drinking, and you know she doesn't make a lick of sense when she starts foolin' with that firewater. It's a damn shame. Now go eat. There's some shrimp and okra in the kitchen."

Claudine was relieved. She had been sure Hattie Mae was going to blame her for what had just happened. She'd been so angry the other night, confronting her about Willy Earl, threatening to slap the taste out of her mouth. Claudine had decided to wait until after the audition to see him again. She'd be eighteen by then, and Hattie Mae would just have to understand that they loved each other. If she won a scholarship, she would be moving anyway. Willy Earl could follow, get a job in Boston. It was a perfect plan. She polished off three bowls of okra, corn, and tomatoes and prepared to practice.

Hattie Mae waited until she heard the music before she went next door. She wanted to strangle Willamina. As soon as Luther Mack had told her that Willamina wanted to see Claudine, Hattie Mae knew something was amiss. Willamina had never taken an interest before, never. Hattie Mae couldn't have gone in there herself or she surely would have broken the woman's neck. So she sent the Deacon to quiet his wife, do whatever he had to do to shut her up. Told him his lavish living arrangements were at stake if Willamina said one more word to Claudine. Stupid woman. Hattie Mae should have seen this coming. She was going to have to send Willamina away, where she couldn't do any more damage. If she had to drive Willamina to the nuthouse herself, with a dishrag stuffed down her throat, she would, and without thinking twice about it. The woman needed to dry out, anyway. It would probably do Willamina some good, and if she started running off at the mouth, no one there would believe her. After everything she'd done for Willamina, this was how she was repaid. As far as Hattie Mae was concerned, Willamina's promises were worthless, just like the rest of her.

WILLAMINA FELT AROUND on the floor for her expensive Chinese wig, which had flown off when the Deacon struck her. She attempted to stand, but her legs wouldn't pay attention, so she crawled toward her room in the rear of the house. The Deacon had long since taken over the master bedroom and kicked her out, along with the pretty blue dresses that she never got to wear because she was too ashamed to leave the house. She adored every shade of blue—indigo, navy, light blue like the sky—and she had hats to match her dresses. When she'd first moved into the duplex, she'd delighted in shopping, coordinating accessories, ordering jewelry from the department stores. Buying pretty things made her feel rich and important. She was a caramel-colored princess. But no matter what she'd worn or how she'd looked in her blue dresses, the Deacon and Hattie Mae never really noticed her. Never said, You look fabulous, Willamina, or What a lovely turquoise wrap, Willamina. She had been practically invisible, a non-person; and then when Claudine started playing that dreaded violin, Willamina nearly disappeared altogether.

Living here was supposed to fix everything, magically transform her life into a gold-plated fairy tale. The Deacon was supposed to love her like a real wife, and she was supposed to be respectable, stand out in a crowd like a ruby that had just been polished. She'd believed Hattie Mae would guide her, spend time with her, love her, but Willamina soon discovered that Hattie Mae didn't even like her. True, the regular influx of cash was comforting at first—a bulging envelope wedged under the mat by the back door every Friday, even when she hadn't laid eyes on Hattie Mae for days. How she used to look forward to Fridays, hoping Hattie Mae would hand deliver the envelope, invite her for lunch, or ask her to the picture show. Ultimately, Fridays became a burden, a day when she was reminded that Hattie Mae would rather drop cash on a dusty porch than be in the same room with her. For a while, Willamina told herself that that was okay; things would be different eventually, when they got to know each other, in a few weeks maybe. Weeks turned into years, and years into pain that crusted her heart and drove her to drink. She fantasized that forking over money was simply Hattie Mae's way of expressing gratitude that she'd moved next door. One day, Willamina would wake up and the Deacon would greet her with a moist kiss, and Hattie Mae would chime in from the screen door: Willamina, Willamina, what shall we do today?

Willamina had thought organdy dresses and hand-embroidered dinner napkins could replace affection. The truth of it was that she would have preferred a warm embrace, a light squeeze of the shoulder to another pair of patent leather shoes. But it soon became obvious that Hattie Mae Jones had no affection to spare. And children, they were supposed to look up to their mamas; instead, Bone and Claudine figured out what the Deacon had realized from the beginning: she was expendable, born to accommodate everyone else's needs. Hattie Mae had everything. Willamina had a husband who ridiculed her, a son who ignored her, and a daughter who thought she was stupid. Yes, Hattie Mae had delivered all that she'd promised, but at what cost? Willamina was thirty-two years old, with a big house, a dresser filled with wadded-up fifties, and still no one gave a damn. And drunk or not, she knew that before the night was over, Hattie Mae would come for her; after what Willamina had tried to do, Hattie Mae probably planned to shut her up for good. It didn't matter. Nothing mattered anymore. She was tired, and all of them could go to hell.

HATTIE MAE WALKED though the house, feeling along the wall for the light switch. She knew Luther Mack was gone. He had services tonight at the church. That's why she never went. Fools like him hissing and hollering in the pulpit, trying to tell decent folks how to live their lives. She knew for a fact that he had three other children by a woman named Cookie over on Sherman Street.

"Willamina! Willamina, I know you in here. Come on out, now. Don't make me come looking for you." Hattie Mae saw a light under Willamina's bedroom door and figured she was passed out, as usual. No matter—this needed to be resolved tonight, so Willamina was just going to have to sober up and suffer the consequences of her big, fat mouth. Hattie Mae went into the kitchen and put on some coffee. Maybe she could make a couple of calls and get her admitted tonight.

"Willamina! Get your ass up!" she shouted. Still no answer. Hattie Mae rolled up her sleeves and opened the bedroom door, prepared to pull her out of another drunken stupor. But Willamina wasn't moving, not at all. There were empty bottles of liquor strewn everywhere. Hattie Mae kicked them disgustedly, trying to get to her. Willamina was wearing a short blue dress with ruffles at the neck, and a straight, black wig that made her look like Cleopatra. Her eyes were open, and she'd taken the time to paint her toes. Something she'd never done. She'd always been a petite girl, but today she resembled a child in an old woman's body. "Willamina," Hattie Mae said, softer this time, and she sat heavily on the edge of the bed. She'd seen this look before, remembered it like it was yesterday. She'd hoped to never see it again. She wouldn't be driving anywhere tonight. She wouldn't have to worry about any more half-drunk confessions. Her secret was safe now. Hattie Mae covered her face with her hands and wept for the first time in twenty years.

CHAPTER 13

"I heard about your sister, Hattie Mae. That's too bad. Pass me a couple of those hush puppies, will you, darlin'."

"I'm gonna need some time off to make some arrangements."

"Well, I already told you to take the day off. Can't the colored funeral parlor across town handle this business in one day?"

"Harlan, I need to make sure my niece and nephew are holding up. Their mama is dead. My sister is dead. That has to mean something to you."

"All right then, five days. That should be enough time. That sister of yours was a burden anyway, always has been. Her death ought to be a relief, if you ask me. And Hattie Mae, those children are grown now, old enough to take care of themselves."

"Thank you, Harlan." Hattie Mae removed her apron and grabbed her purse from the pantry. She wanted to be the one to tell Claudine. She'd had Redd from the funeral parlor come remove the remains after Claudine went to sleep last night.

"Aren't you forgetting something?"

Hattie Mae placed her purse on the counter, unbuttoned

the top of her dress, and waited. She had thought she could make it out of the mansion without obliging him. He finished another helping of hush puppies before he reached for her, stood, and buried his face in her chest like a hedgehog. She was tempted to hold his head there, in her cleavage, until he suffocated. When she felt his stubby little fingers creeping up her thigh, she knew she wasn't going to make it to Claudine on time.

Three hours later, Hattie Mae stood again at Harlan's bedroom door. He'd wanted to watch her bathe, but she kept insisting that he let her go be with Claudine and Bone. She'd rather walk out of that place stinking of him than stay one more moment. Revulsion washed over her, and she felt the bile rising in the back of her throat. She didn't know what could possibly be bothering her. She usually handled this, accommodated his peculiar requests without feeling anything at all. She was a veteran at detachment, seasoned in disassociation. Harlan wasn't supposed to be able to affect her anymore. Today was no different from any other day, except that she had to find Claudine and tell her that her mama was dead.

"Hattie Mae."

She gripped the doorknob, prayed he was too exhausted to want anything else from her.

"You tell that shiftless preacher brother-in-law of yours he has to find other accommodations. Now that your sister's gone, I don't want him getting any ideas. Bone and Claudine can stay, but I want him gone by the end of the week."

Hattie Mae nodded and closed the door behind her. Now, that she didn't mind doing at all.

CHAPTER 14

$\mathcal{C}$laudine watched them lower her mama into the ground. She still couldn't believe Willamina was gone. No one seemed surprised that she drank herself to death. "Alcohol poisoning," someone said in passing. Claudine didn't feel right. She kept her head down. A good daughter was supposed to be distraught during a time like this, but Bone was devastated enough for the both of them. And the Deacon was crying, moaning out loud about his beloved wife being taken before her time. Claudine shook her head in disbelief. Wasn't he just knocking the shit out of Willamina a few nights ago? The Deacon was putting on quite a show for the people who'd come from his congregation. No one attempted to comfort Hattie Mae. They just whispered that she was a fine example of strength and offered their condolences on the death of her sweet sister. Many people attended the service, which surprised Claudine, as Willamina didn't have any friends. She suspected everyone was there for Hattie Mae. Flowers were everywhere, so many that you could barely see the coffin. One arrangement was so lavish that there were rumors flying around about whom it was from.

"Your mama sho' was loved," a fellow had murmured in her ear. It wasn't until she heard him talking to someone else, hours later, that she realized it had been Willy Earl. He'd come to pay his respects in spite of Hattie Mae, and that was good. Showed he had some gumption, some courage, some balls.

Claudine wrapped her arms around Bone. He sunk into her, unable to move. She rocked him like a baby until his sobs subsided into a weak whimper. Folks probably thought that they were feeling each other's pain, being twins and all, but Claudine didn't feel anything but numb. She'd found out about Willamina, coming home the next day, from Adell, who always knew everything—how her mama had sucked down four different kinds of liquor until she passed out and choked on her own vomit; how Hattie Mae had had Willamina's body removed by Redd, the cockeyed undertaker, so that Claudine wouldn't have to see her all crazy-looking and twisted up like that. Someone handed Claudine a tissue. She dabbed at her eyes, expecting to find tears. They were there, but they belonged to Bone, whose face rested next to hers.

After the funeral, people arrived at the duplex with charitable words, delectable foods, and shared memories of Willamina that were generous fabrications. "Remember that time Willamina gave me thirty-eight cents so I could take the bus to work?" Or, "What about when she gave you that dress, Pearl, to go on that interview downtown . . . precious thang." Or, "She was a sweet one, that Willamina, always had a kind word." Claudine laughed at the absurdity of it all. She had no idea which Willamina they were speaking of, but it couldn't possibly be the same woman who had never so much as uttered a Good morning, Claudine, or an I love you, Claudine, in seventeen years. This whole scene reminded Claudine of some bizarre block party, what with people lingering on the sidewalk and the driveway, sitting on the front steps, drinking sweet tea, and consuming countless plates of fried apples and smothered chicken. These mourners, if you'd want to call them that, were talking quietly among themselves, some were even laughing, but no one attempted to walk into the imposing duplex, either side. Women would hand Claudine covered dishes through the screen door, and she would pass them on to Adell, who placed them on a table. Folks were served from the side porch, and no one seemed to mind the oddness of it all. Everyone wanted to make sure that Hattie Mae Jones knew they were there to pay their respects.

It didn't take long for the Deacon to make an appearance, steal the attention from the dead. He was, after all, the husband, a widower with two children to finish raising alone. Claudine spied him approaching from the fancy automobile he'd obviously rented from some back-alley pimp. She hadn't thought he'd show up at all, the way he'd been carrying on at the service, falling out and speaking in tongues, making quite a spectacle of himself. Now here he was back to normal— polished, clean, as if her mama were sitting at the kitchen table waiting for him. In all her life, Claudine had never seen a man wear a suit like that. Adell claimed that it damn near gave her the pink eye just to look at it. Claudine didn't even know the Deacon owned a lime green suit, and unfortunately for him, the glare caused Hattie Mae to drop a piece of red velvet cake.

"What the hell all y'all lookin' at? Ya act like you never seen a nigguh in a silk suit before," the Deacon hissed as folks parted to make room. Annoyed, Hattie Mae wiped her hands and stepped out onto the front porch.

"Well, well, well, if it isn't the grieving husband. What you trying to do? Blind the whole neighborhood?"

"Don't start with me now, Hattie Mae. I'm here to grieve with my children, and then I'm going home and put my head down."

"Oh, did my sister's funeral upset you? Or was it the stop you made on the way home from the cemetery that's got you all tuckered out?"

"I ain't got time for this. I'm going to step in here, real quick like, Hattie Mae, and check on Bone."

"Looks to me like you've got yourself quite a problem."

"And what's that?"

"You're not stepping one foot in my house to do anything, not even breathe."

"Awl, c'mon now, Hattie Mae, I just lost my wife. I don't want to start no mess in front of all these people. I can see that you taking Willamina's passing pretty hard. We both are. We both loved her."

Hattie Mae sucked her teeth. "Please . . . you ain't fooling nobody round here."

"I'll just go on home, then. Stay outta your way until you calm down."

"And where's that?"

"Where is what? Does anybody here know what the hell this woman's talkin' 'bout?" the Deacon yelled behind him.

"Home, Luther Mack. Where is home?"

"Right here, next door to you."

"This was Willamina's home, Claudine's home, Bone's home. I merely tolerated you so Willamina wouldn't get bored. Now, tell me, Luther Mack Tilbo, now that she's gone to Glory . . . where do you think that leaves you?" Hattie Mae leaned over, her breast brushing his cheek, and spoke low, into his good ear. "You don't belong here. You never did."

The Deacon started to laugh nervously and began fishing for his keys to the front door. His hands were shaking, and he didn't want Hattie Mae to notice the effect she had on him, still. He'd never asked if Willamina owned their side of the duplex. He just always figured she did, assumed that Hattie Mae gave it to her outright. She gave her everything else, so why would the house be any different? He tried fidgeting with the front door for at least ten minutes before he realized she'd changed the locks. He fumbled clumsily with his back to her, his back to the crowd, them watching the beginning of his degradation at her hands, once again.

"Come back tomorrow, before noon, and I'll have Adell let

you in to collect the rest of your property. Your property, Luther Mack, not Willamina's."

"Now listen here, I got a right to—"

"You got a right to disappear from my porch before that get-up you wearing gives me a damn headache."

The Deacon turned, seething, and walked back to the white Lincoln with the red stripes painted on the side; his breath was coming in short spurts. He wanted to reach into his alabaster boot, remove his piece, and put Hattie Mae Jones out of her misery for good. He must have thought it a hundred times while he was struggling to open the door, his door for the past eighteen years. He thought about it all right, but her eyes never left his face, and he could feel her picking at his mind like a vulture. He was going to get her for this, if it took him forever. Someway, somehow, Luther Mack Tilbo was going to make her pay.

That night, in her bed, after everyone had trickled home and all the food had been put away, Claudine waited for intense grief to hit her. Everyone had kept asking her, over and over again, how she was holding up. Hattie Mae asked her only once. People had been saying that she was in shock and it was only a matter of time before she started wailing and carrying on like her daddy. She intended to tuck today's memory away. She didn't want to think about it anymore, her crazy mama being gone. She couldn't afford to. Her audition was in two days.

She'd heard the exchange earlier, between Hattie Mae and her father. Claudine didn't care if she ever saw his face again. He could leave now, without saying good-bye, and it wouldn't make a damn bit of difference. She was going places, and she couldn't wait to leave this misery behind. In two more days, she would be eighteen. In two more days, she would have a real future.

"Deeny. Deeny, you in there?"

Claudine reached for a robe. Bone couldn't call her Fat

Deeny anymore. No one could. Several people hadn't even recognized her at the funeral, mistook her for Hattie Mae, of all people. She weighed 138 pounds, and she didn't look like herself. Her features had become more defined since the weight had dropped off, causing stares and unsolicited comments. And to think people actually thought that they were paying her a compliment, comparing her to evil-ass Hattie Mae. It was nonsense anyway. Folks didn't know what they were talking about, just trying to find something to say when somebody was dead.

"Hattie Mae said I could come in, say good-bye. I'm leaving tomorrow, shippin' out."

"What are you talking about? Where are you going? You can still live next door, you know. You'd have the place all to yourself."

"Naw, Deeny. You've always had something I've never had . . . a life. You know I can't stay here. Deacon's moving, Mama's gone, and Hattie Mae . . . well, she ain't never looked after me the way she looks after you."

"No, Bone, that's not true," Claudine answered softly, knowing it was but feeling uncomfortable acknowledging it.

He gave her that familiar look that said she wasn't facing reality. Thankfully, that's all he did. It had always been a painful subject, Hattie Mae's treatment of Bone.

"I'm in the way here. Our birthday's in two days, you know. We'll be eighteen. I'm joinin' the army. Gone go to Vietnam, shoot me some motherfuckers."

"Bone, are you sure? You could get killed over there."

"I could get killed over here. Claudine, will you write me?"

"Of course."

"Even if you get rich and famous up there in snooty-ass Boston."

"I'll write, I promise."

Bone rose to leave and kissed her on the forehead. Tonight, for the first time, she felt like his twin and not just some girl who grew up in the same house. She reached for him and held on tight.

"Bone?"

"Yeah."

"Be careful over there, okay?"

"I will."

"And Bone."

"Yeah."

"I love you."

"I love you, too, Deeny."

"Bone."

"C'mon, already, I have a boat to catch."

"I'll mail you chicken bones, and maybe even pork chop bones if I'm feeling especially generous."

He laughed, she smiled, and for a moment they were a family.

"Deeny."

"Yeah."

"I know you think Mama didn't love you, but she did. For some reason, she just didn't know how to show it."

Now it was Claudine's turn to give him that look. He lowered his head, avoiding yet another painful truth.

"Good luck, Deeny," he murmured before he shut the door gently, careful not to disturb Hattie Mae. Claudine closed her eyes and, to her surprise, felt a tear slide down her cheek. She'd never really liked Bone, but she missed him already.

CHAPTER 15

Claudine awoke to Hattie Mae standing over her, smiling.

"What, what's the matter? Oh my God, did I oversleep?"

"Now, you know I wouldn't let you oversleep, not today. Are you nervous?"

"A little, I guess. Are you coming?"

"I'll be there. You just make sure you're there early."

Claudine was fooling herself. Her hands were shaking at the thought of playing for those people. How in the world was she going to perform without fainting dead away? Hadn't playing all these years while everyone around her, except Hattie Mae, teased her proved that she was foolish, wasting her time? No colored girl was going anywhere playing the violin. She had to remind herself of everything she'd accomplished. And the weight . . . gone. Sometime in the past six months, she'd experienced an epiphany. Claudine had wanted to stop pretending she was that other girl with the normal life and become that other girl, svelte and pretty, with a boyfriend and a future. Still, she was anxious, afraid that she wasn't as talented or skilled as Hattie Mae believed she was. She'd prepared for this recital for months, years. Her whole life had been leading to this very moment. She intended to dazzle the committee with her performance today, prove that Hattie Mae was right and that she was unique, blessed with a gift. A bequest no one had been able to take away from her, not even the Deacon. She was the first chair in the prestigious Colborne Orchestra, and she wanted everyone to know that she had earned it in spite of threats, taunts, and the alienation of being the only black violinist in the school, in Atlanta, in the state of Georgia. She had prevailed to audition for the premiere music schools in the country. She planned to leave them with a musical presentation to remember. The Colborne's music director suggested the material. Something no one else in her class could play—the Sibelius Violin Concerto in D Minor, opus forty-seven. "They'll be impressed," he'd said. "No matter how they feel about the color of your skin, they won't be able to deny your ability." She'd practiced hundreds, maybe thousands, of hours, until the bow became an extension of her hand.

Claudine came out of the bathroom to find the velvet dress draped across her bed. She straightened the folds of her slip and pulled it over her head carefully, gently, like it was alive. She was supposed to be there at 11:00 A.M. The people from the New England Conservatory and Juilliard were going to attend special senior auditions for only one day. Twenty minutes of their time was all she needed to land a scholarship. Hattie Mae had said she didn't have to go to her morning classes. Told her to relax and prepare for accolades. Claudine peeked around the corner.

"Hattie Mae? Aint Hattie Mae? Are you here?" Claudine needed to make sure her aunt was gone before she dialed his number. She had to see him. They arranged to meet at their special place, under the bridge, on Sycamore Street, at 9:45 A.M. He would drive her to the Colborne, let her off in the back. He said he couldn't wait to see her in that dress. She prepared meticulously. Everything had to be perfect.

HATTIE MAE COULDN'T concentrate. The pecans weren't ripe enough. The brown sugar was too dry. The pie wasn't going to come out the way he liked it. He would insist that she bake another one, and she didn't have time for that. She had to get to Claudine's audition, witness years of hard work and sacrifice pay off. She'd waited patiently for this day, prepared for its aftermath ever since she gave Claudine that violin. She yearned to say a prayer, ask God to give her strength, until she remembered she wasn't on speaking terms with the Almighty anymore.

She didn't tell Harlan about Claudine's audition. His dim-witted daughter wasn't asked to perform, for anybody, so knowing about Claudine's good fortune would be enough to put him in a surly mood. He was petty that way. The governor had a mean streak, and she was trying not to see it today. He was in a meeting with the mayor of Atlanta, and she wanted to be long gone before he came barreling in, shouting for his damn pie. He'd order her to make pies for every mayor in Georgia just because he could. Hattie Mae glanced nervously at the clock: 9:18 A.M. She rolled the dough faster. Time wasn't going to wait for her.

WILLY EARL RUBBED Crisco liberally around his neck. He had a touch of eczema trying to creep toward his face. His mama, Mozell, said Crisco could cure anything. He'd been buying cans of it ever since, carrying smaller portions around in tin foil, in case his skin started to scale up. He picked his teeth with an old matchbook he found on the floor and scanned the room for a decent pair of shoes with thick soles. Things were looking up, and the sooner he escaped this shack and got away from his foul-mouthed mama, the sooner life would be the way it was supposed to be . . . easy.

"Boy, where you think you gone? I'm done wiping you ass, you 'ear . . . Cans everywhere. Clean up this mess and stop eating all me damned food."

"Awl, Mama, I was gonna t-t-take care of it when I got back. I'm meeting Claudine, remember? She's got that b-b-big audition today, downtown."

"Aha, stupid boy. Ya think that aun-tee of 'ers gonna let you in de family? She done already bashed your 'ead in once, vexed your tongue. Damn fool you are. I thought that thrashin' would learn you, but no . . . your brain is like de inside of a banana. You 'ave mush for brains, you know."

Mozell slapped Willy Earl on the back of the head disgustedly as she walked by. He'd been a drain, a leech, ever since he squirmed out of her womb. She was tired of looking at him day in and day out, his constantly hanging around, eating her out of house and home, talking like she'd dropped him on his head or something. He always seemed to have money for cars and big-tittied girls but never any for her. "Selfish, stuttering bastard, this one," Mozell muttered under her breath. He reminded her of his useless fathers. The day he was conceived she was so joyful, jubilant even, inexplicably foolish. She'd left Montserrat and all its poverty behind and was thrilled at the prospect of becoming wealthy in America. So thrilled that she had slept with two men—one named Willy, one called Earl. She'd figured that she'd cover all of her bases, in case either one ever became rich and wanted to marry her. That was nineteen years ago, and she was still waiting for an affluent but witless husband who would never come. Meanwhile, since she did have Willy Earl burrowing under her skin like a tick, it was his turn to provide, for a change. His turn to buy the potted meat, the Spam, and those little weenies she adored that came in a can. His turn to bring home some real cheese from the market instead of the oblong kind that she had to stand in line for.

Although she believed him to be a lumpkin, Mozell Jenkins wanted—prayed fervently for—Willy Earl to weasel himself between Claudine's legs and into Hattie Mae's assets, because if he did, Mozell wouldn't be too far behind. A wee one would make her family.

"Willy Earl! Willy Earl!"

"Wha-what, Mama? I'm cl-cl-cleaning."

"That's all right, son. I'll take care of it. You go on, now, and take this 'ere dollar and buy de girl a soda water."

Willy Earl took the money and shoved it in his pocket without question. He refused to let Mozell and her ever-changing moods aggravate him today. He was beside himself. Today was his baby's audition. Hell, he might as well quit his job at Snookie's and start packing for Boston, New York, anywhere. He hadn't been able to see her since the funeral, but he'd anticipated the call. She couldn't stay away from "The Earl." She loved his dirty drawers. Willy Earl smiled into his rearview mirror. As soon as Claudine started bringing in the big money, he was going to get a gold tooth to match his car, maybe even one with his initial on it. She was going to make so much money that he'd be able to spell his whole name out if he wanted to. Willy Earl Jenkins. He had to calculate in his head if he had enough teeth in his mouth to accommodate his name.

He'd never met a girl like Claudine before, someone with real goals and aspirations. Willy Earl didn't know what a violin was until she showed it to him. Now she was looking all fine, too. The boys weren't teasing him anymore, no sir, or calling her Fat Deeny. They all wanted her for themselves, trying to horn in on his gold mine. "Shiesty ba-ba-bastards." Well, Claudine belonged to him, and the sooner he made it official the better. Shut everybody the hell up, including that overly possessive aunt of hers. Always has to tell a brother what to do, like she's the governor or somebody. Willy Earl wanted to see her try that from six states away. He didn't care how much money or influence Hattie Mae thought she had; he was going to be the only person making the decisions for Claudine from now on.

Willy Earl kissed the dash of his antique gold Impala, started the engine, and checked his watch: 9:35 A.M. He'd arrive at their special place just in time. Warm her up some before she played. Give her a little taste of the Willy man. He was at the corner of Denniker and Sherman, eight blocks from Sycamore Street, when he heard an awful hissing sound coming from the radiator.

CLAUDINE ARRIVED ON time at their special place under the bridge. She was immediately disappointed when she didn't see Willy Earl leaning on the Impala, waiting for her, grinning. It was unlike him to be late. She stood on an old crate, closed her eyes, and practiced in her head, making the motions with her hands. Maybe by the time she finished the Allegro moderato, he'd be behind her. Five minutes in, she felt his breath on the back of her neck. She smiled and finished the concerto before she spoke, hoping he was as excited to see her as she was him. But before she could open her eyes or utter his name, she was overcome with trepidation.

"Don't turn around," the man said, pushing her down. She reached for her case, avoiding looking at his face. She wanted to feel the handle in her hand because she intended to run at the first chance she got, fight him if she had to, kick him in the groin as hard as she could, just like Hattie Mae had taught her. She was stronger now. There was no extra weight to hold her back. She could get away. He must have sensed her intention because he kicked the case out of her hand and pressed something hard against the middle of her back.

"Get up."

"Please," she begged, starting to cry as he roughly shoved her forward, toward an abandoned shack on the other side of the railroad tracks.

"Please, I have ten dollars in my purse. Take it, please."

But he didn't answer her. He didn't say anything else while they walked.

"Please don't hurt me. Please, I have somewhere to be. Oh, God, please let me go." She continued to beg. He nudged harder.

"I won't tell anybody if you just let me go. Please."

She looked around, terrified, one last time for Willy Earl, anybody. He grabbed her hair, forced her head forward, and called her by name. No one would hear her scream. No one would admire her black velvet dress with the pearls sewn onto the hem, and no one would listen to her Sibelius Violin Concerto in D Minor and marvel at her God-given gift. Claudine stared straight ahead, fear filling every pore of her body. Everything inside of her said panic, scream, run away, but she knew, without a doubt, that if she tried, he would rape her and then kill her. There was something in his voice that was devoid of any humanity or compassion for a girl who was about to miss the opportunity of a lifetime.

CHAPTER 16

"Please, Mr. Coroniti . . . just a few more minutes. She'll be here. I know she'll be here."

Even as Hattie Mae found the words to plead for their patience, she knew Claudine was not coming. She didn't know how she knew; she just knew everything was falling apart. The people from the New England Conservatory had left more than twenty minutes ago. Waiting for a colored girl to play for them was not an option, nor was it even considered. But Hattie Mae believed she could persuade Mr. Coroniti. He seemed a cultured man, a man interested in true genius. She would get on her knees if she had to.

"We have a plane to catch, Ms. Jones. We can't possibly be detained any longer. Perhaps attending Juilliard isn't as important to Claudine as you'd anticipated."

"No. You don't understand. Playing the violin means the world to her. Please . . . you won't be disappointed. Just give her—"

"I'm sorry. There is nothing more we can do here. It wouldn't be fair to the musicians who were here to audition on time. Now please . . . release my arm."

Hattie Mae continued to appeal to his good nature, urging him to miss his plane for Claudine's sake; she promised him the world. Told him that Claudine was everything he'd heard about and more. He had stopped listening. Hattie Mae had been to the front of the school countless times, peering in every bus that stopped, searching for Claudine, praying she would come running around the corner. It was 11:45 A.M. and there was still no sign of her. How could she do this to herself, to them? All these years of hard work wasted. Hattie Mae would kill her, wring her skinny little neck. Was Claudine lying underneath that stupid boy? Did she risk everything for that boy? No, something was seriously wrong. Hattie Mae could feel it in her bones.

The Colborne music director was trying to pacify her while she watched Mr. Coroniti, the man who was to decide the course of Claudine's future, walk down the steps, get into a rented Lincoln, and disappear with two decades' worth of dreams. Hattie Mae was completely confounded. She hadn't planned on Claudine missing her own audition. This scenario had never occurred to her. She felt nauseous and swayed slightly, almost losing her balance. She started walking to her car, mentally listing all of the places where she would look for Claudine. She'd drive to that boy's house and slap his mama. Thankfully, she didn't need to go looking for Willy Earl, because she spotted his gold Impala speeding around the block, narrowly missing a pedestrian. She snapped open her purse. She would shoot him square in the balls, right here, right now, if he had anything to do with this. Watch him bleed to death in front of all of these people. She should have had him committed when she had the chance, given him more than a stammer to remember her by. He had no idea what he'd ruined. She clutched her finger around the trigger. He was running toward her, yelling her name like a damn fool. He was carrying something familiar under his arm. She released her grip on the small, pearl-handled revolver and reached for the violin.

"Hattie Mae," he said, tears filling his eyes. "I think somebody done hurt Claudine."

"Spit it out, boy. We don't have all day."

"I-I-I was late. My mem-mem-memory hasn't been the same since you cr-cr-cracked my head."

"Did you call her? Did you plan this whole thing?"

"No, she ca-called me. I-I swear. She said she was nervous."

"And then what?" she questioned, her face close to his.

"I was s-s-supposed to drive her to the Col-Colborne, but something was wrong with my ca-ca-car."

Willy Earl continued to explain, almost soiling himself at the thought of Hattie Mae smashing his extremities, limb by limb, if something disastrous had befallen Claudine. He told how he'd known something was wrong when he discovered her violin lying there, in the dirt, like it didn't belong to anybody. He knew she wouldn't have left it. How he'd called out for her, looked around everywhere. "It's my fa-fa-fault," he repeated, over and over again.

Hattie Mae phoned Harlan before she headed down there herself. She demanded that a search party be formed. She wanted the state troopers involved, bloodhounds, whatever it took. She wanted him to use everything at his disposal to find Claudine, exhaust every possibility. He claimed he couldn't organize all that for a colored girl, just wouldn't look right. She would have ripped his heart out with her bare hands if he had been standing in front of her. "Claudine won't be the only one missing if you don't help me," she informed him. Some people would meet her on Sycamore Street, help her look for the girl. He promised.

Hattie Mae and Willy Earl drove in silence, neither finding anything to say that would lessen the tragedy that was unfolding ruthlessly before them. Willy Earl wanted to tell Hattie Mae that he was sorry. He wanted her to know that he was in love with Claudine, intended to marry her no matter what had happened. He tried again to open his mouth. She managed to speak first.

"I'm gone have to cancel the party."

"The party?"

"Ordered a red velvet cake from the best bakery across town, cream cheese frosting, her favorite."

"I don't understand. You mean for after the audition?" Willy Earl asked, bewildered.

"Today is her birthday, you idiot," she said, her words laced with contempt.

"She never told me. I didn't know," Willy Earl whispered, scooting closer to the door, wondering how badly he would be hurt if he jumped out of a moving car.

"That's not gone save you, boy, if we don't find her, 'cause I told you to leave her be. You better start praying, Willy Earl Jenkins. I mean you better start praying *now*."

CHAPTER 17

Claudine finally saw him. He wanted her to. His face was so close to hers that she could count the hairs in his nose. His eyes were unlike anything she'd ever seen. The left one was blue and the other brown. When he stared at her with eyes like that, he looked like something not of this world, a demon in a man's body. He was tall, taller than Hattie Mae, and wore nice cologne, the kind you buy at the department store. He was impeccably dressed and very careful not to dirty his pants when he removed them. He knew who she was, where she lived. He said she should keep the fat off; she looked sexier that way, more attractive. He slashed her black velvet dress with a fancy-looking switchblade. Asked if the pearls were real as he shoved them into his jacket pocket. He couldn't decide if he was finished with her.

"If you lie real still and don't give me any trouble, I won't carve up that pretty brown face of yours," he declared after he'd violated her a third time. She wanted to tell him that it didn't matter anymore, but her voice was eluding her. She thought for sure he could see it in her eyes—resignation, surrender. Didn't he realize by now that she was ready to die?

She could feel blood seeping slickly between her thighs. She ached to move, shift position, but her insides were on fire.

She didn't want to draw any more attention to herself, so she closed her eyes and pretended that she'd passed out. It wasn't far from the truth. She didn't know how long she'd been there, or where *there* was, exactly. Was it still today, or tomorrow? He'd taken delight in waving weapons in front of her face. First the gun, then the switchblade. He'd threatened to fillet her like a piece of catfish if she ever told anybody, described his features. If her voice ever reappeared, she'd tell him that the last thing she wanted to do was remember what he looked like or explain that he wore expensive shoes and was missing two fingers on his right hand. She'd never seen him before and hoped to God she'd never see him again.

They found her hours later, at dusk, in the old abandoned shack, behind the trees, on the other side of the railroad tracks. The dogs picked up her scent from the dented violin case left behind. She lay naked, on her side, curled up in a corner, hugging her knees to her chest, bloodied, disoriented, not moving or responding to her name. The first policeman to arrive thought she was dead until another held a mirror under her nose. Hattie Mae wouldn't allow anyone to touch her. She ordered everyone out, removed her own blouse and coat, and covered Claudine up as best she could.

"Please, sweet Jesus, please, let her be all right. Claudine! Claudine! Can you hear me? Open your eyes, baby. Open your eyes." Hattie Mae gently stroked the side of Claudine's face, repeated her name until her own voice was almost gone, and silently rejoiced when she saw a flicker of the eyelids, a small sign of recognition. Claudine was bruised, yes; time would tell if she was broken.

Hattie Mae had hoped that Claudine would never have to suffer anything like this. She had hoped that she herself had endured enough indignity for the both of them. They were going to get through this. They had to. The two of them had not come this far to be knocked down by another lowlife who thought he'd conquered a woman's soul just because he stole something from between her legs. Everything was going to have to be put on hold, and that was all right for now, because she intended to rectify this situation, for Claudine and for herself. Hattie Mae would find out who'd hurt her baby if she had to lie next to Harlan Tillford for another eighteen years. For Claudine, she could bear it, remaining here a little while longer. This was simply a small setback, and she was more than familiar with those. Nothing ever came easy for Hattie Mae. Escaping Georgia would be no different. Still, she was determined to restore the dream, have the life she'd planned for. Half dressed, she bent over, prepared to lift her daughter and take her home. Claudine reached out blindly. Someone had finally come for her. Hattie Mae held her close and shielded Claudine's face from the glare of the police lights.

"It's all right now, sweet baby, Mama's here."

Part 2

CHAPTER 18

Willy Earl couldn't believe that Hattie Mae was allowing him to be in the same room with Claudine, visit on a regular basis. It almost made him feel like he was significant. He knew she blamed him for what happened to Claudine. Hell, he blamed himself. If only he'd been there on time. Why hadn't he checked his oil the night before? He frequently replayed various scenarios in his head, but the result was always the same. He consistently came out the failure, the one who'd let her down, left her there alone. It had been a month since the incident, and Claudine hadn't spoken to anyone except Adell. Hattie Mae didn't tolerate anybody talking about what happened in that shack on the other side of those tracks, said it didn't do a damn bit of good to dwell on misery.

Hattie Mae and Adell took turns sitting with Claudine, feeding her, bathing her, walking her to the bathroom. Seemed like a different doctor was at the house every other day, some black, some white, one even Chinese; Hattie Mae was trying them all, anything to get that bow back in Claudine's hand.

Willy Earl still wanted to marry Claudine, but a part of him was perturbed that someone got to the goodie box first. He knew Claudine hadn't given it away willingly, but he found himself wondering what she'd been doing before the guy arrived. What she'd said to make that man take what belonged to him, Willy Earl. Maybe it was that dress she had on, or the way she spoke. She'd teased him earlier, over the phone, claimed she looked like a fashion model right out of *Ebony* magazine. She probably shouldn't have worn it. Maybe she'd lost too much weight for her own good. She'd been attracting a lot of male attention lately. He wanted to ask her about these suspicions when she could talk, but he knew Hattie Mae would surely cleave his head from his body. She'd already told him he was living on borrowed time. Claudine wouldn't look at him anyway, turned her face toward the wall when he came to visit; but she never let go of his hand, and that kept him coming back. If anybody could fix Claudine, get her back on her feet, make those biscuits grant her another audition, Hattie Mae could. So Willy Earl decided to wait for her. What the hell else was he going to do?

Hattie Mae observed her every day, waiting impatiently for some sign of improvement. For the past eighteen years, she'd distanced herself from Claudine for the girl's own good. She'd done what she had to do to survive, and one day Claudine would understand that. An explosive dose of reality had passed between them that horrendous night, and Hattie Mae knew that Claudine finally realized to whom she belonged. Whether she'd truly heard Hattie Mae's admission of motherhood or not, the raw truth of it was in Claudine's eyes. Eventually she'd have a whole mess of explaining to do, but not today. Hattie Mae put on her coat, which she'd since bought new, and kissed Claudine on the forehead. She reached for her hand, but Claudine promptly snatched it away. Hattie Mae sighed; enough was enough. She'd allowed this wallowing to go on for too long already. She would tell Adell to leave early today. It was time for Claudine to stand on her own two feet. Tonight, when she got home, if Claudine was still in that bed, like a damn vegetable, she was going to light it on fire. Hattie Mae refused to acknowledge Willy Earl sitting there. She likened him to a bump on a log, a wart on a frog, a malignancy that had spread. The sight of the boy made her want to crush his bones to dust, but she believed his presence was good for Claudine. Maybe she'd heal faster if she believed that she had that bug-eyed fool to look forward to. Hattie Mae stood in the doorway until he got the hint and reached for his jacket. She leaned over and spoke softly, so only he would hear her.

"The best part of you dripped down your daddy's leg."

He swallowed hard and avoided her piercing stare. She made sure that he knew he wasn't allowed to be there unless she was present to supervise his visits. He'd torn his drawers with her, and she'd never give him another pair. "If a man can't keep his word, he ain't worth the dirt he's standing on," she'd told him just yesterday. She continued to ignore his pathetic attempts to speak to her, make conversation like he was a man worth getting to know. She quickly waved Adell in and shooed Willy Earl out the back door, like an unwanted fly.

"HATTIE MAE, I think you've spent enough time with that gal, now. You know I want you here in the mornings. I like fresh pie, not night-before pie."

"For Heaven's sakes, Harlan, stop whining. Pie is pie."

"You trying to sass me, Hattie Mae?"

"I don't want to do this right now. I'm tired. I been taking care of Claudine. She ain't doing too well. I know that don't matter much to you, Harlan, but it does to me. Now tell me what you want, already, so I can get on with it."

"Oh, so now you're trying to tell me what to do? What the devil's gotten into you lately? I think you've gotten a little too comfortable around here, forgotten where you came from."

"How can I possibly? I've had to look at your pasty little face for the past eighteen years."

Hattie Mae worked with her back to him and continued pitting cherries. She sensed him coming for her, so she steeled herself for contact and allowed him to spin her around, to save time. He grabbed her wrists and twisted. She looked down at him, bored by the distraction.

"Maybe I ought to send you back there, revoke your parole. I can do that. I'm the goddamned governor, you know," he said calmly, releasing her arms. "So you think about that the next time you open your mouth."

She could smell his breath, a sickening combination of bacon and bourbon. He was so completely predictable—the same expressions, the usual smells, and always the same threats. She ignored the slight throbbing in her wrists and hoped that he'd go away, leave her be. She was considerably older now. Going back to jail didn't scare her as much as leaving Claudine. He actually thought he could get along without her. She started to hum one of Claudine's sonatas, infuriating him further.

"Folks always said I've been too easy on you. I think that mouth of yours has finally landed you in a whole heap of trouble. Maybe I'll get that sweet niece of yours to take your place here, start baking my pies. Hear tell she's looking mighty fine lately." He licked his lips after he said it, causing Hattie Mae to stop humming and start running.

Governor Tillford never expected her to actually knock him down. He wasn't prepared to defend himself against a woman who was at least a foot taller and thirty pounds heavier. She held him on the ground, like a man, pinning his arms to his sides. It surprised him that he couldn't move. She didn't appear deranged. She looked like the same old Hattie Mae, but with something extra, something the governor hadn't seen in a long time. She was jealous, scared that he wanted to bed her niece. She wanted to keep him all to herself. Despite his confusion about this bizarre exchange, he felt his face flushing and the little buddy down below swelling with excitement. She leaned toward him. He lifted his hips. He'd always known that it would be only a matter of time before she desired him the way he constantly ached for her. The old girl was throwing him down, finally trying to take it. He moaned with anticipation. She slammed the back of his head against the cold granite floor.

"If you ever lay one hand on Claudine, I'll separate your soul from your body with my bare hands."

He wiggled from underneath her. Fury filled him, while pure sexual heat flooded his groin. Was Hattie Mae actually threatening him? She must have woken up this morning and lost her black mind. He walked toward the phone. He'd have Jimmy come pick her up, put her back into the system for a few days. That would teach her to fuck with him. Just whom did she think she was fooling with? The Metro was probably a lot worse now. She'd obviously forgotten what it was like to be in a place like that. She'd be humble enough when she returned, beg his forgiveness, and he'd make her pay for this willful display. And after everything he'd done for her. He started to dial.

"Harlan."

Let her beg. It wouldn't matter if she got down on all fours. She was going back to prison tonight.

"Governor."

He turned around. He wanted to see her cry. He'd never seen her cry.

"If you send me back there, I'm not going alone. Do you think that after all these years I haven't protected myself? I know who you are, Harlan Tillford, and by this time tomorrow the whole world, including your sweet Lavender, will know what you've done, what you're capable of doing."

He stared at her angrily. She wasn't afraid of him anymore. He'd let it go for now, allow her to think that she'd won. He hung up the phone and adjusted his suspenders, his eyes never leaving her face.

"So what'll it be, Harlan?"

"What choice do I have?"

"Apple or cherry."

CHAPTER 19

*T*he relentless pounding on the door startled Claudine from a troubled sleep. She kept her eyes closed, nevertheless, and waited for Adell to answer it. She didn't. Claudine willed whomever it was to go away, leave her be, but they just kept knocking as if they knew she was in there by herself. She glanced through the bedroom doorway for Adell, somebody. There would be hell to pay later if Hattie Mae, her mother, discovered that she'd been left alone. That didn't even sound right, her mother. She'd heard that quiet confession that terrible night, digested it like it was bad fish. For days afterward, she'd believed that the whole occurrence had been some heinous nightmare and she had time to make her audition, create a new page in her life story. She had wafted in and out of reality until lingering pain forced unwanted clarity. Yes, she knew the rape had been real. She could still smell him in her sleep, still feel the rawness between her thighs. But Hattie Mae saying that she was her mother . . . that, that had to be a vicious lie. A delicate admission that Claudine thought she'd heard during moments of delirium when she couldn't even remember who she was. Her mama was Willamina Jenkins, dead and buried. Isn't that what everyone said? Her mama . . . her mama couldn't be Hattie Mae Jones—but instinctively, in her heart, she'd known all along that there was more going on in her family than she had been led to believe. She couldn't put all the pieces together, but she understood why Willamina never really gave a damn about her. She wasn't her mama. She was never her mama. That was what Willamina had been trying to tell her that day, before Luther Mack knocked the truth out of her mouth. How convenient it must have been for Hattie Mae that Willamina had passed away before she could expose Hattie Mae's deception. The woman Claudine had believed was her mother was dying to tell her that her real mother lived next door, pretending to be her aunt for eighteen years. And what about Bone? How could Hattie Mae mistreat him that way, her own son? And Luther Mack? Who knew where he fit into this whole sordid mess? The two of them had hidden their affair very well, pretending that they despised each other. What a show they'd been putting on all of these years. No wonder Willamina was an alcoholic. As far as Claudine was concerned, they could all go straight to hell. She didn't know who she was anymore, and she would never forgive them for that.

The pounding persisted. Maybe Adell had forgotten her key this time. No, that old woman never forgot a damn thing. Adell was the one person to whom Hattie Mae ever really talked, and Claudine suspected that she'd known the circumstances of her birth all along. Adell was the only person whom Hattie Mae trusted. No one understood why, and questions regarding their alliance were not permitted.

"All right, already. I'm coming." Claudine eased out of bed.

"Well, hurry up, then, and open the damn door."

"Who is it?" she asked, now knowing full well who stood on the other side.

"It's yo daddy, and I got something for ya."

He was dressed in a navy blue pin-striped suit, a crisp white shirt, and a tan-colored hat cocked to one side. Claudine searched his face carefully for any resemblance to her own.

She couldn't find any and wasn't surprised. Another mystery for "Mother" to solve.

"You been laying up in here for too long. 'Bout time you get your ass up, get a job, get some meat back on your bones. Told ya you weren't going nowhere behind that fiddle. But see, nobody wanted to listen to the Deacon, though."

Claudine followed him into the kitchen, watched him unload three large bags filled with food.

"Now eat up. You didn't have to worry about anybody messin' with ya when your ass was as wide as the Grand Canyon. Walkin' around here like you some kind of superstar. I bet you won't be prancin' around Sycamore Street no mo', flauntin' some pearl dress. Yes, Lord, I heard all about it. This ought to teach your uppity ainty that she ain't God. She ain't nobody. She wanna act like . . ."

Claudine didn't hear him. The smells emanating from the greasy paper bags enticed her forward. The Deacon and his condemnations didn't exist anymore. Hunger welled up deep inside of her, whispering, Eat, Fat Deeny, and be free. It was calling her, tempting her to remember who she was. In a way, she felt as if she'd betrayed herself by losing all of the weight. Excess had always kept her from harm's way. For years it had been a buffer, a thick shield that kept unsavory thoughts and unpleasant people from penetrating her interior. Now she was thin, raped, ruined, and without the one element in her life that validated her existence, made her feel worthy. No more Betty, no more auditions, no more Colborne. And Willy Earl, why would he possibly want her now? She was damaged goods. Certainty struck her while she stood there watching the Deacon unpack various containers of pan-fried calories. If she had been herself, that vile man would have never wanted her. If she had been herself, she'd be living in another state right now, performing to her heart's content. And in that moment of revelation, the enemy once again became her friend. She started with the honey-fried chicken, moved on to the macaroni and cheese, then a whole catfish with candied yams, and finished with an entire pineapple upside-down cake. She ate, threw up, rested a while, and ate again until two bags were completely empty. Luther Mack watched her intently, with a smug smile of satisfaction.

"Go on, girl, don't waste that food . . . people starvin' in China."

The Deacon left somewhere between the hot-water corn bread and the creamed corn, satisfied that she was weaker than when he had found her. Claudine left a food trail from the kitchen to the dining room for Hattie Mae to discover. There was nothing more for her to do except wait until her stomach settled so she could eat some more. Tomorrow she'd move back next door, sleep in Willamina's bed. The Deacon had been right all along: playing that "fiddle" didn't get her anywhere.

HATTIE MAE WALKED into the dining room to find Adell on her hands and knees, scrubbing barbecue sauce off the hardwood floor. Empty containers of food were piled on the china cabinet, and used, balled-up napkins were trying to make a home on her mahogany table that no one was allowed to eat on. If she didn't know any better, she'd swear that somebody was about to feel pain.

"Where's Claudine?"

Adell shook her head and pointed toward the bedroom. Claudine was sitting up, still in her nightclothes, staring out of the window.

"Claudine! Claudine! What is going on here? You obviously feelin' better, I see. Eating all that damn food like that. You trying to blow up again?"

"I got out of bed. Isn't that what you wanted?"

"Who was here? Who brought you all of this temptation?"

Chicken crumbs littered the imported white bedspread, which meant that grease stains couldn't be too far behind.

Hattie Mae waited for an answer. The girl didn't look right. She was acting like she was touched in the head. Hattie Mae turned and yelled at Adell to bring the broom.

"Tomorrow is a new day," Hattie Mae murmured. Tomorrow they would start over. She'd retrieve the violin from the closet in her bedroom, make the girl start practicing again. She felt Claudine trying to stare a hole in the back of her head. It was unnerving. "You have something you wanna say to me, Claudine?"

Claudine licked a lone piece of macaroni and cheese from her forearm and brushed crumbs onto the floor.

"Well, say it, then. Christmas is coming."

"What's taking Adell so long with that broom?" Claudine asked sarcastically.

Hattie Mae slammed the door. This wasn't going to be easy. Miss Claudine was going to have to get past this, whether she wanted to or not. She was going to have to realize that sometimes bad things happen, but they don't define who you are. They knock you down for a spell, but you have to pick yourself up, start over, make a way for yourself. Hattie Mae wanted to confide in her daughter that she understood firsthand what it was like to have something precious stolen from you while you watched helplessly, to lose everything you worked for your whole life. Hattie Mae wanted to tell her that everything she'd done—leaving her with the Deacon and Willamina, degrading herself every day for nineteen years with the likes of Harlan Tillford, selling her soul to get that violin—everything had been for her. Hattie Mae wanted her to know that she'd kill to protect her.

Hattie Mae was going to guide Claudine back to where she was supposed to be, on stage, exuberant, playing like her life depended on it. It was just going to take a little more time. Meanwhile, there was somebody she had to take care of.

CHAPTER 20

"*S*ee, that's what I'm talking about. Don't let your mouth write a check yo ass can't cash, nigguh."

"Awl, c'mon, man! You done won the last three games. Leave me enough to get a bottle of muscatel."

"You betta run home to yo mama, 'cause I'm fixin' to take her money, too."

Luther Mack slammed another domino on the card table in the living room of one of his longtime mistresses, Beulah. He was rolling now, up two hundred dollars and counting. He knew this fool wasn't going to be able to pay, and that was what he was counting on. He'd make him work it off, doing anything he wanted him to do. That was the American way. He was finally beginning to feel like his old self again. He looked mighty clean, damn near caused a ruckus everywhere he went. He had a pocket loaded with Benjamins, head full of waves, and women lined up around the block, waiting their turn to get a lil' taste. Plus a small derringer stuffed in his left boot, in case one of these sorry suckers got a little too jealous of his hellified winning streak.

There were unexpected perks to being a deacon—access to the collection plate on Sundays; good, steady home cooking; and the women, have mercy. The sanctified depended on his guidance, in the pews, between their sheets, wherever they needed his special kind of counseling. He was always being taken care of by this one or that one. And it was a good thing, too, seeing as how that yellow heifer Hattie Mae kicked him out of his own house. Made him pack up his shit in two days, like he was nobody. Evicted him in front of the whole town on the day of Willamina's funeral. A woman like that didn't have any respect. She ran Bone off, and she was trying to run him off, too. Well, Willamina might be having a highball with the devil, trifling ho' that she was, but Claudine was still his daughter. He felt a twinge of regret that the girl went and got herself raped like that, but she needed something to bring her down a peg or two. She and Hattie Mae got the wake-up call that they deserved. Praise Jesus. Hell, everybody was thinking it, but he was the only one to profess it. And he testified every chance he got—on the street, in the pulpit—anywhere he could make his point about people who thought they knew better than the Lord Jesus. He loathed Hattie Mae, always had, but Claudine was still his child, his seed. He had a right to be heard where she was concerned. He'd never been too fond of the girl; but right was right, and after all, he was a Christian man.

He knew that nosey Adell had spotted him taking food over there. He didn't give a good goddamn, either. The girl had to eat something. She was too damn skinny for her own good. He liked her better fat anyway. She kept her mouth shut then, did whatever he said without giving him all that lip. Lying up in the bed like that, doing nothing. It was downright shameful, but then again, she came by it naturally. She always was lazy, like her mama. Didn't he tell her she wasn't going anywhere? She could have had a good job by now instead of messing around with that stupid fiddle.

"Well, now, Deacon. Looks like I'm on my way to winning my money back. Whacha got? Whacha got? Un huh, should have been paying attention instead of all that daydreaming."

Luther Mack smiled. His teeth were exquisite, gleamed like they came from a factory. Tonight he was going to make one of these fools wax his car, maybe even cut his toenails, clean out the two cabs he owned.

"C'mon, Deacon, quit stalling. I got ya now, boy! I say all or nuthin', mothafucka. If I win this game, I don't owe you shit."

"All right, but if I win, you owe me double, foe hunnerd, plus a night with yo woman."

"Well, come on with it then. I know you ain't got shit."

Luther Mack watched them all watching him. He liked to showboat, leave them something to remember him by. He winked at Benny's girlfriend, who'd come out of the kitchen. Dummyseeds. They didn't know who they were dealing with. He was the original high roller, an accomplished hustler at any game. He rolled the dominos around in his hand, pretended to contemplate his next move, and then he started to laugh, a peculiar, deep-sounding laugh that originated in the back of his throat. He maintained eye contact, nodded at the stragglers who'd come for the show.

"Bam!" he shouted, standing up and smacking the winning domino on the table. "Pay up, nigguh, and tell that fine gal of yours to come on. I'm ready to go for a ride." He grabbed his fifty-dollar hat and motioned for Benny's girlfriend. He always did like them round and brown. Shrieks of "Awl, man," "He got you good," and "He gone work your black ass now" followed him outside. They never saw the spare domino Luther Mack pulled out of his left boot, from next to the petite, coal black pistol. And no one saw the tall figure waiting for him in the dark, three steps outside the door.

Hattie Mae followed Luther Mack as he led Benny's girlfriend to his car. She knew what he had been up to, bringing Claudine all that food, trying to take away any last bit of love the girl had left for herself. He wasn't fooling anybody. She also knew he never expected Claudine to become anything worthwhile. He didn't have much of anything pleasant to say about any female. How had he forgotten that he first saw the light of day through a woman's vagina? She didn't know where he thought he came from, behaving that way, like women were beneath him. Well, he wasn't different from any other man. He was too damn cocky, anyhow. Looked to her like he hadn't had a good ass whipping in a long time. She owed him anyway, for trying to break Claudine's hands. Unfortunately for him, she'd never forgotten about that. She was going back on her own word not to involve her contacts, but a woman had to do what a woman had to do.

"What's the problem, officer? I ain't done nothing." Luther Mack shifted uncomfortably in his seat. They'd waited for him to start the car before they ordered him out, guns drawn. There were two of them. Where the hell did they come from? He couldn't even conceal his gun in its special hiding place under the mat, between the two plastic jars of conk. He was screwed, and he knew it. Benny's woman started to talk, trying to convince these crazy crackers to let her go. He told her to shut the hell up.

"You Luther Mack Tilbo?"

"That's my name."

"You trying to get smart with me, boy?"

"No, suh, just wanna know what ya'll think I done."

"You in a load of trouble, Luther Mack. Turn around, boy. We gone have to search you. Said turn around!"

Luther Mack scratched his brain, trying to figure out what they had on him. He was always so careful, but they knew his name. Somebody had sicced the man on him. If Benny did this, he would slice his jugular good. Nobody knew about his stash buried under the garbage cans in the backyard or the illegal guns that he kept in the pantry, underneath the pork rinds.

They made him take his boots off, then his pants.

"Looky, looky here, Deke. I done found me an illegal firearm. Bend over, boy."

They wanted to know if he was hiding anything else up his ass.

"You want us to go on a fishing expedition?"

The big, husky one named Clyde emptied Luther Mack's pockets and took his new hat. Benny's girl just stood there, scared, staring straight ahead. He started to beg.

"I'm a man of the church. I ain't ever done nothing against nobody. Please, now, officers. I respects the law."

"Somebody's accused you of theft. Where you been today, Deacon?"

"I ain't been nowhere, and I ain't stole nothing. This all some kind of mistake. I been around here all day, down at the church, playing a little dominos. Y'all got the wrong man."

"Is that right?"

Luther Mack nodded his head eagerly. They were mocking him. He hoped that if he went along with the game, they'd leave him alone. He'd play dumb. He was good at that. He reached for his pants. Deke, the one who resembled a pole bean, knocked them out of his hand.

"Not so fast, boy. We got us a bonofied eyewitness. All right now, is this who we're looking for?" he hollered over his shoulder.

Luther Mack turned around, saw someone stepping from the shadows, strained his eyes to see the man who'd sold him out. "Well, I'll be goddamned," he heard himself saying.

Hattie Mae looked him up and down, blew cigarette smoke in his face, and smiled when he tried to cover his peter.

"That's him."

The policemen forced his hands behind his back as Hattie Mae began to walk away. The crazy bitch was actually going to let them take him to jail. He called after her.

"Hattie Mae. C'mon now, Hattie Mae. You know I ain't took nothing from you! Hattie Mae." He breathed a sigh of relief when she stopped and looked back.

"Ms. Jones?" the meaty one called, and then motioned with

his hands to see if she wanted the cuffs removed. Luther Mack eagerly stuck his arms out, but her face was hardened, and she wouldn't look in his direction.

"I'll be down in a few days to press charges." She turned to leave and never turned around again. Luther Mack yelled after her. After a while, he didn't even know what he was saying.

CHAPTER 21

*C*laudine stood across the street from the Colborne. She couldn't sit in that house any longer. It was threatening to swallow her whole. She took a bite out of an apple fritter that she'd shoved into her pocket at home and headed back toward the bus. She didn't belong here anymore. This place, everything she'd accomplished, was in the past. No one was going to give her another chance. She had no idea where she was going or what to do with herself. She just wanted to eat. Of that she was certain. It kept her occupied, and while she was busy deciding what to devour next, her thoughts remained still, didn't wander to other things, tempt her to lose her mind. She rode around for hours, sometimes changing buses when she became bored with the scenery. She didn't realize that she was ringing his bell until he answered the door. He invited her in, and she kissed him first this time.

"G-g-girl, Hattie Mae know you here?"

Claudine scanned the small room. She'd never been in a house so tiny.

"Does your mama live here with you?

"Yeah. She at work."

"I've got my own place now."

"What you t-talking about?"

"I moved back next door, on the other side of the duplex." Claudine looked down at the frayed brown carpet. "It was my . . . mama's, so now it belongs to me." She didn't want Willy Earl to know that Hattie Mae was her mother. She didn't want anyone to know, ever. As far as she was concerned, her mama was a drunk, dead from trying to live somebody else's lie.

"Well, this calls for a sp-special celebration, then. Whacha wanna do?"

Claudine removed her coat. "Whatever you want to do."

"Anything?" Willy Earl said, raising his eyebrow.

"Anything," Claudine responded, her eyes glossing over. She'd dreamed of wrapping her legs around Willy Earl, often fantasized about what their first time would be like. She'd wanted it to be extraordinary, something they'd both remember. Now, what difference did it make? He knew she wasn't a virgin anymore, and they were alone. There was no need to beat around the bush. She needed to restart her life, and now was just as good a time as any.

Willy Earl waited for her to say something else. Tell him that she was messing with his head. But she just sat there, on his mama's lopsided bed, staring at him like she really wanted him to bring it on, use his third leg, and she wasn't acting all shy about it, either. He'd heard of stuff like this happening, girls damn near giving it away, although it had never happened to him personally, until now. He'd lied so much in the past about getting the trim that he'd convinced himself, along with everybody else. Girls always said he looked like a june bug. True, he'd had his share of hair pie, but he was always the one doing the chasing. Times were changing. That was for damn sure. Claudine looked different, though, almost like it didn't matter to her one way or another. She definitely wasn't the same Claudine, but he wasn't going to allow that minor detail to get in the way of a prime opportunity to finally get some loving. He probably wouldn't even hurt her, seeing as how somebody else broke her in first. Willy Earl began to unbutton his shirt. He'd go in to work late for this. Snookie would understand.

Claudine couldn't manage to remove her own clothes, so he helped her. She wanted to go home, tell him she'd made a mistake, but her mouth refused to open. He'd hate her if she made him stop now, and then she'd be alone. He laid her out on the bed, naked, and sucked his teeth.

"Damn, baby, you-you-you sho' look good."

She tried not to peer at his thing, hanging there, resembling a long, fat worm. She closed her eyes, pretended like she was in Willamina's kitchen, eating smothered pork chops, mashed potatoes, sugar snap peas. She felt him climbing on top of her.

"I'm glad you c-c-came over."

Claudine knew he must have been inside of her. It was as if her whole body was collapsing around him. He moved slowly at first, whispering declarations in her ear that she couldn't decipher. With all the stuttering and spitting, he might as well have been speaking another language. She wasn't aware that she began to guide her hips or that she moaned at this new-found state of arousal. Something was happening to her, and she began to whimper softly. She noticed an unfamiliar sensation spreading through her body, experienced intense heat building between her thighs, but was unable to savor it because shame got in the way. And after a while, she didn't feel anything at all but the swelling of her clitoris.

Claudine didn't want him to drive her home, but Willy Earl insisted and she didn't have the energy to argue.

"Are you okay, b-b-baby? Did I hurt you? D-did you like it?"

She nodded. That's all she could manage to do. She'd thought maybe she'd feel different afterward, but she still felt the same, ruined.

"Y-y-you want me to d-d-drop you off at the c-c-corner?"

"No. You can drive me to the front door."

He was shocked at her answer. She obviously didn't care

anymore if Hattie Mae saw them. She was eighteen now. She could do whatever she wanted.

"You want to come in for a while?"

Willy Earl looked at Claudine like she'd lost her mind. He attempted to discuss it, like he had a right to, before she got out of the car.

"When you gone m-m-make up with Betty, start playing again?"

She didn't answer him. She didn't know where the violin was or what had happened to it. Betty had been her companion for years, the one constant she could depend on. She couldn't think about that violin without remembering how he'd kicked it out of her hand.

"I know you hear me," Willy called after her.

Claudine kept walking up the stairs. Hattie Mae had a pie in there somewhere. She was always baking pies.

CHAPTER 22

*H*attie Mae had felt herself slipping into some kind of strange depression. It wasn't like her. She snapped out of it. She didn't have time for one of those hysterical breakdowns that only white women could afford. God help her, she didn't know what else to do with the girl. Most times, she just wanted to sock some sense into her, drag her by the hair, force her to play that damn violin until her fingers were sore and cramping. Claudine wouldn't even talk about it, and if she wouldn't talk about it, Hattie Mae didn't know how she was going to convince her to go anywhere near it, let alone pick up the damn bow. She'd thought about taking Claudine on a trip somewhere, but she herself would be too tempted not to come back. She wasn't prepared to tangle with Harlan just yet. Ever since their tense encounter, when he'd threatened to send her back to the Metro, things hadn't been the same. He was short with her, called himself having an attitude. She wondered how long it would take him to figure out that she didn't give a damn. She'd catch him watching her when he thought she wasn't paying attention. She knew he was up to something, scheming and plotting like the dog he was, and she had to be ready.

That fool Luther Mack was still in the pokey, been over a month now. She'd decided to let him stew in there a few more days before she dropped the charges. It was essential that he knew how far she would go to protect Claudine. She wanted him to experience real apprehension, genuine fear. Trifling-ass man. One day she'd have to put him out of his misery, tell him the truth. Harlan had found out that she'd had him arrested, used his influence to keep that idiot in jail. The governor wanted to kill him, assumed that Luther Mack had broken in to get to her. He went on and on about how he couldn't have anything happen to her. Who would massage his buttocks with warm peanut butter? Who would bake his pies? He'd ordered her to stay over at the mansion for a few weeks, didn't want to let her out of his sight. Sometimes, if only for a moment, he seemed almost human . . . almost. She didn't know how much longer she could go on like this. If only her mama was alive; she'd know what to do. Hattie Mae suddenly felt a lot older than her forty-two years. Exhausted, she reached for the door. Mercifully, he'd said she could go home tonight, sleep in her own bed.

"I'M PREGNANT."

Hattie Mae saw her standing there, heard the words come out of her mouth, but kept asking her to repeat herself anyway.

"What?"

"I said I'm pregnant."

"What?"

"I'm going to have a baby for Willy Earl."

Hattie Mae couldn't believe that Claudine had fixed her face to utter those words and grinned like it was something to be proud of. She folded her arms across her chest to keep from slamming the girl through the wall, shaking her like a rag doll until that baby was a puddle on the floor.

"What about school, Claudine? What about the violin?"

"I'm going to be a mother now. I don't have time for all that nonsense anymore."

Hattie Mae flinched.

"I'm going to take care of my baby."

"And how do you think you're going to do that? I know you don't expect me to take care of it."

"I don't expect you to do anything. Willy Earl has the job at the garage, and I was just offered a job today, a good job."

"This is not right, Claudine."

"Not right for who? You? Why do you care so much, anyway? You never wanted me, and Willy Earl does."

Hattie Mae narrowed her eyes. It was imperative that she maintain control. She couldn't afford to let Claudine see how devastated she was. This would not break her.

"You don't know what the hell you're talking about, Claudine, and no matter how you feel about me, you watch your mouth. You not fooling me, girl. I know what this is about. Don't you stand there and pretend that the Colborne, the concertos, the accolades meant nothing to you."

"That part of my life is over now. I've accepted it. Why can't you?"

"How could you do this? Throw away all these years of hard work for him? Was it worth it, spreading your thighs for him? Did it make you feel better?"

Claudine looked away, unable to hold her mother's gaze, and responded in a whisper.

"He loves me, and that's all that matters now."

"Wake up, girl. That boy doesn't love you. He loves who he thinks you'll allow him to be. He loves everything that you have, sleeping in your expensive bed, rolling around your imported sheets without a roach crawling between his toes. Are you so far gone, Claudine, that you can't see that? Do you hate me this much?"

"Hate is such a strong word, Aunt Hattie Mae."

"Don't you realize that jeopardizing your music career, your life, over this . . . this piece of a man is hurting you more than it's hurting me?"

"You don't have to take care of me, anymore. I'm eighteen now. I can take care of myself and my baby without you."

"Oh, you think so?"

Defiant and nauseated, Claudine remained standing, prepared to feel the back of her mother's hand across her face. She'd never spoken to her like that before, never so much as raised her voice. Now everything had changed between them, and there was no going back to the way things were. She expected more silent fury, threats, another beating perhaps, but Hattie Mae just stood there staring, her face devoid of any emotion.

Hattie Mae watched helplessly as years of planning began to dissipate into nothingness. She wanted to maim that boy, cause him some serious harm again, but she knew she couldn't blame this mess entirely on Willy Earl. It was obvious that Claudine had a hand in this, probably went to the boy willingly, with her legs gapped open. Evidently, Claudine needed to punish her, make her suffer for lying all of these years. All the screaming in the world wasn't going to make this right. What else could possibly go wrong? She grabbed Claudine by the face and held on tightly.

"Girl, do you know what you've done?"

CLAUDINE SAT IN Willamina's old room, the place where she'd died, and rubbed her stomach. She'd called Willy Earl and told him to come over. She wasn't afraid. She wanted this baby. All the times that she and Willy Earl had made love, it had never occurred to her that she might get pregnant. He'd never seemed concerned about it, so she wasn't either. He loved her. He was the only person who had ever loved her. She knew she'd disappointed Hattie Mae, and that somehow made her feel stronger. She was through trying to please her. Hattie Mae was no longer in control of her life. She'd left Hattie Mae over there, staring at the wall. Claudine had informed her that she didn't have to worry. She wasn't going to let her child call Hattie Mae Big Mama or Mudear.

Claudine walked to the back porch. Her future was waiting.

"What are you doing back here?" she asked Willy Earl. He looked around nervously.

"I s-s-saw Hattie Mae's car out front. I almost t-t-turned around. You think she knows I'm here?"

"I don't believe you have to worry about Hattie Mae anymore."

"Wh-why not? You heard what she did to your daddy?"

Claudine ignored him. The Deacon's troubles didn't concern her anymore. For all she knew, he wasn't her daddy anyway. She told Willy Earl about the job first. He couldn't believe her luck.

"Willy Earl, I have more news."

"Bet-bet-better than the job?"

"I'm pregnant."

He just stared at her, eyes as wide as plates. She'd hoped he'd take the news of the baby just as well as she. He did, picking her up, spinning her around until she was tired and out of breath.

Willy Earl raced around the house, moving quickly from room to room. He'd hit the jackpot—not in the way he'd intended, but hit the motherlode just the same. Never in his wildest dreams had he thought that he'd ever live in a neighborhood like this, with these uppity Negroes sipping lemonade and nibbling tea cakes in the middle of the afternoon. He couldn't wait to tell the boys at Snookie's about this. He was in the game now. Shoot, he didn't even mind that she was blowing back up again, getting fatter by the minute. He looked around and grinned broadly. His days of eating potted meat and curried goat were over. This was a long way from his mama's small shack of a house on Hugo Street. Claudine had a real television and a bathroom as big as his whole kitchen. Even if she never became famous or played another note, he still might be able to get those gold teeth, especially with this new job she got herself. He didn't know what kind of drama was going on between Claudine and Hattie Mae, but he liked it. As long as it kept Hattie Mae from going anywhere near that bat, he encouraged the dissension, told Claudine he was the only thing she needed. The sooner he was sleeping in that four-poster bed with her, the better. He had a plan. They didn't call him Willy "The Earl" for nothing.

"Claudine! Claudine! Get up."

"What, Willy Earl?"

"C'mon, b-baby, let's go get married."

CHAPTER 23

*T*he driver, an older man named Cisco, came for her at ten the next morning. He didn't say squat, wasn't much for conversation. She sat stiffly in the back seat, didn't want to wrinkle her new dress. The man who had hired her said that a uniform wasn't required. "Just look real nice, sugar; wear tight dresses and pretty lipstick."

She fumbled nervously with the thin gold band around her finger. Mozell had been so thrilled that she'd put thirty whole dollars toward the ring. Claudine had paid for the rest because Willy Earl said he was saving his money for something special for the baby. He was sweet like that. She'd actually done it, married Willy Earl Jenkins, downtown, just before five. Mozell and a janitor named Punch served as witnesses. The hell with Hattie Mae. They were both of age, didn't need anybody's permission. Now she was everything she never wanted to be— a married woman with a regular job, an ordinary husband, and a baby on the way.

HE WAS WAITING for Hattie Mae in the kitchen, nursing a shot of whiskey at half past ten in the morning, when she arrived. He nodded. He looked glib, like he had a cannon up his sleeve, like he was going to say something that would change her life. Hattie Mae had seen that look before, years ago, when he came to the prison with his seedy entourage in tow. He'd just been elected governor. They stared at each other now, neither wanting to break eye contact first. They had become adversaries. Today was the day he would try to break her again. He spoke first.

"I haven't decided what kind of pie I want today. Maybe I'll have a lemon pie, with a hint of coconut. You think you can do that, Hattie Mae, bake a lemon pie with coconut? As a matter of fact, you know what? Bake lemon pies for everybody in the mansion."

Hattie Mae was annoyed. Was this the best he could do? She would certainly be glad when everything was back to normal. He'd never stayed this testy before. Fool. Coward. Dwarfish freak. Did he actually think that forcing her to make twenty-two pies was going to put her in her place? Make her bow down, cower whenever he strolled into a room? She wasn't that eighteen-year-old girl anymore, scared and naïve, desperate to please him. He couldn't hurt her anymore. She was Harlan-proof. For the life of her, she couldn't figure out how in the world he got decent-minded folk to support him year after year, term after term. Most times, all he wanted to discuss and debate was pie.

She'd never known such a little a man to consume so much pie. She'd baked a pie damn near every day for the past nineteen years: peach, apple, strawberry, sweet potato, lemon, blackberry, and rhubarb. If God made it, she could bake it. Once he even made her bake a pie out of bread crumbs and chitterlings, just to see if she could do it. She baked it, and he ate it, every last slice. Sometimes she even dreamed about pies. She loathed him for that. He wouldn't allow anyone else to make his pies, either, said she had a supernatural gift for crust. She detested pie. Because of him, she couldn't go any-where near it. The thought of eating one made her stomach turn.

"That's a lot of pies, Harlan."

"Governor."

"That's a lot of pies, Governor. Let me get Grace from the laundry. She can help me." Hattie Mae started walking toward the door, trying to calculate how many lemons she was going to need to make twenty-two pies.

"That won't be necessary, Hattie Mae."

"Governor, I need to go to the market. I need—"

"I've hired you some permanent, full-time help. I want you to show this little lady how to make my pies, seeing as how your time here may be coming to an end. Come on in, darlin'."

Hattie Mae watched him guide her into the kitchen, his arm around her waist. She became paralyzed, unable to move, un-able to speak.

"No need for introductions here. I think the two of you al-ready know each other. Well, now, I guess y'all better get to work—got a lot of pies to bake. What was that, Hattie Mae? Did you say something? No? No smart retort? I'll be damned, Claudine. I think I've rendered your aunt speechless."

Confused, Claudine looked from Hattie Mae to the gover-nor and from the governor to Hattie Mae. She'd had no idea that this was where she would be working. The man had said that she'd be working for someone very important. In all the years that she'd known Hattie Mae, Claudine never knew that this was where she came every day. No one did. Now she under-stood where all the money came from, the house, the car, and the private violin lessons. No wonder Hattie Mae never talked about where she went. She was keeping this place all to her-self. What a horrible, selfish woman. She had access to all this wealth and still couldn't raise her own daughter, had to pawn her off on Willamina and the Deacon like she was a piece of unwanted furniture. Claudine waited for some sort of acknowledgment from Hattie Mae, but none came. Hattie Mae just stood there, staring at the governor, her hands gripping the counter, a look of pure hatred masking her face. Willy Earl and Mozell were never going to believe this.

"Where should I put my things?"

No one answered her right away. The governor smiled and reached for her coat and purse.

"Isn't this just wonderful, Hattie Mae?" he said, aiming his lips for Claudine's cheek but gracing her neck instead. "Now we're one big, happy family. And by the way, darlin', that's a lovely dress you're wearing. I think I'm gone have to watch myself around a sweet young thing like you."

Hattie Mae inhaled deeply and heard her mother's voice. "Better to send 'em to Jesus than let one of 'em leave you in pieces."

Hattie Mae was desperate. She'd do anything, even pray to a god who she believed had abandoned her a long time ago. She'd spent the last two decades of her life concealing the truth, keeping Claudine away from here, away from him, and now here she was, waiting for a lesson on how to make lemon pie, his pie, the governor's pie, her daddy's pie. He'd been right about one thing. They were all one big family all right, but nobody in here was happy.

CHAPTER 24

*I*t was Hattie Mae's turn to be silent, introspective. Recently, she'd had nothing remotely kind to say to anyone. No good mornings or good nights, no how was your pie? No nothing. And lately, this maddening inertia, tempting her at every turn. Tribulations were threatening to overwhelm her, and she felt like she was beginning to suffocate from the pressure of it all—the rape, the pregnancy, Claudine working at the mansion, and now this absurd marriage. Did they actually think she was going to sit idly by, baking pies, while the two of them ruined everything? Erasing this marriage was but one more item she needed to add to her to-do list. Liberate herself . . . check, free Claudine from this travesty . . . check, make Willy Earl disappear . . . check, check.

On really dreadful days, she was lured to remain in bed, wrapped in layers of her mama's quilts, until Claudine became the girl she remembered. But she knew that that would never happen without her persistence. She had to protect Claudine, keep Harlan from insinuating himself any further into their lives. She refused to let the girl out of her sight and never allowed her to be alone with him . . . ever. Claudine was getting plumper by the minute, moving more slowly, and that helped.

The baby was making her retch, and Hattie Mae prayed that it would make her even sicker still, too ill to return to work.

She tried to stay out of Harlan's way but smiled sweetly when he sent for her. He'd managed to terrify her, and they both knew it. He hadn't humiliated her in front of their daughter, yet, but she knew that he was biding his time, hoping for her to provoke him, so she kept her mouth shut and baked his goddamn pies. No need to irritate him, cause him to make unnecessary conversation with Claudine. She sent her on every foolish errand she could think of, which caused Claudine to despise her a little more every day. Hattie Mae ignored the icy stares, the monosyllabic responses, and the hateful afterthoughts she heard Claudine mutter under her breath. She chose not to address them then, and that was probably for the best. She was accustomed to folks resenting her, and this was no different. Their time would come eventually; Hattie Mae was counting on it. It was the only thing she had to live for.

Hattie Mae laughed at her own arrogance and presumption. She'd made such detailed plans, and now she'd have to begin again, include a child. Even though circumstances had changed, Willy Earl would never be a part of the equation, a member of her family. He was a cancer that had invaded the nucleus of their family. That's all he would ever be. As far as she was concerned, he was invisible. He assumed, like Claudine, that she was defeated because she wasn't ranting and raving or trying to cause another affliction. He assumed that she'd accepted him, and so he became comfortable in her surroundings. He didn't try to speak to her anymore, and that was a blessing. She itched to beat him down again, expunge him from their lives forever. She noticed the way he sauntered into the house, lying up in the middle of the day, eating fried bologna sandwiches, inviting his hoodlum friends over, pretending like he was a man. He actually thought he'd won something. Leaving him behind would be effortless.

She'd made Claudine go home early today. The girl could barely walk, must weigh close to two hundred pounds with that baby. Claudine was back exactly where she started, minus the violin. She waddled around as if she was enjoying herself, thrilled to be with that dim-witted, frog-eyed husband of hers, but Hattie Mae knew better. As hard as she tried, Hattie Mae couldn't erase his high-pitched voice from her consciousness.

"GET UP, YOU fa-fa-fat ass ho'. You know I have to go to the shop this mor-morning, and you didn't iron my shirt."

"I'm tired, Willy Earl. I'm supposed to stay off my feet. Adell said—"

"I don't care what that old hag said. You ain't the first g-g-g-girl to have no baby. The Deacon told me you-you-you was lazy. Probably d-didn't even want to go to that audition."

"Please, Willy Earl, don't."

"S-s-something you wanna t-t-tell me?"

Hattie Mae had heard them arguing through the walls. She'd heard him call her out of her name. She'd listened to her child crying in the middle of the night, stifled sobs not meant for her to hear. It was happening all over again, a slow metamorphosis. Willy Earl was turning into the Deacon. She'd known it all along, saw it in him the first time he showed his ugly face in the light of day. She just hoped that Claudine would see it before it was too late.

HATTIE MAE SAT down, cross-legged, in the middle of the governor's bed when she heard him come in. He'd been hanging around lately, more so than usual, attempting to engage Claudine in conversation. He'd said that something about her seemed so familiar and asked on more than one occasion if she really loved that simpleminded husband of hers. *"Well, I de-*

clare, Claudine, look like Hattie Mae spit you out herself. Anybody ever tell you that?" Hattie Mae had thought she would faint dead away when he'd uttered those words the first week Claudine started. *"If you were built more like your aunt, here, y'all would look like twins."* For once she had been grateful for the fat that insulated Claudine from his perverse intentions.

Hattie Mae did what she could to make him happy, keep his attention focused on her. She dressed to please him, wore the wine-colored lipstick he'd brought her from Paris last year, and walked with a sensual sway, prompting him to follow. She unpinned her long hair and encouraged him to run his fingers through it. Something she'd never done before, anything to distract him.

Excited and anxious to smell Hattie Mae, Harlan raced home and was pleased to see her perched on his bed. He knelt in front of her and removed his boots. He caressed the side of her face, and no words passed between them. She opened her dress and unfastened her bra, allowing her abundant breasts to gain their freedom. He leaned forward, eyes closed. She extended her hand and placed his head gently in her cleavage, where it stayed for what seemed like hours.

CHAPTER 25

*C*laudine sat on the toilet and attempted for the third time to move her bowels. She'd had to navigate her way through all the mess scattered about the house, his mess. Dirty clothes and empty Coke bottles littered the living room and caused her to wince with pain each time she bent over to pick something up. It was just like cleaning up after Bone and the Deacon all over again.

"Willy Earl! Willy Earl!"

He didn't answer. He never answered her anymore. She didn't even know if he was home, and she started to cry because she realized she didn't care if he was or not. Willy Earl had changed since they were married, and much to her chagrin, he'd become everything Hattie Mae had said he would— lazy, nasty, and downright foul. She didn't know which was worse, the fact that he'd failed her or that Hattie Mae had been right. She didn't want Hattie Mae to be right about anything in her life. Claudine was ashamed and enraged and ashamed all over again. When she looked at him, on the nights he decided to come home, she searched his face, carefully, for the Willy Earl she remembered, the one who told her she was beautiful. He wasn't there anymore, and she wondered if he'd ever existed at all. Her life had deteriorated into this grotesque illusion, and she felt herself slipping into a state of intense denial in order to survive. She wanted to die, finish it like Willamina, but a part of her needed to believe that everything was well, that Willy Earl was caring and loving and Hattie Mae was simply the woman who lived next door.

THE PAIN DIDN'T move her or make her scream out loud like women did in the movies at the dollar matinée. She sensed the baby was coming, felt the small head pressing against her pelvic bone, which was trying to split her bottom in half, but she had no desire to call for help. She was alone again. Claudine crawled into her bed and waited for the inevitable. As the contractions intensified, she imagined how well she would have played at that audition and what she could have been doing right now, in New York or Boston, instead of lying there in agony, wishing for a mama she couldn't claim.

Somewhere in her head she heard voices coaxing her, telling her what to do, but she didn't feel Adell removing her clothes, spreading her legs, or gently wiping her face with a cool cloth. Couldn't they see the crowd was mesmerized? She was performing again, her arm manipulating the bow, causing quite a stir, prompting her very first standing ovation.

"Push, Claudine! Push!" they instructed her repeatedly, but she ignored them and returned to the stage for an encore, playing harder, sweating profusely at her own exertion.

WILLY EARL TOUCHED his nose with the tip of his tongue.

"C'mon, b-b-baby. Looky here. This here is nine inches of pure pl-pl-pleasure."

He considered his unusually elongated tongue to be his best asset, and he wanted to show it off. He'd been out all day, chasing homely, bucktoothed Renee. He loved women with enormous teeth, even if they were pointing in all different directions. Claudine was way too fat and tired to satisfy his needs anymore, so he had to make other arrangements. He flashed Claudine's money, mentioned his new, fancy address, but bucktooth still wouldn't let him have his way. All the fine honeys stayed away from him on account of Hattie Mae, but Renee looked like she might be getting weaker by the moment. She'd said she'd let him sniff it regularly if he paid her light bill. He'd finally convinced her to sample a test lick behind Snookie's Garage when he heard Monkey Man yelling his name loud enough for the entire state of Georgia to hear.

"Willy Earl! Willy Earl! Deeny's about to drop that baby any minute now."

"So?"

"So? Nigguh, you betta slide that freak tongue back down your throat and get on home. Hattie Mae is on the prowl for your narrow ass."

"I-I-I ain't scared of no Hattie Mae."

"Um hmmm. Ain't she the one busted your head wide open?"

"Awl, Monkey Man, you know she s-sucker punched me."

"Ah huh. Well, she liable to kill you dead if she finds out you down here messin' round with that." Monkey Man pointed at bucktooth and shook his head in disgust. He was trying to help the young fool avoid another ass kicking, but Willy Earl seemed intent on getting himself beat down again. Monkey Man's mama, God rest her soul, had always told him there were just some folks you didn't play around with. It didn't take a genius to figure out Hattie Mae Jones was one of them.

"Willy Earl. Git on home now, before I have to scrape your skinny ass up off the sidewalk. And gimme that bottle. You already silly in the head, boy, you don't need no extra help."

Willy Earl began to laugh out loud, took another swig of Thunderbird before Monkey Man snatched the bottle out of his hand. He was a goddamned father, and instead of congratulating him, Monkey Man kept pestering him, trying to persuade him to hightail it to the duplex like some little punk.

Well, he wasn't going home until he was good and ready. He was tired of Hattie Mae and Claudine always telling him what to do, tired of the crew from Snookie's punking him like some sissy, teasing him incessantly about being Hattie Mae's whipping boy. He was the man of the house now, and that ought to mean something. He staggered to Hattie Mae's steps at two in the morning and started yelling, reverting to his native patois.

"C'mon, get de door wo-man. Move yer fat ass, ya heah?"

The least Claudine could have done was wait up for him. She thought she was the queen of Sheba or somebody, like she's the only girl to ever squeeze a baby out of her ass. The Deacon had been right, Claudine was much too uppity for her own good. Wasn't he, Willy "The Earl," entitled to have a little fun, a little merriment, without Hattie Mae getting all bent out of shape? He deserved that, after all he'd been through. Now all he wanted to do was see his baby. Was that too much to ask? He yelled louder, slurring his words.

"Hey, hef-hef-heffa, get up. Open de door before I l-l-lick your backside!"

Hattie Mae took a long drag on her cigarette and reached for an old friend, someone he'd remember well. She opened the door slowly.

"Where's Claudine and me baby? Gwine and fetch'em now, I don't want no trouble outta you. What did I h-h-have anyway?"

"A boy."

"Ha ha! That niece of yours finally done someting right, you know. Willy Earl Ju-Junior. Got a nice ring to it, doncha tink?"

Hattie Mae flicked the cigarette down onto the porch and extinguished it with the heel of her house shoe. She had no intention of allowing him to disturb Claudine and that baby, her grandbaby. She didn't want the child to ever remember his daddy's face. She eyed Willy Earl up and down, standing there drunk, smelling of another woman's twat, completely unaware that they almost lost Claudine during the birth. All of this misery was his doing, and suddenly, he became the reason she went to prison, Luther Mack, Harlan Tillford, and Claudine's rapist, all rolled into one man. She blinked hard and swung low. He lurched back in surprise. This time she wanted to make sure he saw the bat coming and would know right away who'd shattered his knees.

CHAPTER 26

mooth, suave, and superfine—at least that was the way he described himself to anyone that had a free ear and some spare time. It had been a while since he'd seen a fabulous woman, someone truly extraordinary. A woman with a certain jenne se qua; yes, yes, isn't that what the French called it? He was bored with the same old tired twigs he'd been messing around with. They didn't intrigue him anymore. They were just there, sucking up precious air and getting in the way. It was time for him to make a change, secure himself a new jewel in his crown, cement his reputation as the gentleman with the loveliest ladies. Whomever he chose would be damned lucky to be seen with him. He had breeding and class, owned property and drove a sweet automobile; plus, he always smelled good, and this was a plus, with so many brutish, uncouth men roaming the streets. What more could any female want? Hell, it's not like colored girls these days had plenty of options. He could give them a dream life, everything they always wanted and more. He just needed to find the right one, the perfect one.

And he wasn't inclined to drive out of the state, either. Leaving his territory was not one of his favorite things to do. His women became restless without him, mischievous. Crackers stopping him every five minutes, giving him a hard time, jealous of his immaculately tailored suits and matching alligator shoes. Hell, if he wasn't so well connected, he would have been strung up in four counties by now for looking so good. Yes, he would remain in Georgia this time, go on a well-planned hunt. He'd done it before. He could do it again. The last pearl, now she was from New Orleans. Pretty . . . so damn pretty he almost liked her. Light, bright, and damn near white, but with full lips, creamy thighs, and a derrière that made him a very popular man indeed. Heaven, oh, it was heaven when she was acting right, doing what he trained her to do. What a waste, she only lasted six months, two months longer than the skinny heffa before her. He'd be prepared for this new girl, his ruby, his secret weapon, his genie in a bottle. He'd hide the razor blades and lock up the kitchen knives and pills—there could never be any pills. So what if his women never wanted to stay with him. Wasn't his fault that they couldn't hold on to a good thing. He laughed and admired his chiseled chocolate physique in a full-length mirror. He didn't favor them, anyway, and none of them had ever figured that out, not one. They were all beautiful but thick in the head, and he was a genius, a certified ebony prodigy. He was certain of it. And as for his debonair personality, nobody could lay it on like him, make a woman sho' nuff swoon and moisten her panties at the same time. Good Lord, if he'd only been born a white man, the world would be his.

CHAPTER 27

*S*he was seventeen when she met him back in 1943.
He stopped, in a midnight black Packard, to buy fruit
from her mama. The girl couldn't believe that a black man drove
a car like that. He was thirty-six and talked of houses with running water and fine lace curtains. She hung on his every word, allowed her imagination to run wild as he stood in front of her and
ran his hand lightly across her mama's blue-ribbon peaches.

"What's your name, sweet thang?"

"Hattie Mae, Hattie Mae Jones."

"Girl, you so pretty your name ought to be Delilah. You ever
been out of Sparta, Hattie Mae? Ever been to the big city?"

"No," Gracian Jones interrupted. "And she ain't going neither,
so take your peaches and git from around here."

From that moment, Gracian warned her about him, said he
didn't look right, talked out of the side of his mouth, and was
too old, much too old to be chasing after a simple country girl
like her. But he'd mesmerized Hattie Mae with his smooth pecan
skin and finely tailored suits. She'd never seen another man like
him. Unbeknownst to her mama, he found her later, in her bare
feet, milking cows. She knew that she was supposed to send him
away, call for her brothers, but she couldn't resist his charm and
silky conversation. He nestled his hand in the curve of her back,

and her entire body flushed with sensations she couldn't quite describe.

"My, my, my, you are exquisite, simply divine."

Hattie Mae didn't know what that meant, but he smiled so sweetly when he said it.

"Thank you. You know what? I don't even know your name."

"Nathan Lee, and you can call me Nathan Lee."

"You're something else, Nathan Lee. Where'd you learn to talk like that? You not from around here, are you?"

"No, baby doll. I'm from where you're supposed to be."

"And where's that?"

"Where women as luscious as you get everything they've ever dreamed of."

She was spellbound, so hypnotized by his voice that she didn't notice her mother coming around the corner with a pick axe.

"Mister, I done told you to git from around here once. If'n I have to tell you again, my mouth won't be doing the talkin'. Hattie Mae! Hattie Mae! Get your tail up to the house right now, you hear?"

Terrified, Hattie Mae ran without looking back. She knew when not to challenge her mother, and she prayed earnestly that Nathan Lee would walk off the farm with all of his limbs intact. She had never defied Gracian, and she was momentarily ashamed at being caught with Nathan Lee, but all afternoon and night she couldn't help wondering where the "smooth-talking city fellow" was and if he was thinking about her. She tried to busy herself until her mother returned. There was butter to churn, nutmeg to grind, and hell to pay. That night, at dinner, her mother never mentioned catching her with the slick talker, and her brothers just stared at her, like a bolt of lighting was about to fry her at any minute. Something had struck her, all right, knocked her clean off her feet, and his name was Nathan Lee.

For days Hattie Mae and Nathan Lee met secretly, and he taught her to drive his fancy car when her mama thought she was picking tomatoes on the west side of the farm. She believed her *mother to be unreasonable. She didn't understand why Gracian distrusted him so. He was always a perfect gentleman, so sweet, so tender.*

"I can introduce you to a whole new world, Hattie Mae. You don't belong here anymore. See, you're a caterpillar now, but I . . . I can turn you into a butterfly. If you were mine, I'd treat you to gourmet meals at a real restaurant, where somebody else is doing the serving. I'd take you dancing every Saturday night. A beautiful girl . . . no, a beautiful woman like you should have her nails polished the color of a rose and her feet bathed in the finest perfumes."

"Go on, Nathan Lee. You really think I'm beautiful?"

Hattie Mae examined her hands, worn rough from years of hard work. She closed her eyes, tried to envision her short, jagged nails long, filed, and painted.

"I promise, baby doll, you'll never have to work again. Never have to lift another crate or scrape a plate. All of that manual labor, all of this shelling peas and shucking corn is beneath you."

"I don't know, Nathan Lee, I been here all my life."

"Your life is with me now, baby girl. Don't let your mama hold you back."

He continued to tantalize her with seductive tales of life in the big city, where elegant girls laughed all day and lounged around in satin pajamas on the weekends. Hattie Mae was apprehensive.

"I just don't know. I can't leave the farm, abandon my mama, my brothers and sisters, the only home I've ever known, to run away with you."

Unexpectedly, he kissed her full on the lips, caressed the side of her face, inched his hands lightly along her hips. By the time his tongue discovered her ear, everything inside of her said yes.

Gracian knew she was losing her. She could feel it. She had many children to account for, but ever since that hustler showed up, she'd kept her eyes trained hard on Hattie Mae. That child was different from the rest—looked different, acted different—and

Gracian would not, could not acknowledge it for years. But at around sixteen, Hattie Mae started asking a lot of questions, and against her better judgment Gracian answered them. They had a silent understanding: Gracian would answer all Hattie Mae's persistent inquiries about her daddy in one night and then Hattie Mae would never speak of the circumstances of her birth again. All her life, Gracian did what she was expected to do. What she was supposed to do—shell peas and have a baby, plow a field and have a baby, make a meal and have a baby, and so on, until she had an impressive piece of land and a dozen children. They were well fed, well taken care of. She made sure of that. Folks talked about her, said she had to be no good on account of having all that land and no husband to speak of. Well, she had a man once; he'd fathered eleven of her children and died, keeled straight over in a plate of grits. It's not like they'd loved each other or any such nonsense. They'd had an arrangement that suited them both just fine. She inherited land from her mama, and he offered to help her farm it. She barely remembered having sexual relations with the man. Every interaction with him was so methodical, and besides, she didn't require affection. She wanted sons, plain and simple; physical contact was necessary. She thought her children fortunate. At least they would know their father, and a few would actually have a real memory of him. And as far as people stretching their tongues about her, Gracian was accustomed to that. Her mama had prepared her early on, told her that a lot of folks didn't take too kindly to people like them, mulattos, half-breeds. Gracian had never laid eyes on her own father but assumed from people's reaction to her that he had to have been white. Her fair skin and straight hair didn't win any allies in her hometown. It had been a lonely life, one she didn't want her babies to have. For her children's sake, she took up with the blackest man she could find, looked like he came straight out of the Congo. She believed that her offspring would have it slightly easier if she could just brown them up a touch, guide them back to the darker side. He offered to marry her, proper-like, but Gracian's mama had also taught her to keep what was hers, protect it at all costs. Marrying him would have given him rights to the land over her children, and she couldn't allow that. Men come and go, but her children would always be her children.

They worked hard, side by side, lived a sterile, uneventful life, and he was pleasant enough to be around. Everything was moving along just fine until Lucien showed up, Hattie Mae's daddy, and tossed her stable world into turmoil. She was humming "Precious Lord" and wringing a chicken's neck when he happened around the corner, trying to sell her some miracle fruit seeds, claimed they would grow three-pound tomatoes. Ridiculous, she knew, but he cajoled her into buying an assortment. At the end of their conversation, she felt flushed and uneasy, a state she wasn't used to. She couldn't explain what was happening to her, and she didn't like it either—heart racing, cheeks burning, moistness creeping down her thighs. He kept returning to the farm to make conversation, answer questions about seeds and soil, roots and weeds. She knew she should put a stop to his visits, which were becoming more and more frequent, but curiosity held her at bay. She couldn't quite figure if it was love or lust. It was simply a feeling she didn't recognize. Often she thought herself insane for having such wicked thoughts about a white man, but Lucien was unlike any white man she had ever known. He was kind and gentle. He called her Miss and kissed her hand for no reason at all. Before she realized what was happening, she was opening her legs to him one Sunday afternoon in the back field next to the newly sprouting tomatoes. Helplessly, from a fit of something Gracian would never acknowledge, she, like her mother before her, delivered a light-brown baby girl that would be marked forever by her mother's weakness.

"What kind of craziness are you talking, girl?"

"I have a chance, Mama, to go places, see things, not waste my life away here, peeling potatoes."

"You think I've wasted my life here, taking care of this land, raising you and your brothers and sisters? Farm work is good for the soul, gives you character, makes you a woman."

But Hattie Mae had been laboring hard her whole life, sewing quilts, canning vegetables, whatever her mama wanted her to do. She could cook a entire meal by the time she was eight, standing on a footstool to reach the stove, and balance her mama's books without paper and pencil, adding long columns of figures in her head. She was the youngest and also the most responsible. She had always watched over her brothers and sisters, all eleven of them, while her mama ran the stand that was located on the east side of the farm, next to the well, one hundred yards from the outhouse. So the thought of not working intrigued her, made her sneak around like a girl up to no good, beg her siblings to do her chores.

"Girl, you ain't going nowhere, you hear me? I'll tie your hot ass to the outhouse till you come to your senses. You betta come to yourself. That's what you betta do."

Gracian almost had her convinced to stay until Nathan Lee showed up with flowers, daffodils. Her brothers surrounded him. Her sisters tried to offer him corn bread.

"Miss Jones, I'm here to ask for Hattie Mae's hand in marriage. I love her, Miss Jones, and I promise you I'm going to take good care of her."

Hattie Mae started to walk toward him. Gracian pulled her back.

"This man ain't no good, Hattie Mae. I'm telling you now. He ain't worth the dirt he's standing on. Open your eyes. . . . You just a girl. He a full-on man. Something just ain't right here. I can smell it."

"You're wrong, Mama. I love him."

Gracian raised Roscoe, her Stevens double-barreled sawed-off shotgun, and fired, narrowly missing his right foot. He ran but returned that night—and vowed he would return every night until Hattie Mae was his. Her resolve lasted exactly twenty-four hours. When he came back for her the next night, Hattie Mae was ready.

It was hard to leave, the hardest thing she had ever done. It was almost as if she could see her mama's pain reaching out, pleading with her to stay. Her brothers wanted to kill Nathan Lee, bury him in the back field, but Gracian stopped them, said the decision was up to her.

"You have a responsibility, Hattie Mae, to the family, the farm, the land," she said sternly.

Nathan Lee reminded Hattie Mae that she could get her hair pressed once a week and wear real stockings on Sundays.

"You can't ever come back if you leave with him. He gone be the ruination of you, Hattie Mae. I can feel it. You mark my words. You hear me!"

"Mama, why can't you just be happy for me?"

"He gone leave you before a year's time, and then you'll have nothing, and you gone be nothing following behind the likes of him."

Her mama was right. They would be together only nine months before she was charged with his murder.

Hattie Mae chattered nonstop in the perfectly polished Packard, desperately attempting to conceal the butterflies that were swirling around in her stomach. The farm was getting smaller and smaller. He smiled knowingly, held her hand, massaged her shoulder until she felt at ease.

"You a free woman now, Hattie Mae."

"Nathan Lee? You like babies, don't you? I only want two, but not right away, though. After taking care of all my brothers and sisters, I could use a rest. I want us to have fun together, like you promised."

"Yeah, baby doll, we gonna have plenty of fun."

"I'm so excited. Oh . . . I don't have any fancy clothes to wear. I don't have the right shoes. I don't—"

"Shhhh. I said I'd buy you everything you could ever want."

"Nathan Lee, do you think my mama will ever forgive me for running away with you? Maybe we ought to—"

"Hush up about all that now, girl. It doesn't matter. I'm all the family you need."

"But Nathan Lee."

"Lay your head back on that seat, Hattie Mae, and rest those lips. Save your strength, sweet thang, 'cause you gone need it."

They left Sparta that day, drove all the way to Atlanta. He had a house there. He moved her in, set her up in her own room, complete with a real inside toilet and white lace curtains. Two other women lived there, too. He said they were his sisters. They pretty much kept to themselves and usually had somewhere to go. He never touched her while she was there, never attempted to get under her skirt or steal kisses like he did at the farm. She assumed he wanted to wait until their honeymoon, make her first time memorable. She asked often when they would get married. He told her to be patient, good things took time. She tried hard to live up to his expectations. Prepared his favorite meals, polished his shoes, plucked the seeds out of his watermelon so he wouldn't have to spit. But no matter what she did, he didn't seem to notice much, preferring to spend time with his friends. Friends he never allowed her to meet. She became suspicious once and followed him to a bar. She was relieved when she saw that his companion was a man—but unlike any man she'd ever seen. He had the sway of a woman, and they appeared to be very close.

Nathan Lee promised her that her whole life would change. She just had to be ready, he said. He bought her new dresses and gloves with fur to match her coats for when they went out. He rushed her to the beauty parlor, and she felt like Dorothy Dandridge or a black Greta Garbo when they finished unpinning the last curl. He taught her which fork to use and instructed her in the fine art of table conversation. He was very sociable, liked to entertain, and constantly insisted she attend these peculiar parties. Sometimes his sisters were there, but they obviously didn't like her much. To them, she was invisible. It was just as well that they seemed to enjoy being the center of attention. Pale-faced men lolling around the sisters like they were being inspected. She *didn't understand. Her mama had always taught her to stay away from white men, far away. They'll butcher you good, she said, swallow you whole, but Nathan Lee encouraged her to mingle, said it was business. She thought he was grooming her to be the perfect wife.*

CHAPTER 28

"She's got Claudine holed up in there, like some kind of prisoner. Had me thrown in the pokey when I tried to see her, take her somethin' to eat. And Willy Earl, po' Willy 'The Earl' can't even walk around the corner. Hattie Mae wouldn't let him see his own son. I tell ya, she done gone plumb crazy. The light is on, but ain't nobody home."

"Yeah, Pops, you think after she cracked his head, he'd know better than to show up at her house in the middle of the night, drunk. And you. Did you ever get your hat back?"

"How you know about that?"

"I know about everything. I'm going to see about my sister."

Bone finished sucking the meat off his third slab of ribs and wiped his hands. He had been issued a month's worth of leave. He believed his sergeant had made a mistake, thought he was somebody else. He didn't linger around Saigon, waiting for the mix-up to be corrected. The Deacon had picked him up at the train station and had been talking nonstop ever since, blabbering on about things that Bone had now deemed inconsequential. He'd seen a lot, grown some, but the Deacon looked exactly the same. Everyone around this place looked exactly the way they did when he left. He hadn't expected much when he returned, but he'd hoped his sister would be gone, playing her violin up north, somewhere making a name for herself. Old girlfriends wrote to him from time to time, told him what was happening on the home front; that's how he had found out about the rape and Claudine missing her big audition. Now his twin sister was married, somebody's mama, and working for the governor—the governor! What the hell was going on here? he wanted to know. He'd never been right to Claudine, and for the first time he felt bad about it, especially since her life was obviously not what she and Hattie Mae had planned it to be. His mama was gone, and the Deacon was . . . well, the Deacon. Claudine and Hattie Mae were the only real family he had left. He belched and grabbed his duffel bag.

"Are you going to drive me over there or not?"

"I'll drive ya, but I ain't stopping. You gone have to jump out. Pretend like you got a parachute on your back."

"Jump out?"

"You heard me. I ain't going nowheres near that woman, and you betta hope she don't put yo black ass in jail, too."

"She won't. I know how to stay out of her way." Bone laughed, stared hard at his father, and laughed some more.

CLAUDINE TURNED HER face toward the wall after Adell took the baby. Hattie Mae had said that it was a good thing the boy didn't take after his daddy. No bug eyes or a head shaped like a question mark. Claudine barely listened to her anymore. Nothing she said was tangible. The only time Claudine felt worthwhile was when they brought her the baby to nurse. He belonged to her and she to him. That she knew for true. Her body was still feeling the repercussions of a difficult birth. Her back ached, and her insides throbbed with a certain vacancy. Despite Hattie Mae's strenuous objections, she'd named him Willy Earl Junior, after his daddy. Hattie Mae refused to call him that, referring to him only as Baby Boy. Claudine was too drained to fight her. She had closed her eyes but instinctively parted her gown when she heard the door open. Nursing him sustained her.

"No thanks. I just ate."

She remembered the voice, a younger version of the Deacon's, and attempted a smile for him. He came to her and wept for the sister he didn't recognize.

"GIVE HER SOME time, Hattie Mae," Adell persuaded.

"Had enough time. Time for her to open her damn mouth, take a deep breath, move the hell on."

"She been hurt, hurt bad."

"Hell, who hasn't been? Her pain ain't no greater than anybody else's."

"Hattie Mae, she yo chile."

Claudine stiffened when she heard fragments of the conversation between Adell and Hattie Mae. The woman was in the hallway, right outside the door, probably poised for battle, with one hand on her hip and the other on a bat. Anxiety overwhelmed Claudine whenever she thought about having to speak with Hattie Mae, face her again. She'd always been somewhat intimidated, but then again, who wasn't? Discovering that her aunt was her mother didn't make communicating any easier. Truth be told, she'd rather not have anything to do with her at all. But right now, as much as she hated to admit it, being around Hattie Mae was a necessity, especially since Willy Earl had turned out to be such a dismal disappointment. Thus far, Claudine and Hattie Mae had done so well at avoiding the issue, masking the truth, protecting a lie, and for what? When the dust settled, Claudine was only good enough to be a niece, not a daughter. Here and now she would have to take a stand, demand answers for herself and Bone. She couldn't run from her forever, ignore the woman that gave her life. It would take all of the strength she could muster to confront Hattie Mae, make her reveal her true identity to Bone. For her brother's sake, she had to try, put her animosity aside, quell her shitty attitude, as Adell called it. Ask the questions that contaminated her dreams and teased her sanity. Claudine took a deep breath.

She'd told Adell earlier that she needed to talk to Hattie Mae privately, as soon as possible. She knew that would get her home. They hadn't really spoken since the incident. She braced herself when she saw the knob turn.

"What is it? I have to get back to work."

"Bone's here. I sent him next door."

"I know."

"Have you seen him yet?"

"Is this what you called me home for? Do you think I have time to be standing here playing twenty questions with you, Claudine?"

"Are you going to tell him?"

"Tell him what?"

"That you're his mother, our mother."

Claudine searched her face for some maternal reaction, any sign that would make her look real, authentic. Nothing appeared to move Hattie Mae Jones, not even her son's return from the war in Vietnam, alive with both arms and legs.

"I'm not going to tell him a damn thing, and neither are you."

"Why? How could you do this? We have a right to know the truth." She rolled her eyes in disgust. Would there be no end to her lies?

"You have no idea what I've done, what I've had to do to keep you safe. You have never wanted for anything . . . ever. I'm sick and tired of all this whining and complaining. I don't want to speak another word about this again. You hear me, Claudine?" Hattie Mae turned to leave.

"That's it? That's all you have to say for yourself? What about me?"

"You're here, you're alive, you're sleeping on clean sheets."

"What about Bone? I'm going to tell him."

"No."

"You can't stop me. He deserves to know the truth."

"Do you want to deliberately hurt that boy? Are you trying to make him suffer? He's lost his mother already. Now leave it be."

"What is wrong with you? How can you stand there and say that? Ignore your own flesh and blood?"

Claudine was astonished. How could this be happening? Being in the same room with Hattie Mae was making her flesh crawl, and she wanted to attack, lash out, sock her in the eye. Claudine may have been furious, but she wasn't crazy. Still, she hated her—hated her for keeping secrets, hated her for being alive. Now that Claudine knew that Hattie Mae was their mother, her treatment of Bone was even more disconcerting. Mothers were supposed to adore their sons.

"You are his mother."

"No. I am your mother. Bone's mama is dead."

"What? I don't understand."

"The only thing you need to understand right now is that you have a child to raise and a violin to play. Look at you. Chile, you can't even get out of bed, can't go back to work. So until your legs and your brain are working properly, you're going to do exactly what I tell you to do. I don't care what you think about me. The sooner you realize that, the better."

Claudine watched her leave and was more confused than ever. It was the first time since the rape that Hattie Mae had acknowledged the biological connection between them. She and Bone were twins, born of the same egg. She thought of Willy Earl Junior. Nothing on this earth could ever make her deny him. He came through her. And then an inkling, an idea, a twisted notion began swirling around in her mind, and she could barely bring herself to think of it, the possibility of such a monumental deception. Hattie Mae provided for Claudine all of these years and neglected Bone. Willamina worshiped

Bone and most times treated Claudine like she was an annoyance, someone extra she was required to feed. There was an answer here, a revelation hiding somewhere in the mélange that was her life. The sheer weight of the charade caused her to vomit on the new nightgown from Sears and all over the plush, coral bedspread.

IT WAS DISTRESSING for Claudine to sit across from him knowing what she knew. Like her mother, she, too, had become a deceiver. She longed to tell Bone, have someone to confide in, but dared not. She had to think of Junior now, and as much as she abhorred the situation, she needed Hattie Mae. She'd always needed Hattie Mae. She tried to concentrate on the plate of grits and eggs before her, avoiding his eyes.

"So, I heard you done it again."

"Done what?"

"Oh, like you don't know."

"Come on, Bone, I'm too exhausted to play any of your guessing games."

"You really don't know, do you?"

Claudine ate a forkful of grits and stared blankly. After breakfast she would sit next to Junior's bassinet and wait for him to wake. There was nothing else for her to do but tend to him—assure him, during every waking moment, that he was loved.

"Haven't you wondered why that frog-eyed husband of yours hasn't come to see his own boy?"

Claudine shrugged her shoulders. "I try not to think of him at all anymore."

"Well, I'm sure he's thinking of you right about now, and trying not to have nightmares about Aint Hattie Mae."

"What are you talking about?"

"The boy can't walk, Deeny. She busted both his legs this time. He already talks funny, now he gone be walkin' funny, too. He already talks funny; now he gone be walkin' funny, too."

"What?"

"Yeah, she fucked him up good. They say he'll walk again, though, but 'flicted like. He sho' betta watch his back. I believe she gone kill his dumb ass next time."

Claudine was incensed but smiled at the thought of her errant husband in pain, the unmitigated gall of Hattie Mae. She was his wife. She should have been the one to maim him.

"Now, you know you wrong for that. Deeny, I'm sorry about what happened to you. I wish I could have been here. You know you can still—"

She could not allow him to finish. "I don't want to talk about it."

"But what about Betty? When was the last time you—"

"I don't want to talk about that, either. Just leave it alone, Bone. Please, leave it alone."

BONE HELD THE wee baby in his arms, his nephew, his sister's child, and for a moment missed his mother so intensely that he felt his eyes begin to fill. Claudine was not supposed to be like this, live like this. He'd always known, like Hattie Mae, that there was something magical about her. He saw it the first time she played one of those fancy songs on that violin, and he'd hated her for it, for possessing such a talent. He'd wished over a thousand times that an act of God would strike her hands so she couldn't perform anymore; then she would simply be ordinary like him, regular. People had made fun of him, said he'd never amount to much, couldn't believe Claudine was his twin. Told him he'd gotten the short end of the stick. "The Maker was in a bad mood when he got to Bone; just didn't give him much of nothing." He'd heard that from just about everybody, except his mama.

In the beginning, the Deacon, and it seemed the entire neighborhood, constantly expected him to be able to do something spectacular, share his hereditary genius. Folks were constantly waiting for the magic to leap out of him like it did Claudine, but nothing happened. Deep down, he knew he was the reason his mama drank. There were the failed piano lessons, the failed saxophone lessons, the episode with the flute, and the time the Deacon fractured Bone's wrist because he was incapable of mastering any musical instrument. He couldn't do anything that would impress anybody, and after a while, no one expected him to. He'd envied Claudine for being distinctive, unique. Kids, including him, had teased her mercilessly, and most times he initiated the attacks, but she had something to cling to. He knew that playing that violin made her feel whole and made everyone else disappear. Mama had done her best to compensate, make him feel like he mattered, but Claudine's magic engulfed him and whatever gifts he might have been given.

He'd had a lot of time to think in Vietnam, time to sort out who he was and who he wanted to be. Gunfire was as commonplace as oxygen. Men being ripped to pieces, calling for their mamas. GIs pleading with perfect strangers to hear about their families, share their life stories, before Mr. Charlie filled their ass with shrapnel.

One day, while he wrapped what was left of another man's arm, it dawned on him that he was always the listener. No one ever inquired about his family, and he didn't volunteer any information. Even in the jungles of Nam, jealousy consumed him. He had never given Claudine a chance to love him, never allowed her to get close enough to know who he was or what he was meant to do. Hell, he didn't know himself, and that wasn't her fault. He'd put such distance between them with his petty envy, and yet, how ironic that she was the only person he thought of when he feared he wouldn't live through another night. No matter what he'd done to her, she'd never reciprocated, never made him feel like he didn't measure up. She was his twin, the other half of him, and he wanted to love her. He'd been in Nam four months, six days, and twelve hours when he experienced his very first epiphany. Some new fellow, Ronnie from Dallas, possessed a passion for music such as Claudine's, had the same familiar light in his eyes when he clamored on about it, could read and write all those notes and lines. Told everybody his music would change the world and asked Bone if he played an instrument. "No," he'd responded, with a slow grin, "but my sister does. You'd like her, man. She plays the violin like an angel."

Now he was sorry that he'd ever begrudged her. She didn't deserve what had happened to her. The entire course of her life had been altered by one moment, like Ronnie's when he back-stepped on a land mine five weeks later. Bone had shed tears then for his newfound friend, wept for the music he would never play. Now he'd been given a chance to make things right with his sister, and he didn't know where to begin. Claudine was right in front of him, yet still unreachable. He wished he knew of a way to convince her that she still had that magic, that same light in her eyes, but how could he make her believe when he couldn't find it either?

illy Earl cursed his fate. He'd been laid up in his mama's two-room shack of a house with both legs encased in plaster of paris for the better part of six months. Now he could barely take three steps without wincing like a sissy from the pain that seared through both of his knees. He'd lost consciousness frequently in the beginning, almost forgot why he couldn't walk; but her face haunted him, and he had ongoing nightmares about the bat, being chased by a bat, stalked by a bat, dismembered by a bat. He could hardly sleep anymore, what with worrying about what part of his body the bat was going to mangle next. He was so annoyed at his own colossal stupidity that he could cry. Everybody and their mamas knew how she'd had the Deacon tossed in jail over some trumped-up charge, and now here he was, afflicted once again because he'd forgotten who he was dealing with—the devil in a fancy dress. And the worst of it, the absolute worst of it, was that Willy Earl Junior wouldn't even know who he was if Hattie Mae had her way. He scanned the dusty room in disgust. He had to get the hell out. It was cold, and his extremities were damn near frozen. His mama put two pairs of socks on his feet before she left for work, but both pairs had holes large enough for his ankles to get a draft. There was no hot water and never enough food. He'd soiled himself on more than one occasion because there was no one to help him hobble to the toilet, no one to wipe the thick layer of crust that had formed in between the folds of his backside. His mother treated him like dirt because he'd never sent her any money while he was living over on the ritzy side of town, eating off dishes that were a part of a set, drinking from glasses that didn't used to have jelly in them. The door slammed, and he prepared to be berated again.

"Now look at you, boy. You see that. . . . God don't like ugly. That's why your knees all busted up, and now you gone walk like a ole man."

"Mama. Mama, p-p-please, help me."

"Help you. Help you? And what about me? I been waitin' and waitin' over 'ere for an invitation, but no. Got over dere and thought you was too good for me. Neva called, neva bought me a damn ting, not even a can of sardines, and after everyting I done for you."

"I-I said I was s-sorry, Mama. It wasn't my-my-my fault."

"Uh huh. That why you laid up dere like that, stinking of five men. Treatin' your poor mama in such a way, devil boy."

"Mama, it wasn't me. You-you-you know it wasn't me. C-C-Claudine and Hattie Mae d-d-didn't want you there. I tried to talk some sense into them, but they had they m-m-minds made up. Mama, c-c-c'mon, Mama."

"So what are you gonna do now? I have me a grandchild I've neva seen, you know. You better do someting to get yourself back into Claudine's good graces, idiot boy. Don't know how to keep a good ting."

"I will, Mama, and I p-p-promise, as soon as I do, I-I-I'm gone make this up to you."

"How do I know you're not talkin' out of your crusty ass, making lies? I ought to beat you myself."

"I promise, M-M-Mama. I ain't lying, anything you-you

want. I-I-I promise. I just need to get better so I can rush back over there, m-m-make up with Claudine."

"You make sure you keep your promises, you 'ere. And don't be so stupid next time, or that she-devil might put you in de ground. Well, what are you waiting for? Hurry up, fool boy, I have to get back to work, you know."

Mozell helped him up and guided him toward the leaking toilet. She pulled him like he was a little boy, castigating him while he groaned in pain and limped to keep up. After he swore to take care of her, fix her up a room in that big, fancy house, Mama Jenkins let him sleep in her lopsided bed instead of on the cold, hard floor.

Willy Earl despised his mother. He had no intention of ever laying eyes on her again, let alone inviting her into Hattie Mae's house. That would get him squashed for sure. Mozell didn't lie about the obvious, though. He had been a complete idiot, tangling with that . . . that woman while Claudine was under her thumb. He needed a plan. Weaseling his way back into Claudine's and Hattie Mae's good graces was his number-one priority. He'd thought for sure Claudine would have come for him by now, want to nurse him back to health, rub salve on his misshapen knees. At the rate he was going, he'd never get his gold tooth. Today he'd get the casts off, hopefully be able to get around better, walk like a man. Soon he'd reclaim his wife and every luxury that came with her. He'd underestimated Hattie Mae Jones. He wouldn't do it again.

THEY RODE TO work chatting of inconsequential things. Had Claudine received another letter from Bone? What pie was Hattie Mae going to bake this morning? Was the governor going to be in today? They only scratched the surface of their lives and never spoke of untruths, wombs, any subject that mattered. This morning Claudine had watched Hattie Mae fuss over Junior, bounce him on her lap, shower his face with kisses like a real grandmother, and she wondered if Hattie Mae ever adored her like that. She strained to remember.

Claudine had returned to work against Hattie Mae's advice. She might as well have remained home, taking care of Junior, the way that woman followed her around, inspected everything she did. But the pay was good, and in a small way, she felt functional. Her life consisted of three things: taking care of Junior, working, and daydreaming about her wayward husband. She thought of him as they pulled through the open, black iron gate behind the mansion. What was he doing at this very moment? Did he want to see his son? Was he thinking of them, or was he with someone else? She tried not to remember his long fingers or the way he touched her ever so lightly on the back of her thigh, causing her flesh to quiver in anticipation. She hadn't seen his face in so long that she'd created a sweeter version of Willy Earl in her mind to ease the loneliness in her soul and the emptiness in her bed. A Willy Earl who'd make her feel desirable again and feed his son cream of wheat in the middle of the night. A Willy Earl who'd never call her moo cow or cobbler-eating sow and would come home every night, delighted to see her no matter how she looked. A Willy Earl who wouldn't casually insinuate that the rape was her fault or accuse her of leading anybody on. Ultimately, she fell in love with the Willy Earl of her imagination, and before she realized what was happening, she was yearning for the original.

HATTIE MAE AND the governor were talking as if they knew each other's secrets. Standing too closely together, whispering, their cheeks almost touching. Claudine monitored them when Hattie Mae thought she was dusting or coring fruit for pies. The governor appeared to favor her company, and Hattie Mae seemed much too comfortable in his presence. She'd heard

Hattie Mae call him Harlan, and she'd caught him smiling when he answered. The governor spoke to Claudine every day, had attempted to engage her in conversation a few times, but Hattie Mae discouraged her from being hospitable, said that he would hold it against her later. Claudine had so many unanswered questions floating around in her head but couldn't organize her thoughts without feeling nauseated. Every molecule in her body was jumbled. She tried to make sense of what was plaguing her but couldn't focus. It was simpler, less stressful, to remain in the dark and stumble around in a world of confusion.

"Claudine. Claudine."

"Yes?"

"Governor Tillford's asking you a question."

"Oh, sorry. I was . . . I didn't hear."

"I said, are you feeling any better today? Hattie Mae tells me you haven't been well."

"Yes, sir."

"Well, actually she looks kind of poorly to me," Hattie Mae added, hoping he'd order her to go home. She'd get Claudine away from him one way or another. She walked over and placed her hand on Claudine's forehead. "I do believe this girl is running a fever."

"No, I'm all right," Claudine responded, still bewildered, anxious to return to the peaches.

"Hush up now, ya hear," Hattie Mae whispered sternly to Claudine. Then, "She came back too soon. She's liable to infect the entire house."

"I think you should run on home now, Claudine. Hattie Mae can handle things here. I'll get Jimmy to drive you. Jimmy! Jimmy!"

"She can take my car, Governor, and Jimmy can drive me home. Go on now, Claudine. Go on before you spread any more germs."

Claudine dropped her paring knife and turned to leave. She

went to retrieve her coat but realized after fifteen minutes of searching that she'd never taken it off.

Pleased with herself, Hattie Mae took over the peaches while Harlan stood on a chair and licked salt from the back of her neck. He always seemed amazed that she wasn't fazed by it. It irritated her, but today she pretended he was a boil that she was unable to lance just yet. Yesterday he was a plumped-up mosquito. Tomorrow he'd be a dust mite, crawling up her leg, that she could sense but not see. Both heard Jimmy clear his throat. Harlan climbed down and began to rebuke his slick-talking part-time driver.

"Where were you, Jimbo? I called for you over twenty minutes ago. Get the lead out of your ass, boy. I wanted you to drive Claudine home. That's all you have to do, is drive. What the hell good are you if you can't be here when I need you?"

Hattie Mae wasn't listening anymore. She'd walked outside to smoke a cigarette. She'd never liked Jimmy, couldn't respect a man that wouldn't look her in the eye when he spoke. He'd been driving her home, off and on, spying on her for Harlan for the past ten years or so. She wasn't one to judge a book by its cover, but she'd made an exception in his case. He was peculiar looking. In all the time he'd worked for Harlan, he never uttered a word to her or nodded in her direction, and that was just fine by her. Hearing his voice made the hairs stand up on the back of her neck. She never let her guard down around a man like that. Something about him just didn't sit well with her, and every time he slithered into a room, she wanted to reach for her pistol and sentence him for the despicable things she knew he'd gotten away with. She'd go back to jail a hundred times before she allowed him to come anywhere near Claudine.

WILLY EARL WAS careful hobbling through the back door. He'd made sure Hattie Mae was gone before he snuck to Claudine's side of the duplex. Instinctively he knew that he was most likely risking both his arms, but it was a chance he was willing to take. He had to convince Claudine that she needed him, assure her that he was here to stay. He had it all figured out; if Claudine wanted him back, Hattie Mae might let him stick around. He knew Claudine was home; he could smell the liver and onions cooking a block away.

"Is that you, Willy Earl?"

"C-c-course it's me. H-h-how many other Willy 'The Earl's' do you know?"

"What are you doing here?"

"You been eating g-g-good, I see. Where's my b-b-boy? Where is he?"

Claudine pointed to the sleeping bundle nestled in the middle of the bed and watched her teetering husband dodder awkwardly toward Junior. He was leaning on crude, uneven sticks, hand-fashioned to look like real crutches, for support. He resembled a cartoon character, the way his knees strained to point in opposite directions, and he'd lost a lot of weight, which made his eyes appear even larger than they actually were.

"You wanna hold him?"

"Naw. I wanna h-h-hold you."

"Me?"

"You."

Claudine scooted over, allowed him to wrap his spindly arms around her, and breathed deeply. She was anxious for something else to fill her up, keep her mind from wandering. Red velvet cakes, smothered pork chops, and endless plates of Adell's crispy catfish weren't satisfying her anymore. The glorious feeling of fullness always subsided, no matter how much she consumed. She weighed more now than when he met her, and he continued to want her. He was still her husband. That had to count for something.

Hattie Mae found them like that, wrapped tightly in each

other's arms. Willy Earl was so panicked by the sight of her that he nearly peed on himself. Claudine held on to him, reassuring him without words to hold his ground. Hattie Mae was livid, and she wasted no time letting the both of them know it.

"I wondered how long it would take you to creep back in here."

"Hattie Mae, j-j-just g-give me a chance. I-I-I . . ."

Hattie Mae rolled her eyes in disgust and refused to answer him; instead she directed her fury toward Claudine.

"What the hell is wrong with you, Claudine? You must want to flush your future down the toilet. Why else would you allow this fool back in here? Willy Earl is a bonofied leech, baby. He's going to hold you back, keep you down, suck the life right out of you like a Hoover."

"He's my husband," Claudine interjected softly.

"Girl, it's only a matter of time before he puts his hands on you and steals the food from Baby Boy's mouth."

Claudine nearly faltered during Hattie Mae's tongue-lashing. She almost told Willy Earl to go, in order to regain some measure of peace, but he squeezed her hand and whispered everything she longed to hear while Hattie Mae prattled on about his endless faults.

"I m-m-missed you so much, baby. I'm sorry I wasn't here for you. You-you know how much I loves you. I-I-I came as soon as I heard, but Hattie Mae b-b-busted my knees befo' I st-st-stepped through the do'."

Hattie Mae glared at them both and stormed out, promptly slamming the door.

"What about Junior? You love him, too?" Claudine whispered. She didn't wipe the spittle from the side of her face; his response was more important.

"Course I-I-I love that boy. He my-my boy. I-I'm gone be a good father. I need you, Claudine. I miss b-b-being inside of you. Baby, d-d-don't you want me?"

Claudine sensed that he was toxic, knew he wasn't what he

claimed to be, but she didn't have the energy to escape his tight embrace. He hadn't really even looked at his son, didn't know that the boy had a birthmark on his left foot or that he favored the sound of running water. Willy Earl confessed his devotion while he stroked her, warming places inside that had grown cold. He told her again and again of his dedication, until the crutches slipped to the ground and his hand found its way under her dress. Claudine wept quietly as she felt her legs open. Maybe this Willy Earl was better than having no Willy Earl at all.

CHAPTER 30

She was lonely. He'd leave on trips and not return for days, sometimes weeks, at a time. His sisters had moved out some months ago. He'd said that he found them good jobs. He discouraged her from making any girlfriends and forbade her to have anyone over when he was traveling. He claimed he wanted her all to himself. She thought he was sweet and remained in the house, eating imported chocolates and reading fashion magazines. He always left her more than enough money and told her to relax and enjoy herself. Hattie Mae missed her mama and her brothers and sisters. She longed to show them the sophisticated lady she'd become, but she couldn't go back home. She was a different person now. New hair, new clothes, and a sexy new voice, demure and understated, the way he liked it. When Nathan Lee was around, there were new people to meet and more gatherings to attend. He liked to show her off, always introduced her to each gentleman in the room. It had been exciting in the beginning, but surprisingly, she became bored and found that she wanted to do something, had to do something. She wanted him to get her a job, also, and complained that he was leaving her alone too much. The next day, he announced that he'd found her some work, asked if she was ready for a thrill.

He said they were going to another party, a special party for a

*very important man. She was to look her best and mind her man-
ners. She wore her finest dress, one that accentuated her volup-
tuous figure. They were stopped by the police on the road, and she
immediately began to pray. It was twilight, and Hattie Mae was
terrified. She'd heard enough horror stories from her mama and
brothers about white sheriffs stopping black folks in nice cars and
committing unspeakable acts. But Nathan Lee never broke a
sweat. He got this sly smile on his face and handed the police a
brown, folded piece of paper that he kept taped under the dashboard. He and Hattie Mae were told to move along. She marveled
at all the magnificent houses and manicured lawns. It was obvious that they were in a white neighborhood. Anything could happen to them, and no one would ever know. It was a long drive,
and she wanted to talk, ask what was on that folded-up piece of
paper, but Nathan Lee was unusually quiet. They arrived at a
grand house that had no lights, no cars, no people, and no music.*

"Nathan Lee, we must be at the wrong address."

"Shut up," he hissed, something he had never said.

*He blew his horn three short times and led her along a path
lined with dogwood trees and delicate azaleas.*

"This is a beautiful yard, Nathan Lee. Can we stop for a
minute, smell the pretty flowers?"

He didn't answer her, and he wouldn't let go of her hand.

*A very short man met them at the back door with a bourbon in
one hand and a model 12 Winchester clutched in the other like
he was expecting to use it. He eyed her up and down before he allowed them inside and guided them up the stairs. Nathan Lee
called him Your Honor and enunciated her name like she was a
foreigner. Then he never looked her in the eye as he ordered her
to remove her faux fur wrap for the judge and stand in the middle of the room.*

"This here is a tall one, Nathan Lee. You know I like the tall
ones."

*The stubby little man circled her like she was prey and tried to
bury his head in her chest. Startled, she pushed him away. He*

seemed to like it. She waited for Nathan Lee to defend her honor, quickly usher her from this place that reeked of sin.

"She'll do; she'll do nicely. Damn near looks like an amazon."

"And did you check out these big, juicy melons, Your Honor?"

"Noticed those right off, Nathan Lee; but you know I'm an ass man, too, and this little gal right here, or should I say big gal, has enough to keep me grinning for at least a week or two."

"Yes sir, Judge, I knew you'd appreciate this precious gem. Went out quite a ways to find her. She's mighty fine, ain't she?"

"That's one good thing about y'all's women. They do protrude in all the right places. I'll take her. I'll definitely take her."

"This diamond's gone cost you though, her being so well proportioned and all."

Hattie Mae listened to them discuss her body parts like she wasn't there, and it dawned on her that she had nothing. He'd bought the clothes on her back, the shoes on her feet. She had no money of her own, and he always kept hold of the keys to the car. Nathan Lee and this stranger were negotiating a deal. And suddenly, the past nine months became a dream of deceit. He'd never wanted her. Fragments of various conversations kept popping in and out of her head. She struggled to justify his actions; but in the end, reality prevailed, and her heart was crushed with the awesome weight of the truth. She saw their mouths move and satisfied smiles spread across their faces, but she couldn't hear them anymore. She was concentrating on the keys she heard jingling in Nathan Lee's jacket pocket and the large wad of money he was placing in a brown paper bag. The stubby one began to remove his clothes. It didn't take her long to realize that she had been sold. She was the party.

Nathan Lee tried to leave her there.

"I'm not staying here, Nathan Lee. Take me home right now."

He slapped her while the judge watched in amusement.

"I thought she was ready," the midget said. "You assured me she was ready."

Hattie Mae began to shake when she remembered her mama's words: "He'll be the ruination of you."

"Please, Nathan Lee, don't leave me here."

He stared at her like he didn't know who she was.

"Why so sad, baby doll? You ought to be grateful that someone as wealthy and powerful as the judge here wants you at all, seeing as how you so inexperienced, so green, so fresh." He winked at the judge and started to brag that he had other clients lined up, waiting their turn to sample the curvy hayseed that looked like a caramel-colored movie star.

"Looka here, Hattie Mae, if you behave yourself, the good judge here won't hurt you. Treat him extra nice, he might even keep you around for a while."

"Please, Nathan Lee, don't make me do this."

He pushed her away.

"You owe me, Hattie Mae. You've got to repay my generosity somehow. I've spent a lot of my time and money getting you ready. Did you actually believe I bought you all those fine things because I loved you, because you were special? His Honor here has paid good money to be in your company. Don't you get it yet? I deliver girls like you to men like him. I don't marry you simple bitches. Females don't interest me."

"What? What are you saying?"

"My God, girl, you dumber than I thought. Face it, baby doll, you have nowhere to go, so spread 'em with a smile and introduce the judge here to some of that famous country hospitality."

She heard her mama's voice as they advanced toward her: "Better to send 'em to Jesus than let one of 'em leave you in pieces. Ain't no shame in protecting yourself, keeping safe what God gave you."

Hattie Mae backed up and blinked back tears because she knew somebody was about to die.

Part 3

*C*laudine felt an urge to clean. She started with the bathroom and planned to scour her way to the parlor. She'd been going to her job sporadically, and no one seemed to give a damn. It was obvious that Hattie Mae didn't want her there. Claudine didn't care; she wasn't feeling too well, anyway. She usually didn't have much of a desire to do anything anymore, so when the urge came to disinfect, she took advantage of it. These days she was frequently tired. Willy Earl claimed that it was because she was hauling around all that extra weight. He was starting up with her again, slowly, deliberately. Taunting her, teasing her about her ever-expanding behind.

"That ass get any b-b-bigger, Deeny, we gone have to reinforce the t-toilet." It was almost as if he waited until she was calm to then disrupt her peace with petty insults.

"Cl-Cl-Claudine. Bet you thighs feel like they gone catch on f-f-fire."

Her fragile state of mind didn't deter his nasty disposition. When she was weak, he thrived. Tormenting her had become a hobby, which he perfected in his spare time. She'd insulated herself well from his attacks. He couldn't hurt her anymore. No one could. Her heart was numb, and she didn't feel anything at all. She wasn't disappointed in him, either. For some reason, she'd expected him to revert back to his original self. She ignored him most times. Ever since she'd told him that Hattie Mae was going to let him stay, he'd been acting like she'd never cracked him over the head in the first place or re-arranged his kneecaps. Claudine didn't know how in the hell anyone could forget something like that; but then, he was a moron, and morons needed reminding every once in a while. At least that's what Adell always said. Some days, Claudine wished Hattie Mae had cut his tongue out. Today he was getting on her last nerve.

"Brang me some more d-d-devil eggs, and I wants another Dr Pepper."

"What? Did you call me, Willy Earl?"

"Naw. If I-I'da called you, I'd h-h-have a pork chop in my hand."

She tried to erase his voice and concentrate on scrubbing the tile. Annoyed at his constant interruptions, she decided to mop Hattie Mae's side first. He wouldn't dare step foot over there, and she could use the peace and quiet. She started in the kitchen, washing the floor on her hands and knees until she found herself scrubbing in front of Hattie Mae's closet. She jumped up. She wasn't supposed to be in this room, cleaning or otherwise. How convenient, Claudine thought; Hattie Mae can rearrange everyone else's life, but no one was allowed a peek into hers. Claudine reached for the doorknob and turned it. What could Hattie Mae do to her that hadn't already been done?

Claudine stood gaping in disbelief, barely able to breathe. She hadn't thought that she'd ever see it again. She'd never wanted to, or at least that's what she'd told herself when her arms ached to hold Betty. She fingered the clasps on the case, and before she knew it she popped it open. Betty was whole and intact, nestled inside blue velvet. Claudine began to wring her hands like a junkie, bite her lip in frustration. The violin, her violin, was imploring her to reclaim it, caress it, remember it. She sunk to the floor and pulled her knees to her chest. It had been here all this time; and there was nothing she could do, no magic that unclenched her fists or directed her arms toward the bow. A black garment bag was hanging there, keeping the violin company. She unzipped it, careful not to let her arm brush the violin by mistake. It was a new dress, more ornate than the last, long and flowing, with intricate designs in the material. Claudine ran her fingers over the smooth fabric, one she'd never felt before. She began to weep at the absurdity of it all. Why had Hattie Mae done this? Had she kept these things to torture her, as a constant reminder of who she could have been? Claudine could no more fit into the fancy dress than she could stroke the violin that lay in the closet pleading to be played.

Hattie Mae discovered her there, sprawled out in front of her closet, holding on to that dress like it was a man. She had been hoping Claudine would find her way to that closet, open it, and get her memory back. In a way, she believed that the girl was suffering from a freak kind of amnesia. Claudine just needed something familiar to jar her memory. Hattie Mae had been waiting for the right moment to reintroduce her to the violin, but now was just as good a time as any. The spirit had led Claudine to find it on her own, and that had to be a good sign. Months ago, Hattie Mae had ordered the dress made from the House of Chanel, in Paris, the same size as the previous one. She'd written to those music schools on Harlan's personal stationery and inquired about another audition for Claudine. They were delighted to accommodate anyone handpicked by the popular Governor Tillford, the people's governor. They said that all she had to do was get there on time.

Hattie Mae had even gone to the courthouse and bribed Eulabell, in records, to destroy Claudine and Willy Earl's marriage license, supposedly per the governor's orders. She'd also had Willy Earl's filthy name deleted from Baby Boy's birth certificate. As long as she was walking this earth, Willy Earl Jenkins would have no claim to Claudine or that boy, ever. After all this time, Hattie Mae was still calling him Baby Boy. She couldn't bear to call him Willy Earl Junior. The name felt like a disease. Hattie Mae knew from experience that if she tried to keep them apart, Claudine would gravitate to Willy Earl out of spite. Keep your friends close and your enemies closer was a lesson she'd learned early on from Harlan Tillford. When Willy Earl had crawled back into Claudine's bed, Hattie Mae knew that he'd know better than to let her lay eyes on his scrawny face. They hadn't acknowledged each other once in six months, and she was grateful to have a respite from stupidity. Hearing his voice oozing through the walls was enough. Claudine would have to learn the hard way that a man like that couldn't change, couldn't magically transform into someone kinder or smarter. Being trifling was in his bones.

Hattie Mae slid to the floor and placed Claudine's head in her lap. She stroked the side of her daughter's face, and for once the girl didn't brush her hand away or curse Hattie Mae under her breath. They stayed that way until Claudine could get up on her own. When they finally stood, Hattie Mae wanted to knock her back down to the floor. She threw her hands in the air and shook her head in disbelief. She knew what kind of sickness the girl had. It was seeping out of her pores.

"One step forward. Three steps back. That's all you know how to do."

"What are you talking about?" Claudine asked, confused at the sudden coldness in her voice.

"You're pregnant . . . again."

Claudine glared hard at Hattie Mae. Instinctively her hands flew to her stomach.

"No."

"Yes."

"No."

But it was definitely possible. Claudine couldn't remember

the last time she'd bled, and more often than not she was in a daze, half asleep, when Willy Earl climbed on top of her. She shrugged her shoulders defiantly, avoiding Hattie Mae's piercing stare, and sank deeper into a relentless depression.

Hattie Mae stomped around in a fury. If Claudine didn't already look like she was pounding on death's door, she'd strangle her for getting herself knocked up again by that degenerate. Willy Earl wasn't remotely interested in the first one. Had to practically threaten him with a split skull to get him to wipe the boy's ass. Hattie Mae would have to handle Willy Earl permanently before he made a whole house full of big-headed, bug-eyed babies. Baby Boy came out fine, looked just like Claudine, thank the Lord, but who knew what the next one would look like? Man should have his pea-size balls cut off. Trying to multiply like a damn jackrabbit just so he could keep his lazy ass laid up in her house, eating Spam sandwiches and playing tonk with his dim-witted friends. She'd tolerated his ugly ways long enough, allowed him to remain on her property because Claudine halfway wanted him there. The sight of him literally turned Hattie Mae's stomach. He reminded her so much of someone she didn't care to remember.

The girl was just going to have to learn to take cold showers and use her imagination, like every other woman in Georgia. Hattie Mae had gotten rid of the Deacon, and Willy Earl was next on her to-do list. It amazed her that he lived a wall away and was still breathing. She was constantly surprised at her own restraint. Claudine kept saying that he pleased her, but Hattie Mae figured that was the dementia talking. And since Hattie Mae didn't listen to anybody crazy, arrangements had to be made. After this baby was born, Willy Earl had to disappear from their lives for good.

HATTIE MAE HAD made her come to work today. Demanded Claudine comb her hair, leave the house, get some fresh air. The governor was supposed to be away at a luncheon, so she didn't have to worry about him nosing around her and Claudine. She'd left Claudine in the kitchen, making pie crust, while she sat in the courtyard and smoked a cigarette. She was trying to figure out what in the world they were going to do with another baby when she heard Harlan's voice and Claudine's blood-curdling scream. Hattie Mae ran faster than she'd ever run in her life. The governor was squatting on the floor, trying to reason with Claudine, calm her down, but she kept screaming "Mama" and reaching for Hattie Mae, until it became apparent that "Mama" and Hattie Mae were one and the same. Initially, Hattie Mae thought Harlan had harmed Claudine in some way, provoked this hysteria, but he looked baffled and just as surprised. She held Claudine's shoulders tightly.

"Claudine, what's the matter, baby? What happened?" She knew Harlan was watching. She knew he'd heard every word that came out of Claudine's mouth.

"Did I just hear her correctly, Hattie Mae?"

Claudine's screams subsided into a soft whimper.

"Did she call you Mama?"

A strained look passed between them when Hattie Mae remained silent. Harlan waited for a verbal confirmation that would never come. She turned her attention back to Claudine. Hattie Mae didn't owe him any explanations. She didn't owe him anything. Harlan stood over them, refusing to leave, wanting to hear it all.

"He's here," Claudine whispered, shaking.

"Who's here?" Hattie Mae asked.

Claudine tried to tell her that she'd seen him outside the window, leering at her, and that he'd smirked when he saw the familiar terror in her eyes. He'd put his finger to his lips and waved to her with the other hand, the hand with the missing fingers. She began to hyperventilate when he entered the kitchen to ask the governor a question. She pointed at his feet, but Hattie Mae and Harlan didn't understand that he still wore the same tan shoes; and they didn't understand that his one blue eye still woke her in the middle of the night. He must have followed her that day. She'd always wondered, during moments of madness, how he knew her name, knew where she lived, and was able to recite personal information about her life.

The governor spoke first.

"Jimbo, what in the world is going on here? Do you know this gal?"

Hattie Mae didn't need to hear the whole answer. The panic on Claudine's face when he opened his mouth spoke volumes. It had been a long time, but Hattie Mae remembered how to kill a man. She leaned over and whispered in Claudine's ear.

"Mama's gone take care of it."

She felt Claudine grabbing frantically at her dress as she stood and walked toward the pantry. She heard Harlan calling her name. She watched Jimmy mumble and pretend like he didn't know what all the commotion was about. But the voice in her head stood out from the rest: "Better to send 'em to Jesus than let one of 'em leave you in pieces."

"Hattie Mae. Hattie Mae, where are you going?"

The governor nearly tripped on his own feet when he saw the gun in Hattie Mae's hand, the determination on her face. He'd seen that look before.

"Now, Hattie Mae, come on now, darlin', put that down now. I'm sure we can work this thing out. Jimmy, is there something you want to add here?"

Hattie Mae raised her pistol. Harlan looked from Jimmy to Hattie Mae and from Hattie Mae to Claudine cowering in a corner.

"Oh, good Lord, Jimmy, you didn't do what I think you . . ."

Unable to finish his question, Harlan took several steps backward, moving quickly out of the line of fire.

Jimmy had no time to respond and no place to run. The first bullet struck him directly in the right temple, before he could formulate a lifetime of denials.

CHAPTER 32

*N*athan Lee had underestimated her. He'd hoped she was broken, ready to deliver her soul to the devil because she was deceived, alone, and had nowhere to go. He'd assumed that she'd allow him to sell her body to the highest bidder without creating a scene. He'd believed she was incapable of defending herself, much too ladylike now to fight for her life. Nathan Lee ripped her favorite dress. Hattie Mae snatched the condensed little man's Winchester. All of a sudden the judge wasn't as interested in her cleavage anymore.

"All right, I've just about had enough of this," the little man hissed. "Go on now, get the hell out of here before you wake up the entire neighborhood."

His Honor couldn't have anybody knowing that he had two coloreds in his parlor, rabble-rousing in the middle of the night while he stood on the sidelines, naked as a jaybird.

"And I want my money back, Nathan Lee. She's just too much for me to handle. I don't have time for this. Do you understand me, boy?"

Things were getting out of hand. "Hattie Mae! Hattie Mae! Drop the Winchester now. C'mon, before you get yourself in a whole mess of trouble. Baby, this was all a misunderstanding. You know I would never leave you here. I just wanted to see how you'd handle a situation like this. Baby, you know I adore you. The judge here and I were just playing a game. You're so sexy when you get mad, Hattie Mae, did I ever tell you that? You gone make a good wife. Goddamnit now, Hattie Mae, put it down now. You hear me?"

Nathan Lee took a step toward her. She tightened her grip on the Winchester leveled at his heart. When the pseudocharm failed, he became angry and spiteful.

"What you think you gone do here, Hattie Mae? You think you gone shoot me? Huh? You know what I'm gone do? I'm gone drive back to Sparta and tell your highfalutin mama and your brothers what a worthless cock-sucking whore you've become. Miss Gracian's gone be so proud of you when I tell her how you routinely spread your thighs for a few cents on the dollar. Drop it now, Hattie Mae, or you won't recognize yourself after I get done with you."

There seemed to be no way out. She was humiliated and ashamed that she'd allowed him to lull her into such a false sense of security. She'd believed that he actually wanted to be her husband. She'd left her family behind to follow Satan. Had thrown away everyone and everything she loved just to end up standing against the wall holding a gun on the man she'd thought she'd be with forever.

"Did you ever love me, Nathan Lee? Were those other girls really your sisters and nieces and cousins?"

He just stood there, looking her up and down like she was stupid, like she was the one who'd lost her mind. And in that moment, he'd almost convinced her she had. This was a long way from the west side of the farm, a long way from canning peaches and harvesting the earth with her bare hands, now scented with expensive French perfume.

She glanced over at the petite judge rushing to clothe himself and wondered if he knew she'd been tricked, if he realized she wasn't supposed to be here, or if he cared that she had nowhere else to go. Nathan Lee lunged for the Winchester. They struggled *fiercely, and she didn't realize he'd struck her until she felt her left eye starting to close and a warm slickness spreading over her bottom lip. He managed to wrench the gun away from her, and she grabbed the car keys from his jacket pocket. She wasn't in the dark anymore. Maybe she had a chance. She'd take his car and drive as far as it would take her.*

"For Christ's sake, you stupid nigger," the judge exploded. "You can't even control your own whore. Give me my gottdamn gun; and from now on, I'm going to start buying my refined black tail from somebody else. You and I are history, you understand? I don't ever intend to lay eyes on you again."

"Your Honor. I'm sorry about all this commotion. I'll take care of her, believe me. Please reconsider your position and think about what you're saying. After all, I do have your express permission to be in this fancy neighborhood, doing what I'm doing. Got your handwriting taped under my dashboard for everybody to see."

"Are you threatening me, boy? Do you know who you're dealing with?" the petite judge asked Nathan Lee while Hattie Mae listened, horrified.

"All I'm saying is, I know you. I know all about you and your special preferences. I know how to get certain information, certain documentation, in the right hands if I have to. Tell me, sir, you still plan on running for governor next year?" Nathan Lee inquired coyly.

She waited for an opportunity to flee while they fussed back and forth, each trying to intimidate the other. When Nathan Lee attempted to return the Winchester to the judge, she bolted through the parlor, down the stairs, and out the back door. She was fumbling with Nathan Lee's keys when she heard the first shot. She froze, unable to move. Lights went on everywhere, and someone was calling her name.

CHAPTER 33

"My God, Hattie Mae, what have you done? You've killed him. I'm the governor, for Christ's sake. I can't be a party to a homicide."

"I didn't kill anyone," Hattie Mae answered, her face devoid of any emotion. "You did." She walked calmly to Claudine, warm gun still in hand, and guided her toward the door.

"Where do you think you're going?"

"I'm taking my daughter home. It's your turn to clean up the mess."

CLAUDINE WOKE UP in her own bed, startled and confused, soaked with perspiration. She'd dreamed that Hattie Mae had killed him for her, the man in her nightmares; shot him dead right in front of her face. Claudine reached out blindly for Willy Earl but brushed against something soft and firm instead. She pulled Junior close and held on tight. It had all seemed so real. She remembered what she was doing, what she was wearing, and how the governor was standing over her, peering into her face like he was searching for something familiar.

When the bedroom door opened, Claudine knew it wasn't

Willy Earl, and when she saw Hattie Mae's face, she was sure it hadn't been a dream at all, but a memory. Hattie Mae was standing in the doorway, normal as could be, not trembling or worrying about the police or instructing her on what she should or shouldn't say. She just leaned there casually against the frame, smoking a cigarette and cooing at the baby.

"You sleep all right?" Hattie Mae asked softly, avoiding her daughter's eyes.

"Yes," Claudine answered.

"You gone be okay now." It was more of a statement than a question.

Claudine nodded her head, dumbfounded, and handed over the baby as Hattie Mae continued like nothing out of the ordinary had happened to either of them.

"You stay here and rest awhile, get some sleep. One of us has to get back to work."

For a brief moment, Claudine thought that Hattie Mae would say something more, reassure her somehow that everything was going to be all right. Embrace her and promise the world. But when Hattie Mae grasped the doorknob without missing a step, Claudine realized that they would probably never speak of what had happened in the governor's kitchen that morning. Never acknowledge that that diabolical man had existed at all. Claudine was still stunned at how Hattie Mae had ended his life with such ease—it never appeared that she would question that monster or that she wavered in pulling the trigger—while Claudine sat completely petrified, unable to move again. Even now, in the aftermath, words escaped Claudine, and what she needed to say became lodged in her throat. She wanted to thank Hattie Mae for risking everything, for being there, for protecting her when she couldn't protect herself. The woman she'd believed had thrown her away had killed for her without blinking an eye. Claudine had been wrong about Hattie Mae; she knew that now. She didn't know all the answers, but forcing a confession out of Hattie Mae was no longer important. Claudine had a real, live, breathing mama, and that was the only thing that mattered. She wanted to tell Hattie Mae that she loved her, and she didn't care what she had done in the past. Claudine wanted to ask for forgiveness and reach out to the mother she was just beginning to know. Claudine wanted to be held by her, once, before she closed the door and disappeared on the other side.

"Mama."

Hattie Mae paused, her back to Claudine.

"Please be careful."

And then she was gone, and Claudine felt a small flicker of faith. For the first time since that dreadful day underneath the bridge, she experienced a reawakening, a healing from the inside out. She was alive again, and in the darkest corner of her soul, she finally believed she was loved.

Willy Earl was hiding behind the bathroom door, waiting for Hattie Mae to leave. He'd heard her come in while he was taking a leak. She hadn't pummeled him lately, and he didn't want to provoke her by being in her direct line of sight. He was terrified of her and knew way down deep that she'd love to see him take the big dirt nap, and there'd be nothing he could do about it. But he had been listening and peeking from behind the hinges of the bathroom door. He'd heard Claudine call her Mama, saw the expression on Hattie Mae's face. Could it be that Hattie Mae was actually Claudine's mother? Now, this here was a secret worth knowing. His mouth began to salivate at the thought of having something on Hattie Mae Jones. But on the downside, if Claudine was making nice with the evil old witch, it was only a matter of time before they tried to get rid of him, stomp him into the ground. Or, worse yet, send him back to Mozell and endless days of potted meat slathered on stale white bread decorated with green specks. Well, well, well, this little piece of information might get him a gold tooth after all. He had to keep a tight rein on Claudine, remind her

again just who was boss. He limped through the door, keeping
his right hand on his good knee.

"So, Hattie Mae's y-y-yo mama."

Claudine refused to answer him. She was still reeling at the
thought of Hattie Mae returning to the mansion, dealing with
the governor alone, working there like it was an ordinary work-
day. She replayed the scene in her mind again, heard the shot,
saw him stumble and fall forward. She recalled the way Hattie
Mae spoke to the governor. It was familiar, way too familiar,
and the manner in which Governor Tillford reacted, like he
was accustomed to it. It was as if he knew she was going to
shoot. He hadn't even tried to stop them when they left. And
she could swear that she'd heard Hattie Mae mention something about him, the governor of Georgia, cleaning up the
mess.

"Don't ma-matter if you won't answer. I-I-I knew it all along.
You hear me, Fa-fa-fat Deeny. I betcha if I had a bucket o'
chicken you'd talk to me."

Claudine didn't see him. She was someplace he couldn't
reach with his insults and accusations. There was so much to
process, so many new feelings to absorb. A man was dead because of her. Another baby was growing inside of her, every
day, and the hatred she'd felt for Hattie Mae over the past two
years had vanished, along with her obsession for Willy Earl.
She crawled out of bed and began to dress, completely unaware that he was still attempting to engage her in conversation.

"Where you think you going now, hef-hef-heffa?"

Willy Earl said everything he could think of to antagonize
her, nudge her into a confrontation, but she continued to ignore him, treat him as if he didn't exist anymore. It was eerie
the way she looked through him, like he wasn't there. She reminded him of Hattie Mae. Frustrated, he decided to go in
search of answers elsewhere; and when he returned, some-

body was going to give him the respect he deserved, dammit. He was Willy "The Earl" Jenkins, and he was back in the game.

Claudine stood again in front of Hattie Mae's closet, this time sure of what she would find. It was two hours and eighteen minutes before she could open the door. She removed the black case and closed her eyes. If she concentrated real hard, remained focused, maybe the music would begin to flow and remind her who she was. She ached to open it and hold Betty now, smell the wood, slide her fingers across the strings. She wanted to remember what it felt like when the bow worked its magic and became a part of her hand.

CHAPTER 34

When she didn't come, the judge found her, marched her back up the stairs and through the parlor. He made her look at Nathan Lee, what was left of him. Blood and chunks of flesh were splattered on the walls, the floor, and all over His Honor. He'd obviously wanted to make sure Nathan Lee was truly dead.

"You want to kiss him good-bye, or perhaps you'd like to get a shot in yourself? Go on, it'll be our little secret. It'll make you feel better."

Hattie Mae shook her head no and implored him to let her go.

"I promise I'll never tell a soul what happened here, please," Hattie Mae pleaded. But she knew he wasn't going to take that chance.

"You know I can't do that, darlin'. Somebody's got to take the fall for this. Somebody's going to have to clean up this mess. You're probably going to have to do some hard time; but if you keep your mouth shut, I'll put in a good word for you, make sure you don't get thirty years to life for trying to murder an elected official. And besides, no decent person would ever believe a woman like you anyway, a woman who consorts with a notorious nigger pimp. I, on the other hand, am a respectable citizen, an officer of the law. I have a future to protect and a high-society wife to support. This is an awful shame, too; you mighty pretty for a colored girl."

He told her that he intended to inspect her mounds of glory one last time before they shipped her to Constitution Street. She stood stoically while he stepped carefully over Nathan Lee and advanced toward her. He expected her to wail hysterically, fall down on her knees. But Hattie Mae refused to beg him. She'd never beg anyone for anything again.

He informed the police that the prostitute and the pimp had been trying to rob him, had intended to shoot him with his own gun and steal the precious treasures of his Confederacy collection. Everybody knew he had coins that once belonged to Jefferson Davis himself, even dumb, uneducated niggers like them. The authorities applauded him and patted him on the back for his courage and quick action. They leered at her, each lining up to run his hands under her dress and across her bare breasts, pretending like they were searching for contraband. They examined her in the open and took turns probing her again in the privacy of the judge's opulent foyer. She wouldn't remember how many of them violated her with their hands and their tongues or hurriedly ripped the bodice of her dress, exploring her roughly, stealing her virginity. They all began to merge into one face, and after a while, she stopped counting.

Someone downtown asked her if there was anyone she wanted to call. Saying no was effortless. It would be better if her mama never heard from her again, believed she was married now, with one on the way, than found out she was going to jail behind Nathan Lee. Hattie Mae felt enough shame, for everybody she'd ever known. Later, a different judge sentenced her to twenty years and sixty-two days. Twenty years for attempted murder and sixty-two days for being mixed up with a known criminal. That same judge asked her if she had anything to say for herself or any apologies she wanted to make to the Tillford family. She didn't hear him anymore. She was back on the farm, peeling sweet potatoes and showing her sister Viola how to jitterbug. She was still twirling around, snapping her fingers to the music, when the court declared her insolent, placed her in contempt, and gladly sentenced her to another year for good measure.

She'd served five and a half years before she saw him again, peering at her like she was a long-lost relative. Although she feigned like she didn't know who he was, her flesh began to crawl the moment her name passed his lips. She tried to keep busy in the prison kitchen, but they came to fetch her, told her she had no choice. He'd requested a private visitation.

"You still mighty pretty. Good to see that prison hasn't dirtied you."

She remained silent, confused as to exactly what he wanted but knowing he wanted something. He puffed his chest out, and it was obvious he had lifts in his shoes.

"I'm the governor for the whole state of Georgia, and I require someone to run the kitchens at the mansion. I heard you were handy with a frying pan. Of course, one of my aides could have taken care of this very important selection, but you know I'm extremely particular."

He moved toward her and whispered an offer she couldn't refuse.

"I'll arrange for a conditional parole, possibly get your sentence commuted, if you come to the mansion and take care of things, whatever I need you to take care of. You'd never want for anything, I assure you. You'd have your own house, your own car, and I'll let you go a lot sooner than the Metro ever will. I'll be keeping tabs on you, though. I can't let a woman like you run wild. You've done well, Hattie Mae; consider this a reward for keeping your mouth shut. I've never met another colored gal like you, Hattie Mae. You're one of a kind."

She didn't need time to ruminate over the offer in her cell or weigh the pros and cons of remaining in jail versus getting a chance to live again. He advised her in no uncertain terms, before they sealed the deal, that he wouldn't tolerate any willfulness or trickery.

"I'll send you back here lickety-split before I allow you to make a fool out of me. After all," he reminded her for the nineteenth time since he'd entered the small, rectangular room, "I am the governor. Do we have an agreement?"

She maintained eye contact and offered her hand. He didn't want that. He wanted to do something else to secure their new, mutually beneficial arrangement. She'd suspected what he wanted all along. She could see it in his eyes, the way he stared at her. It reminded her of that awful night in his house, when he was a judge, before the police arrived. He motioned for her to remove the hair net. She followed all of his silent instructions, unsnapped her prison-issue slate gray dress and prepared to seal the deal with the devil.

CHAPTER 35

"Boy, you talkin' crazy." The Deacon inspected his nails. One of the busty usherettes had just given him a manicure. He didn't believe in a man having grimy nails. No telling where you might find your fingers later. Manicured nails and shined shoes were what separated the men from the boys, the players from the two-bit hustlers.

"I think she must have knocked out part of yo brain along with yo mangled knees. Get on outta here with that mess."

"I'm telling you, Deacon, I heard everythang. I heard Claudine call her Mmmmmama. Hattie Mae had a tear rolling down her face. I'm talkin' 'bout a real tear. Think about it; k-k-kind of make sense, don't it?"

Luther Mack straightened the cuff of his sharply creased trousers and waved the gimp-legged boy toward the back door of the church like he was a gnat. Willy Earl was silly in the head, just like his slick-talking mama. If Luther Mack didn't believe Willy Earl to be such an dummyseed, he'd give this ludicrous claim a little more attention. Damn fool was going to get his eyes plucked out next time, messing around with that evil-ass Hattie Mae. Wasn't too long ago that the boy's head resembled one thick scab. The Deacon sighed and shook his head. It was his duty to try to counsel the simpleminded, up-lift the half-wits of the community.

"Listen here, boy. I don't care what you think you heard. There's no way Hattie Mae could be Claudine's mama. I'm Claudine's daddy, and I'd recall, believe you me, if my peter had ever been inside that behemoth woman. Damn fool."

"H-h-how you-you know?"

"How I know what? You gone have to speed it up, boy. All this stuttering and slow talkin' is beginning to irritate me."

"How you know you-you-you Claudine's daddy?"

"Watch yo mouth in here. You in the Lord's house. Don't you be bad mouthin' Willamina, either, God rest her soul. What did I just say? You deaf now, too?"

"Okay, Deacon, h-h-how many children you have by Willa-mina?"

"What you trying to say, boy?"

"How many?"

"My twins, Bone and Claudine."

"H-h-how do you know?"

"How do I know what, boy?" the Deacon yelled, aggravated.

"How do you know they was twins?"

" 'Cause Willamina, 'cause Hattie Mae . . . 'cause I . . ."

The Deacon stopped speaking for a moment and started fig-uring and remembering. He was going to say because Willa-mina told him so. He hadn't been there when those babies were born. He was on the other side of town making a new one. He'd met Hattie Mae around that time. She was there, in the room, when Willamina showed him the babies, told him she'd had two. He didn't think anything of it at the time; after all, they were sisters. But his mind was spinning with memories, days he had felt like something wasn't quite right. Hattie Mae letting piss-poor Willamina move into that big house like that, knowing she didn't have any money, buying furni-ture for Willamina and anything Claudine ever wanted.

Taking Willamina shopping and giving her money for Bone whenever she needed it. Never even asked for it back. Wasn't that what sisters did for each other? Hell, he'd never so much as bought his sister a ham sandwich. Come to think of it, Hattie Mae had always done more for Claudine than she did for Bone. Willamina never needed him for anything after Hattie Mae mysteriously showed up. At first he enjoyed the lack of responsibility, even bragged about his special arrangement, spent his money on other avenues. It didn't take long, though, for him to become a joke, feel like an outsider. He wasn't the man of the house, the king of the castle. His final word was no longer the final word. Hattie Mae had completely taken over after those babies were born, and he'd hated himself and everybody else for allowing her to assume a role that was rightfully his. He was a respected deacon once, preaching the gospel, and she was the head of his household. Hattie Mae Jones was an abomination; that's what she was. He called after Willy Earl, who was teeter-tottering down the steps.

"Hey, boy, what else did you hear?"

Willy Earl grinned widely and sat down. He had no idea how thick the lies were, swirling around in that duplex, but after seeing Hattie Mae's face, he did know that she was definitely Claudine's mama. And if she was Claudine's mama, then this old fool standing here, scratching his head like a monkey, couldn't possibly be her daddy. It took the Deacon long enough to figure that out, and people called *him* dim-witted. He needed the Deacon on his side. He couldn't go after Hattie Mae Jones alone, and he intended to go after her, all right, make her pay for his knees, his head, and everything in between that wasn't working right.

"You told anybody else about this, Willy Earl?"

"No, suh."

"What about Claudine? She know you know?"

"I-I guess. I don't know . . . wouldn't even talk to me before I left. What we gone do now, Deacon?"

"We gone hatch us a plan, but we got to be careful, though, real careful. You know that woman works for Governor Tillford, found that out in the clink. If you play your cards right, you'll get a lot more out of her than a gold tooth."

CHAPTER 36

"*The governor was true to his word, Hattie Mae was released two days later and picked up in a fancy Chevrolet. It was all very hush-hush, her conditional parole. The other inmates wouldn't know she was gone until weeks later. In the back seat of the car, she pressed her legs together tightly and tried not to remember the feel of him or the way he clung to her like a parasite. Briefly afterward, she'd contemplated making a run for it when she got out; but he must have sensed her uncertainty, because he swore he'd find her, have her family arrested and jailed until she surrendered. She cringed at that thought and knew this was only the beginning. He had told her things when he'd wedged his head between her breasts. How her mother suffered from arthritis and Viola was running the farm, and did she know she had sixteen new nieces and nephews? Soon, she hoped, he'd become bored with her and encounter someone else to capture. In the meantime, she would make the best of it, attempt to have a normal life, forge a new path for herself.*

She was dropped off in front of an elegant white duplex and handed a large envelope and two sets of keys. One for the house, the other for the gleaming new Plymouth parked in the garage. The house, the car, every luxury was in her name, like he'd promised. She was reminded that everything would remain the way it was as long as she abided by the rules. Rule number one: report to work on time every day. Rule number two: be discreet about where you're employed and for whom. Rule number three: never allow anyone into the house without his permission. Rule number four: no one was to step one foot in her bedroom, ever. She understood he intended to control her, monitor her every move.

She was sent directly to his office the first day and asked again if she understood what was required of her. He enjoyed flexing his power, lording it over her like some ravenous emperor. She accommodated him, his bizarre requests—eating slices of strawberry pie from various orifices of her body, lapping pure maple syrup from her toes, wedging his upper torso between her legs like he was trying to reenter the womb. As distasteful as she found his nasty predilections, she gratified him for fear of jeopardizing her freedom. Freedom—although she wasn't behind the bars anymore, she might as well have been. From the moment he walked into that prison, her life revolved around his needs and his life of aberrant details.

It didn't take long for Emily Tillford to discover Hattie Mae barefoot in the expansive kitchen, making pies. She would come and sit and stare for hours, never saying a word, always with a look of envy etched on her narrow face. Hattie Mae did everything she could to show her that being there was not her choice. The governor was the master puppeteer. Unbeknownst to him, it paid off. The governor's wife spoke one day, out of the blue, after months of silence.

"At first I thought you liked it, being here, lying with my husband, and I've hated you for it. But I was wrong, wasn't I?"

"Yes," Hattie Mae responded, her eyes focused on the flour that needed to be sifted.

"It's no wonder; I'm always wrong. I guess I should be grateful; ever since you came here, he's been remarkably decent to me, almost kind. I wanted him to look at me just once the way he looks at you."

"No, you don't, Miss Emily."

"He talks about you in his sleep, you know. You've been in his head a long time now, Hattie Mae; but I've been watching you, and you don't strike me as a woman who would lie with him willingly. I see that he disgusts you."

"Yes."

"He has you trapped like a rat in a cage, doesn't he? He has something on you, something that's kept you from running."

Hattie Mae didn't have to answer; Emily Tillford saw the pain spread across her face. As much as she tried to despise the black woman her husband lusted after, she couldn't muster any hatred. They were two very different women with the same dilemma. Both were stuck with a man they wished was dead. In the beginning, Emily Tillford had tried to love Harlan, be a model governor's wife, but deep down she sensed he never really wanted her, never desired her the way a husband should desire a wife. He had moved from one black whore to the next, often flaunting his distaste for her pale skin and waiflike body in her face. "Go sit outside, Em, your skin looks like a peeled potato. Look at me when I'm talking to you, Em. When you turn sideways, I can't see you at all, ass flat as a pancake. You know, that striped bass I just caught has bigger lips than you." Her life was a carefully designed concoction, a pieced-together production. He had married her for show. If he could have wed one of those black tramps, he would have. How ironic that the one he fancied, the one whose name he called out when he was bucking inside of his wife, wanted nothing to do with him. Emily Tillford thought it poetic justice that Hattie Mae would just as soon slit his throat than live as his merry mistress. They both knew he was in love with Hattie Mae. She was the wife he wanted but couldn't claim in public. Emily was his window dressing, his alibi, and she loathed him for it. So there were no afternoon luncheons or giddy conversations about life and love. Emily Tillford and Hattie Mae Jones became unlikely allies and invisible friends. They developed a silent understanding and stiffened simultaneously whenever he entered a room.

He gave extravagant gifts to Hattie Mae and sometimes ordered her to wear her hair down and paint her lips the color of a cherry. He knew she didn't like to draw unnecessary attention to herself, but that didn't stop him from presenting her with form-fitting dresses and several tubes of imported lipsticks, always delivered to her in a plain brown bag. The help didn't bother with her too much. She saw the way they turned their noses up when she walked by, heard the whispers when she arrived early and left late. She continued to hold her head high and tried to exist in a house that threatened to suffocate her.

It took three months for her to realize that she was pregnant, remember that she hadn't seen her flow since the Metro. Concealing her swelling abdomen was essential, and confiding in him was never an option. He constantly reiterated that no one must ever know of their arrangement, or his political career would be ruined; and if she ever found herself in a family way, he'd make sure she'd be well taken care of. He knew of a special doctor that handled such vicissitudes. He'd used him before. Hattie Mae abhorred Harlan and vowed to protect the child growing inside of her, keep it from him at all costs.

She started to eat excessively in his presence, began to comment on her own weight. She wore oversize aprons covering her snug dresses. When she couldn't manipulate the seams anymore, she knew it was time to throw her plan into action. It was storming outside on the morning she went looking for Miss Emily, who was heavy with child herself, and initiated their first real conversation—Hattie Mae cried on cue. She claimed she'd received an urgent telegram informing her that her beloved mother was ill, on her deathbed, about to meet her maker. She said she was afraid the governor wouldn't allow her to leave. She asked tearfully for Miss Emily's assistance in convincing him to let her go, spend some time with her family. Thanks to Miss Emily's persuasion, he reluctantly granted her a leave, ordering her to call once a week. Miss Emily made sure that he kept his word and sent her packing the very next day. Hattie Mae suspected that his delicate wife knew about her condition yet yearned for the chance to deceive him and be rid of her at the same time, if only for a few short months. Emily was integral in keeping him occupied, sustaining his attention, sticking to his side like a dutiful wife, as Hattie Mae knew she would.

She rented a room three towns over, found a midwife named Adell to help her bring life into the world. It was difficult for Hattie Mae to trust anyone, but severe contractions left her no alternative. She delivered Claudine on a Wednesday and marveled at the baby's sheer perfection, the best thing she'd ever done. The first time Hattie Mae held her, she knew the child was destined for greatness and realized right then that she couldn't leave her behind for someone else to love. There had to be a way to keep her near, supervise her upbringing, make certain that she received everything she needed to thrive. It could be done, but she couldn't pull it off alone. For both their sakes she was forced to ask the midwife for guidance. In a leap of faith, Hattie Mae divulged her life's story: Gracian, Nathan Lee, Harlan, the Metro, working in the governor's mansion, and everything in between that brought her unwillingly to this moment of clarity. Adell graciously opened her heart, and Hattie Mae wept profusely, finally able to unburden her soul.

Adell said she knew of a girl heavy with child, due any day, who desperately needed money. She was young, fourteen, and had been put in the family way by some two-faced, fork-tongued preacher man from over in Atlanta. He'd abandoned the poor girl when he found out, said she didn't have a pot to piss in or a window to throw it out of. Claimed he was somebody big in his town, needed a girl with substance. The child was some scared and alone, didn't have any kin to help her, and was looking for somebody to adopt the baby. Her name was Willamina, and Adell was convinced that she'd jump at the chance to flee this place where most folk pointed at her tattered clothes and yelled Hussy when she stepped into the light of day.

The promise of a fine house to live in, real food to eat every day, and money for her baby whenever she needed it persuaded Willa-mina to accept Hattie Mae's offer. Six days later she delivered a scrawny baby boy, barely clinging to life. The three women made a pact that night, vowed never to tell another soul the true cir-cumstances of Claudine's birth. Adell agreed to return to Mari-etta with Willamina, keep an eye on things when Hattie Mae wasn't around. And as far as anyone would ever know, Hattie Mae and Willamina were sisters, and the two-faced, fork-tongued preacher man from Atlanta was now the father of twins.

Hattie Mae watched the governor carefully when she returned to the mansion, saw the things he gave his daughter, and became an expert mimic. She bought the same dresses, ordered identical shoes, and found a colored charm school for Claudine to attend so that she would be well taught in social etiquette, like Laven-der. When Hattie Mae overheard Miss Emily tell Lavender that a proper young lady should master an instrument, she followed them to a music store and returned the next night to buy the exact same violin. What was good enough for his daughter was good enough for hers. Claudine would have everything his money could buy and more. And as the years passed, Hattie Mae watched Lavender struggle with the violin and melted inside when her child played like an angel, played like it was the only thing she was ever meant to do.

CHAPTER 37

She walked gracefully through the throng of police officers who were moving about the grounds, questioning members of the staff. She overheard the gardener say that no one really heard or saw anything because the shooting occurred so early in the morning. She wanted to tell the police that they were wasting their time. Even if anybody had seen her pull the trigger, they'd never talk. Anyone who was close to the governor knew he protected Hattie Mae. Folks around these parts loved Governor Tillford. The man had been elected to six straight terms, always beating his opponent by a landslide. She'd never understood how such a repugnant little man could be so loved, so adored. She couldn't imagine what the governor had said about how Jimmy got that hole in the side of his head, and she didn't care. Someone tapped her on the shoulder.

"Hey there, Miss Hattie Mae. We just need to ask you a few questions. Good thing you were out sick this morning, or you might have witnessed the shooting. We're doing our best here to keep this thing pretty low-key. The big guy doesn't want the press catching wind of this one. Can you believe it? Somebody he handpicked tried to off him with one of his own guns. Sick bastard, that Jimmy Dulan, planning to assassinate the governor. Did you know he was an ex-con, had a prison record as long as my leg? Did you ever notice any suspicious behavior toward the governor? Did you—"

"No. And I didn't even know his last name until now. . . ."

"That's enough of this mess, now," Harlan interrupted from the background, anxious to speak to Hattie Mae alone. "Hurry up and get the hell on outta here."

Still they had questions for him, so many questions. Policemen were crawling everywhere, dusting for prints, refusing to give him a moment's peace. They wanted to protect him, they said, in case Jimmy Dulan had any accomplices. Why did Dulan do it? What was his motive? Was he working alone? There was even talk of an FBI investigation. Harlan's press secretary had managed thus far to keep this whole nasty business out of the papers. Hopefully this spectacle would die down fast, and everything would be back to normal by the end of the week. The governor told them he wasn't answering any more goddamned questions.

"The reprobate simply wanted money. He tried to kidnap me. We got as far as the kitchen. We struggled, and I managed to get my gun back and blow the son of a bitch away. End of story."

Alone, Harlan Tillford leaned back in his overstuffed leather chair and downed his fourth scotch. He couldn't even laugh at the irony of this situation. He'd gifted Hattie Mae with the twenty-five caliber, pearl-handled baby Browning to protect herself. He owned a slew of them, gave one to his daughter when she left for college and made his late wife, Emily, carry one in her purse, just like Hattie Mae. He'd run and gotten a gun after Hattie Mae left and fired it outside, wrapped Jimmy's limp hand around it so the prints would match. It had never occurred to him not to interfere, not to protect Hattie Mae. She'd gone to the Metro for him once. He owed her, and they both knew it. They'd known each other a lifetime, he and Hattie Mae, and he was certain she'd realized from the first moment she left his bed that he intended never to let her go.

She'd always been a thrill ride for him, something new and exotic. She was an intricate labyrinth he had to solve, a sensual enigma to ponder again and again. As the years passed, he tried to discover her secret, unlock the mystery and figure out why he could hardly make love to another woman, including his own wife, after he'd been inside of Hattie Mae Jones. She loathed him. He felt it, and that kept him on his toes, allowed him to maintain a practiced indifference whenever she was around. He'd never thought that he'd come to depend on her, and he didn't realize he was in love with her until he told the police, without a second thought, that she was never there.

And now, deep down in his gut, he knew she'd managed to keep something from him. He didn't know how. He'd watched her constantly, and when he wasn't around, he usually had somebody else watching her. He knew where she went and with whom. He knew where she purchased her salt pork and the special Madagascar vanilla she used in her sweet potato pie. He knew where she shopped for shoes and which attendant serviced her car every Sunday. He knew to the day when her monthly came, and he was informed every time someone new crossed her path, even if it was to light her cigarette. He assumed he knew her like the back of his hand. He was sure he knew everything about her that there was to know. He prided himself on holding her close to the vest. How had she managed to have a child, his child, and he not know? Harlan threw his tumbler against the wall and reached for a new one. When? When had this happened? Damn her. And then he remembered, years ago, when she said that her mother was dying. She had gone crying to Emily, and Emily insisted he allow her to go home for a while, spend some time with her family. His wife always suspected something was going on between them. He'd had to let Hattie Mae go then, keep Emily off his back, pretend like her presence didn't matter. Somehow Hattie Mae Jones had outsmarted him, and he didn't have to turn around to know she was there.

"It was Sparta, right? You had her when you went to Sparta that time, to see your mother." He didn't turn around. He couldn't face her, not yet.

"I never went to Sparta."

"Then when, then where? How?"

"Does it matter?"

"It matters because she's my daughter, goddamnit, and you've kept her from me! How could you do that?"

"Do what? Protect my daughter from you? You who didn't want to put together a search party to look for her when your driver murdered her dream? You who sent me to prison for something you did? You who for the past twenty years have kept me here for your own twisted purpose, promising me freedom, knowing you were lying every time you opened your filthy mouth? I don't owe you a damn thing, Harlan Tillford. I never have."

Harlan stood abruptly and turned to face her. God, she was still so beautiful. She'd shot a man in the head a few hours ago, and apparently it hadn't affected her at all. She was his kind of woman. In a different time, he would have married her, started a family. Her arms were folded across her chest, and her hair was pinned on top of her head. Twenty years had passed, and she didn't look like she'd aged a day.

"I didn't know, Hattie Mae. I didn't know she was our daughter when that happened."

"Should it have mattered, Governor?"

"Yes, goddamnit. Does she know? Does she know that I am her father?"

"No."

"Are you going to tell her?"

"No."

"What gives you that right? She's my daughter."

He swayed slightly, paced around when he spoke, slinging driblets of scotch from his glass wherever he walked. He noticed she didn't move at all.

"No, Harlan. Lavender is your daughter. Claudine is mine and only mine."

"We'll see about that."

"What are you going to do, Harlan? Announce to the world that you have a half-black daughter, out of wedlock, by an ex-con you got released from jail because she was serving time for a crime you committed?"

"You shut up. Shut your mouth right now, ungrateful little tramp. You'd probably be dead by now if it wasn't for my intervention. I've given you everything."

"You've given me pain."

"I ought to . . ."

"You ought to what? Send me back to the Metro? No. I've served all the time I'm going to serve for you, Harlan. Today I'm paroling myself."

Hattie Mae looked around his office. She wasn't planning on ever seeing it again. She hadn't intended that her departure be so revealing. She'd never wanted him to find out about Claudine, but now that he had, leaving was painless. Maybe it was better this way, him knowing, hurting, desperately wanting something he couldn't have. She left him there, wobbling, ranting about Sparta and slick-talking whores. She was in the pantry, reaching for her shawl, when he caught her off guard and spun her around to face him. He hissed up at her, scotch-flavored saliva spraying her face, his nails digging into the flesh of her wrists.

"You are not leaving me, woman. Not today. Not ever."

In his drunkenness, Harlan Tillford believed the rapid breathing belonged to him. He hadn't noticed the kitchen door opening or heard the footsteps clicking across the linoleum. Nor did he feel the baby Browning nuzzled behind his left ear.

"You take your hands off my mama."

CHAPTER 38

Luther Mack Tilbo drove erratically over to Hattie Mae's house, narrowly missing two pedestrians. He had no idea what he and the stuttering wonder were going to say, but he intended to get some answers out of that tight-lipped woman one way or another. He felt the cold steel resting nicely between his sock and his boot. Conniving witch. She would tell him the truth today or die lying.

"Listen here, boy, you let me do all the talkin'."

Willy Earl had been bombarding him with questions ever since they left the church. How long did he actually know Willamina? Didn't he ever wonder why Claudine didn't look like him? Just how much money had Hattie Mae given Willamina? After each question, Luther Mack became even more determined to get to Hattie Mae, because he realized he didn't know any of the answers. His mind was racing.

"H-how we gone get in, Deacon?"

"Don't you have a key to your own house, you damn fool?"

Luther Mack remembered that he almost hadn't recognized Willamina when she'd strolled into his church all dolled up. He remembered the crisp new bills she'd placed in the collection basket. He remembered the way she'd looked at him like she knew something he didn't. He'd asked around for days before he found out that she was Hattie Mae's little sister. The same Hattie Mae Jones who owned that big white duplex on Norfolk, the Hattie Mae Jones who always seemed to have an endless supply of liquid assets. He showed up a week later, with flowers for Willamina and candy for Hattie Mae, who he'd never seen in person. She wasn't at all what he'd expected. She was tall for a woman, stunning, and took his breath away when she opened the door. He observed the surroundings and quickly discovered that Willamina lived on the other side of the duplex, all by herself. They had some crotchety humpbacked woman hanging around, taking care of the house. He didn't like the way she eyed him up and down, snorting loudly when he attempted to make conversation. It dawned on him now that Hattie Mae had never left the room when he was there that first time, never allowed him and Willamina to speak alone. It took three glasses of lemonade and a nose full of smack, which he conveniently sniffed in her enormous bathroom, before he asked to see the baby. He was surprised when they handed him two, a scraggly little baby boy and a plump little girl whose skin was lighter than it should have been. It happens that way sometimes, the old humpback had piped up when she saw the confusion on his face. She'll brown up soon, Willamina had added, look at her ears. He'd believed them then, after they convinced him that he, too, was the color of a ripe walnut instead of a raisin. Willamina had already named the children Luther Junior and Claudine. He expressed to her that he wasn't too partial to the girl's name, but Hattie Mae said he'd better get used to it, just like that, right to his face. And before he left that day, she told him if he ever wanted to see those babies again, or step foot in that house, he best return tomorrow with a ring and marry his own damn self. He didn't know, then, that she would rule him for the next twenty years.

Bone grew to look like him. However, Luther Mack never thought about Claudine's appearance before because she was fat in the face, and Hattie Mae was always doting on her. He gave all his attention to Bone. Now he recalled how Claudine had looked suspiciously familiar at Willamina's funeral. People surprised at her thinness remarked how much she was beginning to favor her aunt, and when she'd stood next to Hattie Mae after the service, their profiles were the same. It was so obvious; the truth had been staring him in the face, and he never would have known it if this imbecile hadn't been eavesdropping in a crapper. One thing still left him confused as they opened the door and sat on Claudine's French provincial living room furniture. If he wasn't Claudine's father, then who was? And then it hit him, hard. Why hadn't he figured it out before? Everybody in the whole town knew no man had ever stepped one foot in Hattie Mae's bedroom. There was only one man who saw her every day, one man who'd been around her for the past twenty years, as long as Claudine had been alive, one very powerful, wealthy man. He slapped his thigh at his own deduction.

"Wh-wh-what's the matter, Deacon?" Willy Earl asked nervously.

"Hot damn, boy. We's about to be rich."

CHAPTER 39

*H*attie Mae clutched her purse tightly and stared out the window while Claudine drove. In a twist of fate, the daughter had become the protector, the liberator. As long as Hattie Mae lived, she would never forget the look on Harlan's face when Claudine held that baby Browning on him, the very same one he'd given Hattie Mae years ago, forced her to carry. She'd stashed it this morning in the violin case, never thinking her daughter would open it anytime soon. Hattie Mae and Harlan had been shocked to see her standing there strong and defiant. He'd cried like a baby when she'd threatened to shoot him, commanded her to consider his position. He must have thought she could understand him, decipher truth and parentage from his slurred speech. He'd called after them as they were leaving, refusing to accept the inevitable. He was sinking to the floor when Hattie Mae glanced back at him for the last time. He held her gaze, and they both knew that for once in his life all of his power meant nothing.

Something warm slid down Hattie Mae's face, and much to her surprise, it was tears.

"Don't worry, Mama. We'll leave this place. We can go anywhere. I'm ready to play again. I can hear the music in my head."

The tears began to flow faster, and no matter how hard she tried, she couldn't hold them in as she'd always done. She wept out loud, long, stirring sobs, causing Claudine to pull the car onto the side of the road.

"Mama, what's wrong?"

Hattie Mae was without words. She didn't cry because her only child called her Mama like it was the most natural thing in the world or because she'd have to tell her that that crumpled-up old man on the floor back there was her father. She didn't wail because she was afraid of what the future held for them. She didn't collapse into Claudine's arms because of all the wretched things she'd done to survive. She allowed Claudine to hold her close because Hattie Mae had glimpsed perfection again, witnessed the woman she'd sacrificed a life-time for her daughter to become.

CHAPTER 40

As they waited eagerly for Hattie Mae to return, Luther Mack and Willy Earl decided that one of them would clock her if they had to, tie her lofty ass up even, to obtain the information they needed. They'd lock Claudine in the closet if she got in the way, shove a cold biscuit down her throat. Willy Earl suggested that he'd hide behind the door and startle Hattie Mae, catch her off guard. He was desperate to be the one doing the bullying, giving the orders. He was tired of loud-mouthed women like Mozell and Hattie Mae deciding his future, dictating who he was supposed to be. Today they would both know he was the man with the plan.

The Deacon rubbed his hands together greedily. He could already feel the plump bulge in his pocket from the rolled-up hundred-dollar bills he was going to bilk from Hattie Mae. She would pay. The governor would pay. Somebody was going to pay for his misfortunes. All these years he had to work so hard, numbers running, messing around with small-time hustlers when he should have been relaxing, living the high life, like Hattie Mae. Own a couple of businesses, come and go as he pleased, work when he felt like it. She had everything—money, cars, the house, fancy clothes. He had a son that laughed at him and a no-account greasy daughter who wasn't his daughter after all.

"You reap what you sow," the Deacon murmured under his breath. He relished beating that wicked woman at her own game and had fantasized often about choking the life out of her with his bare hands. He imagined caressing her ample breasts, kissing her mouth while she gasped for air, but reckoned that her lips were probably just as poisonous as the rest of her.

"Amen to that, Dee-Dee-Deacon."

Willy Earl closed his eyes and saw Hattie Mae bound and gagged, tears streaming down her face, that fancy hair all over her head. He wanted to switch houses and sleep in her bed for a change. She was going to beg him not to beat the shit out of her, beg him not to deliver an old-fashioned ass whipping. Wh-wh-wh-where's your bat now? he'd ask over and over again. He scanned the room quickly; he'd have to hit her with something good, like a tire iron or a tree limb, for the blow to have any effect. She was a healthy woman, big boned, and his fists just wouldn't do the job. By the time he got through with her, he was going to be driving her Caddy with a mouth full of gold.

Willy Earl and the Deacon were so consumed by their respective revenge fantasies, so busy plotting and scheming that they didn't hear the footsteps coming through the back door.

"Well, well, well, looky here, Deke. I believe we've caught us a career criminal."

Luther Mack didn't need to turn around to figure out who was prodding him in the rear. He remembered the name, and he recognized the voice. His palms begin to sweat immediately with the memory of their last encounter. He still wasn't over it, the embarrassment, the humiliation, the revulsion he felt as they probed his private parts and laughed at his manhood.

"Couldn't just leave well enough alone, could you, boy? Why . . . this oughta get you a good twenty years in the pokey. Don't you think so, Deke?"

"Un huh, and he has an accomplice this time, Clyde."

"No. Wait a minute. He-he-he's with me. I live here with my wife," Willy Earl interjected, looking from one cop to the other in confusion. "This here is my fa-father-in-law."

"That right."

"Yes, sir."

Willy Earl watched the burly policeman flip through a small pad of paper. He wasn't worried. This was obviously a simple misunderstanding. All he had to do was keep calm, be cool, get rid of the law before Hattie Mae and Claudine returned. He nodded at the Deacon, who was strangely silent.

"You find what you were looking for, Clyde?" skinny Deke asked as he circled Luther Mack. "You awfully quiet, Deacon. What's the matter, don't have a sermon handy?"

"I'm with him. This is my daughter's house. We're waiting for her to come home; that's all. We don't want no trouble." As the words slipped from Luther Mack's lips, he knew *trouble* wasn't enough of a word to describe what they'd gotten themselves into trying to put the squeeze on Hattie Mae Jones. He had a sick feeling in the pit of his stomach, and all he wanted to do was run, get the hell out of there as fast as he could. These hillbilly cops were taking their time, toying with them. Of that he was certain. He glanced over at Willy Earl. The boy had no idea that the hammer was about to fall. The Deacon thought quickly. Somehow, someway, she'd played him again, but he had one last card to play.

"I want to speak to Hattie Mae."

"You trying to give me orders, boy?"

"Tha-tha-that's okay, Deacon," Willy Earl said. "I live here. We don't need to b-bother her. What's all this about?"

"Shut up, boy," the Deacon hissed.

"You hear that, Deke. This one says he lives here, in this grand old house."

"Yeah. Appears like he really believes it, too. Ms. Jones was right. The sickness has taken ahold of his brain."

"I-I don't understand. My-my wife . . . Claudine. She'll be back soon," Willy Earl added, utterly confounded.

"Your wife?" Clyde questioned. "Did he just say his wife, Deke?"

"I believe he did, Clyde. You know, I bet them fancy doctors got a special name for this kind of *in*sanity."

The Deacon located every possible exit in the house within his line of sight. He would claw his way out if he had to. They weren't taking him back to the Metro, no way, no how. If he could only get to Hattie Mae, tell her he'd figured it out, demand that she and that sawed-off runt of a governor pay for his silence, everything would be all right. He cleared his throat.

"Just call Hattie Mae. I have some information that she'll be interested in, she and Governor Tillford."

"Listen at this, now, Deke. Now this one here thinks he knows the governor. You want us to phone the president for you, too, boy?"

Luther Mack watched them slap their knees, laugh at his expense. They seemed so calm, too calm. Why weren't they arresting them? What were they waiting for? He took a chance and started to walk toward the door. Big Clyde blocked his exit and removed his billy club from its holster.

"We got a call this morning. Two darky nutcases, fitting ya'll's description, busted out of the loony bin a little while ago."

"So wha-what's that got to do with us?" Willy Earl asked, suddenly feeling very confident. Mistaken identity. He looked at his watch. He'd have this mess cleared up in five minutes. He grinned reassuringly at the Deacon.

"Well, one man is running around town pretending like he's the deacon of some big colored church, and the other, well, the other is just plumb crazy, with a . . . what ya call it, Deke?"

"Speech im-pe-di-ment."

"Yeah, what he just said, and this guy genuinely believes he's married to Miss Hattie Mae's niece. Thinks he lives in this house. That sound like anybody you know, Luther Mack? What about you, Willy Earl?"

Voices could be heard coming from the kitchen. Luther Mack tried to reach for his piece.

"Run, Willy Earl, run!"

Three men in white barreled through Claudine's parlor and grabbed them, bending their arms behind their backs. One went straight for the Deacon's gun like he expected it to be there.

"Hey, Deacon," Clyde called as they were wrestling Willy Earl to the floor, "you like my hat?"

Luther Mack lunged. Rage welled up inside of him, and he fought with everything he had, knocking over lamps, jumping over furniture, struggling to make it to the door, any door. He bit, clawed, scratched until Clyde cracked his ribs with the billy club and shoved a dishrag in his mouth. He heard Willy Earl whimpering like a puppy, and there was nothing more he could do. They were hopelessly outnumbered.

Willy Earl began to plead for mercy when he looked out the window and saw a van with small, black lettering on the side that read MILLEDGEVILLE CENTRAL STATE HOSPITAL.

"I'm sorry, I-I-I didn't mean it. Pl-pl-please let me go."

He managed to scream Claudine's name twice before they gagged him. Desperate, he strained to get the Deacon's attention. He wondered if he knew yet where they were going.

Luther Mack was still trying to put together all the pieces of this elaborate takedown while they were dragging him off the porch, trussed up like a turkey. Somehow she'd found out that they were coming for her. How had she beaten him again? How was she constantly able to stay one step ahead of everyone else all the time? How? She didn't trust anyone, and a woman like that couldn't afford to have any friends. Exasperated, defeated, he fell to the ground. She had to be around somewhere lurking, cackling at his defeat. Hattie Mae Jones loved to gloat from the sidelines, revel in her victory. He peered up and down the street, scrambling to get one last glimpse of her face. Instead he spied someone across the street pointing at him, laughing from behind lavish lace curtains. It was her. It had been her all along. She was the one who knew all the answers. She could have revealed the truth years ago. She'd been there from the beginning, like a hawk, observing, reporting back to Hattie Mae, protecting her interest, informing her of every single occurrence. He railed against the straitjacket and cursed her name. The last thing he saw before they shoved him into the van was the hump of her back and the shadow of his fifty-dollar hat sitting atop big Clyde's head.

CHAPTER 41

"This be all of it. You done finally lost your mind," Adell chimed from the parlor.

"I can't believe you're leaving all of your nice things, Mama. We can still put this stuff in storage somewhere. Come back for it later."

"We can't ever come back here, and stop calling me Mama."

"What are you saying? What about Bone?"

"Least give it all to the church or something," Adell added, incredulous at Hattie Mae's decision. "This is just crazy. Young folk nowadays don't have a lick of sense."

Hattie Mae rolled her eyes and ignored the frequent interruptions.

"Bone will find us. I'll make sure of that. This isn't our home anymore."

Hattie Mae detected Claudine's uncertainty, recognized the confusion in her eyes. They'd shared something sacred after Jimmy's death, experienced a moment that would bind them forever. Now she had to keep Claudine focused, guide her to where she deserved to be. The five of them were deserting this place—Hattie Mae, Adell, Claudine, Baby Boy, and the unborn child, whose feet would never touch the red soil of Georgia. It had been two days since the shooting—two days that

Hattie Mae Jones didn't have to prostrate herself before the governor; two days since she'd baked a single, solitary pie. Enjoying this newfound freedom was somewhat disconcerting, but she was slowly adjusting. No more absurd demands on her time. No more assinine conversations, no more unwanted advances. She would forge her own path and erase the past, leaving Nathan Lee, the governor, Jimmy, the Deacon, and Willy Earl behind. She was back in control, and she intended to stay that way. Claudine's sudden adoration had temporarily distracted her. She didn't have time for the release of all this repressed affection, kissing and hugging every five damn minutes. She had a daughter to refine, lives to transform, grandchildren to raise. She'd already spoken to the people at Juilliard, and Mr. Coroniti was only too happy to oblige the governor of Georgia. He'd granted Claudine a new audition in three weeks' time. They'd be comfortably settled in New York City by then. This place, this house, would become a distant memory and fade away into nothingness.

"Well, if you don't like what I have to say, I can stay here, keep the dust mites company," Adell mumbled under her breath. "I'm 'bout dust myself anyway, be dead and stinkin' in a minute."

"Stop talking such foolishness, old woman. We started this together. We'll finish it together."

"But Hattie Mae. Baby, just because that four-foot cracker gave—"

"Adell, I don't want to hear another word about it. I mean it, not another word, you hear?"

Claudine watched her mother carefully. She'd returned, the Hattie Mae she'd always known, unconquerable and in complete command of her surroundings. It was as if the moments they'd shared in the mansion, in the car at dusk on the side of the road, never happened at all. Claudine smiled; she knew better. She walked around one more time, from room to room, back and forth between houses. She'd grown up here, married, had a child, and survived multiple nightmares. She noticed that all of Willy Earl's belongings were gone. There was no trace of him anywhere. His toothbrush, all of his clothes, three half-used cans of Afro Sheen had been removed. No one would ever guess that he'd resided here at all. His unexpected departure was a blessing.

Claudine felt a flutter dance across her middle. She was four months along now, barely showing, excited and terrified at the same time. What if she couldn't perform like she used to? What if they didn't have enough money? What if Willy Earl decided to come looking for her?

"What about the china? We gone take the china?" Adell asked loudly, aware that Hattie Mae was ignoring her.

"Here, take Betty and wipe that frown off your face," Hattie Mae said, handing the violin to Claudine. "Stop worrying so much. Play Adell and Baby Boy something nice while I finish up in here."

"Now?"

"Now is just as good a time as any."

"Well, I'm packing this china," Adell stated, "and I'm packing the silverware, too, unless you want me to eat with my fingers. I ain't eating with my fingers. I don't care what you say."

Claudine ran her hands over the case's blue velvet. Her fingers began to tremble at the thought of embracing the instrument once more. She closed her eyes and caressed the bow, prompting Adell to think out loud.

"Lord have mercy, Jesus. The girl acts like it's a damn peter."

"Shhhh," Hattie Mae scolded. "Give her time. She and Betty just need to get reacquainted."

"If you ask me, both of y'all touched in the head. Apple don't fall far from the tree, I'll tell you that."

Hattie Mae busied herself closing up the house, draping expensive sheets over sofas and chairs, bureaus and armoires. The duplex was to be sold fully furnished. Taking a loss was not important. Being free of any possession that connected her with Harlan was. She'd refused to pack one linen, one dish, one dress, or one tube of lipstick that reminded her of him. She left cultured pearls, Persian rugs, and paintings of white women lounging on sandy beaches for the new owner to discover in the hall closet. Harlan had always told her what she liked. Those days were over. Leaving so quickly was surprisingly hassle free, but then she'd always anticipated leaving in a hurry. She sensed her daughter's apprehension, her fear of the unknown. Hattie Mae had been preparing for this escape since she felt Claudine growing inside of her. She'd listened to the governor when he spoke of money, stocks, bonds, and certificates of deposit with his cronies. Asked Miss Emily to explain to her the terms she didn't understand. Ordered every book she could find to educate herself about the exchange market. Used the governor's influence to secure information and buy property, always making sure her name was buried in the fine print. She'd perfected his signature in case she ever needed it, held his letterhead and duplicates of other personal documents in a safety deposit box. Over the past eighteen years, she'd accumulated more than four hundred and fifty thousand dollars, all willed to Claudine. She already owned a brownstone in the Park Slope section of Brooklyn, bought six months before Claudine's audition. It had been sitting empty since the rape, waiting for a family, waiting to be christened by Claudine's magic. The sweet sounds of the Barber Violin Concerto were beginning to float through the house, validating Hattie Mae's determination. She dabbed her eyes and inhaled her daughter's joy, listening intently for any mistakes. After fifteen minutes she was convinced there weren't going to be any. She'd always known it would be this way. It was as if the bow had never left Claudine's hand.

CHAPTER 42

*D*isoriented, disheveled, and abandoned, Harlan attempted to stand. He had been sitting in the same spot for hours and hours, trying to figure out where he'd gone wrong, how she'd managed to slip through his fingers. She was a mystery, that woman, a silky temptation, a waterfall of passion; and he would be lost without her. She knew him, the decency of him, the wickedness of him, all of it, every crevice of his character. She was the one he yearned for, the woman he always had to have. Hattie Mae Jones was under his skin, trapped in his soul; and she would remain there until he took his last breath.

He hadn't really begun to digest the parentage of Claudine yet. The weight of that revelation would assault him later, after the Jack Daniel's had worn off and he could think clearly. Every time Claudine crept into his consciousness, he filled his crystal tumbler quickly and tried to locate his mouth. He succeeded and earned himself a brief reprieve. Hattie Mae could not leave him, period. It was that simple. He had to make her understand that he loved her. He *loved* her. Sweet Jesus, how he loved her. It was the first time he truly allowed himself to feel the gospel of it; and it washed over him, causing his stomach to swirl, his hands to shake, and his heart—his heart was threatening to fly out of his chest and go get her. Somehow he would make this right, make her cherish him. They would all live together in the mansion, eat blueberry pie, have dinner in the Sherman room when the staff was gone. No one would ever guess their secret; he hadn't. They could hide it forever. He reached for another bottle at the mere thought of Claudine, his child, his and Hattie Mae's child. How could he possibly explain Hattie Mae and Claudine to Lavender? What would she think of him bedding a colored, fathering an illegitimate half-breed baby? He inhaled deeply. Her reaction was of no consequence; she barely spoke to him anyway, never called, never wrote. Truth be told, he'd lost her a long time ago, right after Emily passed away. Lavender abhorred him, and they both knew it, accepted the inevitable like rain. It was as if she saw through him the moment she was born. He coughed until his sides ached and took another drink. The shameless, lecherous things he'd thought and said to Hattie Mae about Claudine, his own daughter. He'd fantasized countless times about Hattie Mae and Claudine in his bed, disrobed, one wrapped around each leg. He began to retch uncontrollably. He was going to hell.

Before he realized what was happening, he was behind the wheel of his black Cadillac with roses he'd clipped from the cutting garden; Hattie Mae adored roses. And on the way, he intended to stop and buy some perfume for Claudine. He vaguely remembered that Claudine had a boy, a boy that he hadn't even seen. He was a grandfather—a grandfather—and it was a damn shame no one would ever know. Well, he was still the governor of Georgia, by God, and nobody was deserting him, especially his Hattie Mae. He'd order them both to return to the mansion immediately, and that was all there was to it. He'd assign roadblocks if he had to, place troopers at the state line. He started the Caddy with renewed vigor. He was not coming back alone.

CLOTHES WERE PACKED, furniture was covered, and Baby Boy was dressed for travel. This is too easy, Hattie Mae mused, glancing at the clock. She'd anticipated upheaval and prepared mentally for a battle. Adell and Claudine had reassured her that he wouldn't try to stop them from leaving, but they didn't know Harlan like she did. He didn't like to lose, and he was accustomed to being in control, informing other people what they were supposed to be doing. She'd destroyed one weapon but had another tucked discreetly in her handbag. Harlan had always made sure that she was well armed, in case some degenerate should accost her. She narrowed her eyes. She was ready. One of them would be sucking concrete if he came for her or Claudine.

"Claudine! Claudine! You ready?"

"Ready as I'll ever be."

"Well, you better be, 'cause it's time to go."

"How we getting to the station?" Adell asked.

"I called a taxi; that should be him pulling up right now."

Claudine ran and looked out the parlor window. She didn't see a taxi. She saw the governor struggling to get out of a big car with an armful of flowers. She glanced nervously at Adell, Adell looked at Hattie Mae, and Hattie Mae casually grabbed her purse.

"Ya'll go on now and wait out back. The taxi should be here any minute, and when he gets here, tell him to hurry up and start tying these bags on top of the car. Claudine, take this cord."

Claudine couldn't move. Hattie Mae walked over to her, opened the girl's hand, and closed her fingers tightly around the spool of thick white rope. "Here now, take this. I'll meet you in the taxi."

"Mama, let me go with you. Maybe I can . . . maybe we can . . ."

"No," Hattie Mae snapped. "This is between me and him. Get on out back now and put Baby Boy in first. And Claudine."

"Yes?"

"I told you to stop calling me Mama."

Claudine felt her eyes beginning to fill. If the governor tried to stop Hattie Mae from leaving, she would surely kill him. This could not happen. She'd just gotten her mother back; she couldn't lose her again.

"Adell, do something! We can't just let her go out there alone."

Adell squeezed Claudine's elbow and guided her toward the back of the house.

"Hush now, sweet baby, and let your mama handle her business. It's in God's hands now." Adell nodded at Hattie Mae as she steered Claudine out of the parlor and into the kitchen. "You hear that horn, girl. Taxi's here."

Hattie Mae couldn't believe he'd come with flowers, roses at that. She hated roses. The man was touched in the head. He was actually smiling as he teetered toward her, barely able to put one foot in front of the other. She held his gaze. His brain must be deteriorating, she thought. She was anxious to be finally done with it, done with him.

"I brought you these flowers, Hattie Mae. I cut them myself."

"And?"

He lowered his head, and when he looked back up at her, she saw the familiar coldness in his eyes.

"Just where do you think you going, Hattie Mae?"

"Away from here, away from you."

"I can't let you do that. You know I can't. So you go unpack all of your things and come on back with me where you belong. And bring Claudine with you, and the boy of hers."

Hattie Mae knew time was being wasted. There was a train on track number nine that wasn't going to wait for them. She didn't have time for this nonsense.

"Well, say something, for the love of God."

"God doesn't have a damn thing to do with this here. Harlan, I'm only going to tell you this once."

Harlan raised his hand to silence her. "Hattie Mae, please don't do this. Don't leave me."

"What?"

"It'll be better. I'll be better."

"You don't own me. You never did. Go home, Harlan."

"I can't go back there without you. I can't be without you, don't you understand? Somewhere, Hattie Mae, you have to feel something for me. We've been together too long, been through too much. Listen to me, now, can't nobody love you like I do."

Hattie Mae searched his face for some sign of derangement. He astounded her because she knew that he actually believed what he was saying. He had been in her life for more than twenty years. They had eaten together, slept together, breathed the same foul air; and in all of that time, his fantasy never once became her reality. Yes, she knew that he loved her in his own twisted way. She hoped he knew that she would still kill him in spite of it.

"I'm turning around right now and getting into that taxi with my child. You hear me?"

"Wait! You want me to beg, Hattie Mae? You want me to get down on my hands and knees for you? All right, all right, I'll do whatever you want me to do. I'll say whatever you want me to say. I'll do whatever I have to do to make you stay."

"Harlan, please, get up. The sight of you hurts my eyes. I'm finally free of you, free to go and do what I please. I have erased you from my mind, removed your life from my memories. I have already forgotten the smell of you. My daughter will have the best life, I promise you, and she will never know you, remember you, or think of you at all. As time passes, Harlan, this place, this way of life, and your connection to us will be lost entirely, buried so deep she'll be dead long before she even remembers your name."

Harlan watched Hattie Mae turn her back to him as if he wasn't someone to be reckoned with. His head felt like it was going to explode, and he wanted to holler like a newborn wails for its mother. He wiped his moist face with the back of his hand and reached for her arm. She turned around with the reflexes of a cat, and she had a gun in her hand, another baby Browning he had given her.

"Don't make me kill you."

He saw it then, that look in her eyes. He'd seen that look before, decades ago when he'd tried to buy her from Nathan Lee and two days ago when she'd sent his driver to hell. "Well, you're going to have to kill me, then, because I can't let you go. God help me, I can't let you go." He could barely get the words out without wheezing. He was sweating, and his heart was pounding, and he was having difficulty breathing. Suddenly dizzy, Harlan eased down onto the porch and tried to focus on the grinning figure behind Hattie Mae. Emily was laughing at him, pointing her finger, celebrating his shame. "Hattie Mae, help me, I'm dying. I know I'm dying," he panted, barely able to get the words out.

"Good then—one less thing I have to do."

When he heard the door of the taxi slam, Harlan grabbed his chest and waited for his heart to stop beating. Dying would be preferable to living without her. She was gone less than a half hour when he realized there was nothing wrong with him that being inside of her wouldn't fix. His heart wasn't shutting down; it was simply aching for the woman he'd lost and the daughter he would never know.

"ALL ABOARD! LAST call for number 326 to New York City."

Claudine heard the announcement and watched Hattie Mae flip through the pages of a *Jet* magazine she'd brought with her. Adell was roaming the train in search of the dining car. Claudine was in a daze. Everything was happening so fast. Their lives were changing forever, and she seemed to be the only one who was affected by it. Junior played on the floor, oblivious to the lurching train or deluxe sleeping accommodations. The porter had smiled when he took their tickets. Hattie Mae had purchased three roomettes, all with private toilets. "I don't want ya'll pestering me," she'd said. "This is a long trip, and don't act like you never been anywhere before, either. We're not moving to New York so y'all can embarrass me." New York. It sounded like a dream, and Claudine repeated it over and over in her head until she could think of nothing else. Not Willy Earl or the Deacon and Willamina, not the governor of Georgia, left in a heap on her mama's porch, or that man sprawled out on the checkered linoleum with a hole in his head.

"Well, me and Baby Boy are going to our car to get some rest now. We'll see you in a while for dinner."

"I thought Junior could sleep here, keep me company."

"I don't know who the hell Junior is, but Baby Boy's going to be spending a lot of time with me in New York. He might as well get used to it now." Hattie Mae lifted up her daughter's child, now fussing for his mother, and left.

Claudine stared out at the scenery that was rapidly shifting. Her life would never be the same again.

CHAPTER 43

*T*all buildings, people dressed in odd-looking clothes, and cars, so many cars, startled Claudine as she exited the terminal. New York was unlike anything she could have ever imagined. It was different; it was cold; it was a city made of steel.

"Look at all these people," Adell mused as they waited for a taxi. "They sho' look like they in some kind of hurry."

Claudine inhaled the crisp New York air. Hattie Mae had been right again; it did smell different from the country, although the smells and the excitement of exploring a new city weren't enough to keep her from throwing up on the sidewalk in front of Penn Station.

"Good Lord, Claudine, you couldn't wait until we got home?"

"Leave her be, Hattie Mae. Baby's probably jumpy from the train ride."

"Where to, ladies?" the cab driver asked.

"Park Slope," Hattie Mae answered.

"Park Slope, in Brooklyn?" he countered. "Are you sure that's where you want to go?"

"Do I look confused to you?" Hattie Mae shot back.

"What the devil did he just say?" Adell interrupted. "Boy talkin' too damn fast."

Claudine tried to ignore her queasy stomach and concentrate on the scenery unfolding before her—boats, water, trains that seemed to come up out of the ground. Twenty-five minutes later, she was standing in front of the enormous brownstone that was to be her home. It looked like two complete houses stacked on top of each other.

"Well, this is it," Hattie Mae said, grabbing some luggage and heading up the long walk to the front door. "Come on. What are ya'll waiting for? It's cold out here."

"YOU ARE AWARE, Ms. Jones, that Claudine is pregnant, and under those circumstances, maybe she should defer her admission for a year."

"Mr. Coroniti, I assure you that Claudine's pregnancy will not interfere with her studies here."

"We were all sorry to hear what happened to her. I'm sure that in time—"

Hattie Mae cut him off. "She's just fine now. That's all in the past, and we'd both like it to remain there."

"Very well, then, she can begin this spring, and please thank Governor Tillford for interceding on her behalf. His letter of recommendation was quite impressive."

"I'll be sure to let him know."

"I think our business is concluded here. Tell Claudine that I look forward to seeing her and I believe she'll make a great addition to the Juilliard family."

Hattie Mae floated to her car. Claudine would be thrilled. She'd been waiting for this decision for weeks, waddling to the mailbox, running to the phone. Hattie Mae and Adell were constantly telling the girl to calm down. They both knew that Claudine's audition had to have left that man speechless. Hattie Mae stood outside, in front of her car, for a long time. Things had not gone as smoothly as she'd planned, but she was here nevertheless, with her daughter, Baby Boy, Adell, and a new one on the way, soon enough. Maybe she'd go to the Fulton Fish Market and get something special for dinner, or stop by Prospect Park and sit a spell. She thought to stroll around Manhattan and purchase more sheets, more dishes, more of everything for the house. Discovering what she liked was a new experience for her; shopping had become somewhat cathartic, and these days she was always buying something for the house. It was so large, and Hattie Mae hated to see empty rooms. Lately she'd been thinking of Gracian and her brothers and sisters back on the farm. Was her mama still alive? How many nieces and nephews did she have? Did the tomatoes still grow the size of grapefruits? She didn't know what had come over her. She hadn't thought of the farm in years. They were all lost to her, and she was suddenly saddened by the memory of them. How had she ended up with another family? Maybe there was a God, after all. She understood her own mother so much more now and wished for a moment she could tell Gracian how sorry she was and how much she missed her banana pudding. She opened the car door and got in. "Enough of this," she said aloud. "Enough of this."

CLAUDINE STRUGGLED TO get comfortable. She was eight months pregnant, and she was ready for this child to come out, crawl out, fly out. She didn't give a damn how it got out; she just wanted it out. She was tired of being the size of a farm animal, and she ached to play Betty. She'd had a nasty attitude all day and was planning on having another one tomorrow. "I can't take much more of this," she whined to Adell. The sharp contraction seconds later took her by surprise.

"Looks to me like you won't have to," Adell chuckled as she

went to fetch her birthing bag. "This baby's gone come early. Runnin' it outta the womb with all that complainin'."

"When is Hattie Mae coming back?"

"Don't worry 'bout her none. She'll be on directly; probably out opening her purse. Woman don't know what to do with herself, buying up everythang in sight. And Claudine, watch all that screaming, hear, so you don't wake Baby Boy."

Claudine was perplexed; the old woman was getting senile. She was seventy going on a hundred and two. "I haven't been screaming, Adell."

"Don't worry. You will. As evil as you been. Hmph, this baby's gone wear you out."

Hattie Mae arrived to find Claudine hollering loud enough to wake the whole neighborhood. She flew up to Claudine's bedroom, taking three steps at a time. Baby Boy stood at the doorway, eyes wide as an owl's, staring at his mama thrashing about on the bed.

"Baby's turned, trying to come into this world feet first. Hattie Mae, go put Baby Boy back in his bed. No sense in scarring the boy for life."

Claudine called out for her mother. She didn't remember all of this pain and distress. To tell the truth, she didn't remember much about Baby Boy's birth at all. She could feel this child writhing inside of her. She could feel Adell's hand mingling with her insides. It had to be a girl; only a female would give another woman this much hell. Another contraction spread across her abdomen, and she called Willy Earl Jenkins every horrible thing she could think of, even though Hattie Mae had forbidden her to ever contaminate the crisp New York air with his name.

"Adell! Adell! Can't you give her something to make her stop screaming like that?"

"Hush now, Hattie Mae, and let me do what the Lord put me on this earth for." Adell never panicked, even when Clau-

dine thought she was going to die from one prolonged contraction, or when Hattie Mae raced to fetch the big-city doctor. She chatted on calmly, about inconsequential things, and
turned the child around while it kicked to escape Claudine's
womb.

DAYS, WEEKS, MONTHS had passed and still no word, no phone
call, no surprise telegram. Harlan knew that she'd meant
everything she said, but he couldn't believe she was truly gone.
A part of him expected her to be at the foot of his bed each
morning, with a smile and a fresh pie. When he awoke hope-
ful and she wasn't there, something inside folded into nothingness and disappeared. Everyone else around him seemed
invisible or moved in slow motion, and he was left alone to
contemplate over and over again how he'd let her slip away.
The whole damn state of Georgia was looking to him for guidance, and all he could do was fantasize about her. He lurched
around in a daze, scratching his head and muttering to himself
incoherently. It was disgusting. Working, speaking, signing
documents took entirely too much effort. Georgia's fiscal crisis
was the least of his problems. Harlan was content to destroy
everything in his path in order to obtain information that he
believed would return his sanity, restore his manhood. Although he was creeping toward madness, he knew people
were talking about him, insinuating that he'd caught some
kind of old person's disease, claiming that he was touched in
the head. He heard his own doctor, Rory Jessup, confiding to
Lavender, who had probably flown in just to pick over his rusty
bones.

"He just hasn't been the same since the shooting. Killing
that rascal took more out of him than we thought. He's in a
state of shock, that's all it is, what with his driver trying to kidnap him. He'll be fine in no time at all, spitting vinegar and
raising hell."

Harlan wanted to scream at the top of his lungs, Everything will get back to normal when I find Hattie Mae!, but he couldn't, and no one would understand anyway. So, Get out, you waste of skin, and leave me the hell alone! sufficed for quite some time. Much to everyone's dismay, he committed a kind of social suicide, staying holed up in his room with a case of flour, rancid butter, and his endless, fabricated memories.

It took him exactly four months in a semidelirious state to figure out where she had gone. He could have ripped himself a new one for being so stupid. Everything she'd done had been for that girl. Straight away he hired a private detective named Dicky and sent him to New York to take photographs and gather pertinent information of a personal nature. When the first set of pictures arrived in the thick manila envelope, he felt the blood begin to percolate in his veins, prompting him to finally brush his teeth, wash his rear end, and unlock the deadbolts on his bedroom door.

CHAPTER 44

JANUARY 1971

*T*he first day at Juilliard was difficult. Her nipples were leaking, her thighs were rubbing together, and she was fat again, very fat. She stood in the hallway with a schedule in her hand, confused as to which way to turn. She was caught up in a whirlwind; people were swirling past her, and still she remained leaning against the wall of a music history building, dumbfounded. She was lost, sweating enough to cause a small flood, and too nervous to ask anyone for help. She felt it, though, an ill wind tampering with her nerve, tempting her to run home. She saw the stares, the pursed lips. She heard the hurried whispers.

"She has to be lost."

"She must be looking for the cafeteria."

She knew what they were thinking. She held on to Betty and kept searching for her class. Since she was starting in the spring, she'd missed many of the auditions for ensembles and placement in the school orchestra, a coveted position for any Juilliard student. She was prepared to work for her seat. She was prepared to play any piece that was asked of her. Much to her dismay, no one asked. No one seemed to notice at all that she carried a violin. For the time being, she was back to being invisible.

The privileged students didn't speak to her, the professors looked through her, and the men, if you'd want to call them that, snickered behind her back. They all laughed at her, considered her a nonentity, an insignificant outsider. None of that mattered; she had two children at home to raise and a mama who had killed for her. The students' opinions about her were of no consequence. All she needed was a chance, an opportunity to show everyone at school that she belonged at the forefront, in the first chair. It was, after all, everything that she had ever known. Riding home on a crowded subway, she didn't think the day could get any worse. She was wrong.

Claudine stiffened instinctively when she arrived at the brownstone. Something wasn't right. She sensed it as she walked up the stairs. The air seemed thicker, heavier, and she could swear it smelled different. Baby Boy and Lula Mae weren't frolicking on the front porch; short ribs weren't simmering in the oven; and there wasn't a light on anywhere, in any of the rooms in the brownstone, no illumination to guide her steps. Hattie Mae sat in the kitchen, smoking a cigarette, staring out of the window at nothing in particular.

"She's gone."

"Who's gone?"

"Adell."

"Where did she go?" But as Claudine asked the question, she realized by the twinge in her heart and the look on Hattie Mae's face that gone meant gone.

"When? How? Where are my babies?"

"This afternoon, around three. Baby Boy went in to wake her up from a nap and couldn't. I'm telling you, I knew it even before he ran out of that room hollering and carrying on. Death's been in this house all damn week, skulking around, just waiting for the right moment to snatch her away."

"Oh my God. Is Baby Boy all right? Where is he?"

"The babies are with Miss Petula next door. I didn't want the boy to see Adell like that anymore, her soul gone, her face frozen. And don't worry none, I had her picked up already. I didn't want you to see her either. Bad enough one day you gone have to see me like that."

"Stop it! I hate it when you talk like that. Adell was fine this morning. I played scales for her. She made cocoa, scrambled eggs, and bacon. She was fine this morning." Claudine whispered, "She was fine," over and over again, half expecting Adell to walk around the corner and tell them both to shut the hell up. Hattie Mae extinguished her cigarette and sighed heavily.

"Baby, she was over seventy. For all we know, she was over a hundred. It was bound to happen sooner or later. I just thought it would be later, the way she carried on, fussing about every damn thing. In all of the years I've known her, she's never so much as had a sniffle. That's been a lot years, you know. We've been together as long as you've been alive."

"Why didn't you call me at school? I would have come home right away, been here with you."

"There was no need to; and besides, Claudine, there was nothing you could have done, and you know how Adell hated when we made any kind of fuss over her."

"Are you all right? I know how much she meant to you. I just can't believe it."

"I'm fine. All of this commiserating ain't gone bring her back. I'm gone go lie my head down, borrowed myself a headache behind that woman. I'll make the arrangements first thing tomorrow. You can pick the kids up in the morning. I checked on 'em about an hour ago."

Claudine splashed her face at the kitchen sink. She still couldn't believe Adell was dead. Just like that she was gone—no warning, no furtive signs, no nothing. One day she was frying bacon, sipping tomato juice, and the next they were placing her remains in some crypt. She'd always expected Adell to be dragging her feet around for years, complaining about one thing or another. Claudine began to cry silently; she'd never thanked her for anything, not even for delivering both of her children safe and sound, not for her compassion after the rape, not for who she was, not for anything. She felt guilty for the omission and ashamed of herself, simultaneously. Without Adell, where would Hattie Mae be? Where would she be? She didn't even know the woman's last name. Claudine slid to the floor, wondering if she should try to talk to her mother, find out what she could do to make this difficult time easier to bear. She washed her face and climbed the stairs to her mother's room. Claudine waited outside of Hattie Mae's door, wrapping her arms around her knees, until she nodded off from exhaustion. Hours later, she dreamed that Lula Mae was crying, and Claudine was running, practically sprinting, searching for her, but the hallways kept getting longer and the crying sound farther and farther away. Damp and frantic, Claudine awoke and rose quickly to rescue her child, then remembered that Lula Mae was safe next door. And yet she heard it still, soft and rhythmic. She pressed her ear against her mother's door and listened as Hattie Mae wept softly for Adell, now gone from their lives forever.

HATTIE MAE COULDN'T let her see that she was in pain. It was imperative that Claudine believe that everything was well and as it should be. But Hattie Mae was scared in an orphaned-child sort of way that she found difficult to explain, though she knew she would never share her feelings with anyone, especially Claudine. Adell had been with her for more than twenty years, treated Hattie Mae as if she'd sprung from her own womb. She would never encounter that kind of loyalty again, of that she was certain. Adell had been a stand-in for Gracian, a temporary replacement, a willing substitute who kept Hattie Mae's secrets and defended her decisions without question.

Hattie Mae had to be strong for herself and Claudine now, and that she could do. That was who she was. Adell's passing had rattled her to the core, knocking her soul from its familiar resting place, and she struggled to maintain control of herself.

She could handle this. As much as her insides ached, she could handle this.

"HOLD YOUR GROUND, baby. Hold your ground," Hattie Mae said before she left for school every morning for a year. Claudine practiced, studied, waited, and practiced some more. In orchestra, she was immediately placed in the back, far from the conductor's line of sight, the place where the inexperienced played, the place where virgin violinists picked their noses and discussed Saturday matinées that were showing in Times Square.

The following Christmas, the orchestra class was assigned a modern piece to learn for the spring recital, a violin concerto in F-sharp that had been composed by one Francesco Giovanni Romano, a master violinist from Italy. As soon as Claudine grasped the score from the lanky professor, she felt alive, invigorated, and ready to throw her heart into what she knew would be a defining piece of wonder. The notes were filled with passion and pain, hope and joy, and Claudine longed to fill her pores with the same, encompass the very essence of the melody until she and it combined. She mastered it in two days, playing constantly, refusing food, sleep, and sticky kisses from her children. When Francesco Giovanni Romano arrived twelve weeks later to audition each musician personally and observe a practice run of his concerto, she was ready to make love to his masterpiece in front of the world.

CHAPTER 45

"Claudine Viola Jenkins. Congratulations."

She heard the words, shook his hand, and still couldn't believe she was actually standing in front of the chair of the violin department and receiving her diploma. Hattie Mae had been right; Marietta seemed like a lifetime ago. Claudine had played intensely the last four years, practiced harder and longer than she'd ever thought physically possible. She had no social life and rarely saw her own children. Hattie Mae made it so easy for her to excel, raising Baby Boy and Lula Mae single-handedly, tending to their every need, allowing her the freedom to practice until she collapsed from exhaustion. Her instructors and classmates thought her insane. No one understood her desire, her need for perfection, except Hattie Mae. Playing again, immersing herself in the arias and the concertos, was all that she'd known it would be. In four years' time, Claudine Jenkins had transformed into an exceptional virtuoso, eclipsing anyone who thought they could perform on the same stage with her. Even now she didn't appear to be a threat—black, rotund, unassuming—but she'd captivated them all, leaving a trail of enchantment and unanswered questions.

"Congratulations, Momi," Baby Boy and Lula Mae screamed at the top of their lungs.

"Congratulations, Claudine," Hattie Mae added.

"Thank you. I only wish Adell could have been here to see it."

"Yes, indeed."

"I miss her still."

"Pick your face up off the ground, now. We've got things to do before we leave for Tuscany, and you need to go on a diet. I'm not packing all of those big dresses, you hear?"

"I know, Hattie Mae. I know."

Hattie Mae thought of Adell every day, but she was gone. Getting all emotional again about her passing wasn't going to do anybody a damn bit of good. They had to keep on living, and that is just what she intended to do. Claudine and the babies were the only family she would ever have. Their success was her priority, their happiness her reason to breathe. Upon reflection, she'd decided to sell the brownstone in Park Slope. It seemed the logical thing to do. Claudine had been invited to study under master violinist Francesco Giovanni Romano in Italy minutes after he heard her play. It was an offer she couldn't refuse. Initially, she'd wanted to remain in the States after graduation, try to secure a booking agent, but was persuaded to broaden her horizons, develop her technique. As fate would have it, the prestigious Husch agency learned of Claudine's invitation and signed her right away, assuring her bookings all over Europe as she enhanced her repertoire. They would represent her, they said, as long as she kept their alliance confidential. Old man Husch, with Hattie Mae's cooperation, created a long-term plan for Claudine's future. She would leave America as Claudine Viola Jenkins and return as someone else.

Harlan Tillford stood in the shadows of the auditorium and watched her stroll across the stage, the spitting image of her mother—beautiful and confident. Pride swelled his chest and was immediately followed by an intense shame that turned his stomach and colored his face bright pink. He had a plan, a very detailed plan, carefully concocted when he'd locked himself away and swatted at imaginary flies sent in by Lavender to drive him mad. Lavender had tried reasoning with him in the beginning, eventually resorting to shrieking at him through the keyhole like he was some kind of half-deaf retard, but he'd ignored her. She wasn't real. She wanted something from him; they all did, constantly intruding on his thoughts, interrupting his planning every five damn minutes, trying to force some blasted pill down his throat. He'd fixed them good, though, referring to Lavender as an imposter and firing a Winchester at Doc Jessup—damn near made the man piss his pants. And of course, Lavender didn't know what the hell he was yapping about, and he didn't care enough to explain it to her. Everyone pretty much had left him alone after that, leaving food outside his door and clean underwear whenever he requested it, which wasn't too often. Nothing was ever right, and he wasn't about to pretend like it was, not even for his firstborn, who couldn't bake a simple apple pie to save her life. He'd deduced, during one particularly long nap, that she'd most likely try to poison him, anyway.

When it all had been said and done, he realized that he didn't exist without Hattie Mae, couldn't peacefully go from one day to the next. She haunted him relentlessly and cursed his dreams from afar. Claudine would be his way out. With enough time, he was sure he could convince Hattie Mae to take him back, but he would have to go through Claudine. Claudine—his Claudine—was salvation. If he could just get her alone, win her over, Hattie Mae would come to him.

He saw them a few feet away, standing together laughing, and he was emotionally paralyzed, unable even to open his mouth to speak or put one foot in front of the other.

Claudine's boy, his grandson, had grown considerably, and the girl baby was holding on to Hattie Mae's leg for dear life.

He'd had Dicky track their every move since he discovered that Claudine was attending Juilliard; he kept photos of the house, Adell's grave, and everything in between stuffed in his pockets. Initially he had counted on Hattie Mae calling him for money but, upon further investigation, learned that he'd hopelessly underestimated her. He'd had no idea Hattie Mae was that clever or Claudine was really that good. His life had changed dramatically since Hattie Mae left, twisted into some-thing pathetic and grotesque. The lieutenant governor, a slip-pery weasel named Rufas Bell, had run his state into the ground while Harlan forgot, or refused to do, the simplest of things that governors were supposed to do; he remembered only the smell of French vanilla on Hattie Mae's skin in the middle of the afternoon.

Harlan strained but couldn't see them anymore, though he sensed Hattie Mae was near. She was oblivious of him, and yet he longed to reach out through the crowd blindly, grab her, and hold her close; but it was not to be. She would have killed him those many months ago on her front porch, and she would cer-tainly kill him now. Hattie Mae looked exactly the same, stronger even, and he could scarcely wipe the spittle from his own chin. Harlan Tillford was sixty-eight years old, and seeing her was almost more than he could bear. He began to wheeze uncontrollably and fumbled around in his jacket pocket for a handkerchief, dropping crinkled photos and hundred-dollar bills. Horrified, he fell to the floor in a panic as a parade of anx-ious feet trampled his treasure. He began to whimper while grasping at nothingness and slapping bills out of hands trying to help collect the money that was now scattered in many dif-ferent directions.

CHAPTER 46

First the train, now a ship because Hattie Mae refused to fly. Siena, Italy, seemed so far away, but experience reminded Claudine that life took quick turns and yesterday became today in the blink of an eye. The ocean was vast, but she knew Italy would be staring her in the face by tomorrow morning. For the first time in three years she was a bundle of nerves, unsure of her abilities, frightened of failure. What if he didn't like her? What if he thought he'd made a mistake? What if she contracted leprosy on the boat and her fingers fell off when she tried to play? Thousands of twisted thoughts floated though her mind and caused her to retch every few minutes the closer they got to their destination. Baby Boy and Lula Mae thought she was crazy, hanging over the rail like a rag doll, and Hattie Mae kept handing her Ritz crackers and Alka-Seltzer, claiming they would calm her swirling stomach and soothe her frazzled nerves. They didn't understand who she was. They didn't know that her entire career depended on whether or not Francesco Giovanni Ramano thought she was worthy to be called a violinist. No one knew that the mere thought of him made her entire body sweat and plead for some kind of reassurance.

Claudine, Hattie Mae, and the kids boarded a train and

then later a private car, stopping often to sample food from each region. Claudine fidgeted the entire way, until she saw the city of Siena whispering her name from a Tuscan hilltop.

CLAUDINE STRAIGHTENED HER dress, bit the inside of her bottom lip until it bled, and waited patiently for the master violinist's arrival. Sleep had eluded her the night before. It was midafternoon, and she was more than an hour early for their scheduled appointment. She prayed that he would still want her. She and Hattie Mae had rented an apartment in Siena, not far from the glorious Accademia degli Intronati, founded in the sixteenth century. They'd been in Italy a week and a half, and already Claudine adored it—cobblestoned streets; balconies covered in exotic-looking floras; grand structures standing side by side, some centuries old, some newly built. Visiting the Mangia Tower; experiencing history as they toured the magnificent rooms of the Palazzo delle Papesse, a real live palace. Both she and Hattie Mae lost some weight, constantly climbing the three flights to their walk-up. They noticed that Italian people walked everywhere. The food took them a couple of days to get accustomed to, calamari and every shape of pasta imaginable. Baby Boy and Lula Mae, now six and four, loved polenta and cheese, a northern Italian treat. Hattie Mae said to eat up because polenta was the closest thing any of them would get to grits in a long time. To Claudine's delight, Hattie Mae had recently discovered wines—Chiantis, Baberescos, and every regional table wine in between. Hattie Mae couldn't get enough of the food, the people, the music. It was the first time Claudine had ever seen her laugh. For that gift, she would cherish Italy forever.

Siena took Claudine's breath away. It was majestic, so full of history and tradition. She marveled at the wondrous combinations of fabrics the people of Siena wore. After church, the Sienese strolled about in their Sunday finest, window shopping, admiring what everyone else was wearing. She thought them to be very similar to black people in that way, so conscious of their appearance on a church day. And despite the language barrier, no one was unkind to her. No one called her hateful names or commented on the size of her thighs. People appeared to be happy in their own skins, and in a short time she became happy in hers.

"Are you ready for me, my dear?"

He was all that she remembered—olive-hued complexion, salt and pepper hair, and skin that smelled of basil and freshly baked bread. Now that she had the time to really pay attention to his features, she guessed he was around the same age as Hattie Mae: older than forty, younger than sixty. She was intimidated by his reputation and acutely embarrassed for thinking that he was the most beautiful man she had ever seen. She excused herself and sat down, momentarily grateful for the distance. Claudine didn't want him to hear her heart beating wildly or feel the unwanted heat coming from her body.

"Master Romano. I'm honored you wanted to work with me. What would you have me play?"

He waved his hand in the air and closed his eyes. "Play your best thing."

And so she played for him a Bartok violin sonata, a most demanding piece of music. She wanted him to know that she was willing to take risks. She needed him to understand that she wasn't afraid of hard work. Long after she retired her bow, exhausted, he sat with his eyes closed and offered nothing. Three hours passed, and Claudine was wondering if he was still alive. The silence, the not knowing, was killing her. When he finally spoke, dusk was upon them.

"We must do two things, my dear. First, you must practice with me four hours every day, no excuses. And second, you must call me Francesco."

As the months passed, Hattie Mae noticed the subtle changes in Claudine. She was thinner, softer, and smiled more.

She allowed her hair to grace her shoulders, and men were beginning to appreciate her beauty out of the corner of their eyes while they walked with their wives or girlfriends. Hattie Mae could tell the attention pleased her. Coming here was a good decision, and Hattie Mae smiled at her own foresight. She kept old man Husch informed of Claudine's progress, had notified him just yesterday that she was ready to take the stage professionally. The children were thriving with their tutor, and Hattie Mae often had to pinch herself to make sure she wasn't dreaming. Harlan hadn't attempted to contact her, and the moron twins, Luther Mack and Willy Earl, no longer posed a threat. She'd bribed enough people at Milledgeville to make sure they were never released, never allowed to see the light of day. It was strange to have no worries. Odd not to be afraid. She still tensed when she sensed someone close behind her, had nightmares on occasion about blueberry pie, but she was free. Free to do and say whatever she pleased, without fear of repercussion. Claudine was living the life she was destined to live, refining her repertoire one concerto at a time. What more could any mother want for her child? Hattie Mae had met Master Romano and initially approved of his influence. He intrigued her, and he seemed a passionate man, a man of some honor. Hattie Mae and he had meals together often, sipping red table wine, eating hot bread with garlic-infused olive oil, and lounging on the terrace, listening to Claudine practice. Their affair took Hattie Mae by surprise.

CHAPTER 47

"More, Claudine! More!"

Francesco walked around his studio, furiously waving his arms, conducting a class of one. He had been with her for hours, and still she played like she was possessed. She was unlike any student he had ever trained, and he found himself thinking of her in ways that frightened him. She was a girl, and he was an old man, and yet he wanted her still. Her music seduced him. If only she would make more mistakes. If only she didn't work so hard. If only she wasn't so beautiful. He often kept his eyes closed when they worked, because he knew if he looked at her, he would be lost, and then where would they be? Imagine him, Francesco Giovanni Romano, falling in love with a student. He cringed at the thought of it. Today he was especially weak, and he tried to find the strength to tell her that that was enough for the day; but the words escaped him, so he allowed her to play even though he knew she was worn out. Her dedication impressed him, and he remembered fondly the first time he'd heard her play. He was auditioning members of the school orchestra for his concerto. He'd written it as a favor for a longtime friend from his *contrada* at Juilliard, Alberto Coroniti. Juilliard needs something special, Coroniti had said. He'd agreed out of boredom and resigned himself to working with ordinary students, devouring some American hamburgers, and going home. As was his custom, he wanted to hear every member of the orchestra play, so he could weed out the ones who were tone deaf and inconsistent. He was half asleep, dreaming of a robust merlot, when the back row began to play, one by one assaulting his ears with their fledgling attempts at music. And then he heard her, everyone heard her, playing his score like her life depended on it. He couldn't remember anyone else's audition after that. He thought her too young and too female to have such passion, too inexperienced to play with such fervor. Why, he had asked the pimply faced instructor, why was she in the back and not in first chair where she obviously belonged? Was he deaf? Was he so stupid that he did not realize she was so obviously misplaced? So Francesco had moved her himself, ordered her to her rightful place, directly in front of him. She'd captivated him then. She captivated him now. The wait for her to finish Juilliard had been difficult. But if she was that magnificent in her second year, he could only imagine how well she would be playing by the time she got to him two and a half years later. And now here he was, an old man, smitten with a caramel colored prodigy. He would have to be careful, very careful indeed.

"Master Romano. Master Romano."

"Yes, Claudine, I'm listening."

"I'm not playing anymore. I'm sorry. I know I stayed longer than I should have. I wanted it to be perfect."

Francesco had his back to her and did not want to face her. He wished she would just go, leave him to his libidinous fantasies.

"Master Romano, are you all right? You seem a little distracted today. Should I begin again?"

"No, just go, *bella,* go home now. I'll see you tomorrow, no?"

"Please, if I have played something wrong, I can do better." Claudine began to open the violin case and was startled when he rushed over and slammed it shut.

"Did you not hear what I said? Go. Now."

Claudine could not move. She could not leave thinking that he was disappointed in her. She would stand and play all night if she had to, the same aria fifty times, until he was satisfied. She was confused and hurt by his reaction. He had never used that tone of voice with her before, had never been so cold.

"Master Romano, I will keep practicing. Please allow me to—"

"It was perfect, *bella*. You are perfect." Francesco turned around slowly and succumbed to all that she was and all that he felt. He gently took the case from her hands and kissed her until he felt her pelvis arch and her knees grow weak. He would have her today, honor be damned.

For Claudine, it was as if she was in another woman's body. No emotion had ever compared with this, and as she lay there on his studio floor, writhing with pleasure, with his head buried deeply between her thighs, it was inconceivable that she was capable of feeling this way . . . erotic, light, insatiable. She reached behind her for something steady to grab on to as his tongue titillated and teased her again and again. She moaned uncontrollably, and at the moment she felt her insides quiver, he entered her, and she thought for sure the world was coming to an end.

CHAPTER 48

"*Bella,* it is time for you to move on. All of Europe will throw rose petals at your feet."

"How can you be so sure, Francesco? What if they can't accept me?"

"What foolishness are you talking? What about your Leontyne Price and Marian Anderson? Our audiences have seen your beautiful brown faces excel at Italian opera at the highest level imaginable. We do not care who's playing the music as long as they are playing it well. You must have faith, my *amore.*"

Claudine pressed her breasts against his chest. She ached for him in a way that unnerved her, craved his tender affections as well as his approval. With him, she had no inhibitions, no shame in enjoying the pleasure their bodies created. He caressed her the entire length of her body after every practice, and that always led to their fervent lovemaking. Now she practiced regularly in the nude. That was all he desired of her—hair down, no makeup, no clothes, just her and the violin. Head thrown back, legs wide open, and music filling the room like warm summer rain. Sometimes he would sit across from her and weep at the sheer beauty of it. He longed to play her the way she played that violin.

"I would die a thousand deaths if I couldn't make love to you," Francesco murmured.

He had taught her how to love. She wondered if Hattie Mae had ever felt this way . . . adored, satiated, replete.

"Tell me, *bella*. What was your life like there in America? Were you as happy as you are now?"

"My life began here. My happiness began with you," Claudine whispered, wrapping her legs tightly around the man she adored.

HATTIE MAE WAITED up for her. It was time they spoke about these illicit rendezvous, force the nasty business out in the open. Although she was fond of Francesco, handing Claudine over was not part of the plan. He was turning into a complication, another unwanted distraction she would have to eliminate. She had to be careful, handle Claudine very delicately. They'd come too far to be thrown off course by another man. The girl's nose was so wide open, she could drive one of those I-talian meat trucks right to her brain. Hattie Mae nursed her tepid cup of coffee and opened the door when she heard Claudine tiptoeing up the stairs.

"Looks to me like you're learning a lot more than you supposed to."

"I'm sorry I'm so late again. Our practice keeps going over."

"What do you call the kind of practicing y'all doing? Is there some fancy I-talian word for screwing your teacher and playing the violin at the same time?"

"What are you talking about?"

"Who do you think you're fooling, Claudine? You know damn well what I'm talking about."

"Hattie Mae, I—"

"End it, Claudine. We don't have time for this. You play the opera house in two days. Two days."

"I cannot. I love him, Hattie Mae. Don't you understand? I—"

"I understand you came over here and lost your damn mind."

Claudine held her gaze. "He makes me feel like a woman."

"You already a woman. Go on, look in the mirror if you're still confused about it."

"That's not what I mean."

"End it, Claudine, or I will."

"No. No, I won't let you do that."

"Francesco is in the way. This thing with him is a mistake, and it won't be the first time I've rectified one of your mistakes."

"What are you saying? I thought . . ." Claudine responded quietly.

"Girl, did you think it was a coincidence that Willy Earl Jenkins disappeared when we needed him to be gone?"

"Oh my God, Mama. What did you do?"

"Don't worry about what I did. You just fix your lips on saying good-bye."

"Please don't make me do this. I love him."

"We're moving to Paris after your performance. Love him from a distance."

IT WAS WRENCHING to face him knowing this afternoon was all they would ever have. She had no alternative; she knew that. Claudine refused to be a part of his demise at the hands of Hattie Mae. She would never forgive herself if some harm befell him because she couldn't let go. She'd surrender Francesco before he became someone too painful to remember. He'd uncovered something buried deep inside of her and ultimately reminded her who she was, who she had always been.

He was watching her, waiting for her to begin. She removed

her clothes and played for him for the last time, putting her heart, bleeding, into every note. Getting through the sonata was almost unbearable. She was to make her professional debut tomorrow, and today she could barely put one foot in front of the other. How could Hattie Mae make her do this, turn away from the man she yearned to be with so desperately?

"You played for me so passionately, *cara mia*. I have never heard a more beautiful sonata than yours."

"Francesco."

"You have something you wish to tell me, no?"

Claudine struggled to speak. He placed his fingers gently on her lips and pulled her close.

"You do not have to say. I can see it in your eyes. I am but an old man, a faded memory to most; and you, I fear, have only begun. *Li amerò per sempre.*"

"I, too, will love you forever," Claudine answered, reaching for him, falling into his embrace.

"I know, *bella,* I know. Promise you'll never forget me, even when you're famous and live in your own palace."

"Never," Claudine murmured, still clinging to his every word.

CLAUDINE INHALED DEEPLY. Today was the day. This was what she'd been waiting for, practicing for, living for. She tried to muster up some enthusiasm for her performance, tried to appear poised and regal. Didn't they know her heart was broken? Hattie Mae fussed over her while the promoter looked on amused. Claudine could only nod in his direction. She was incapable of speaking, attempting small talk, when all she wanted to do was run to Francesco, leave everything and everyone behind. The promoter expected her to astonish the crowd, and she expected Francesco to stride through the door and profess that he wouldn't live without her, would fight for her, do something. Old man Husch himself walked in. He'd arrived twenty minutes before curtain to witness the debut of his secret client, gauge the reaction of the foreign masses.

"Claudine, dear, I think now would be a good time to consider a pseudonym—a nom de plume, if you will. We've drawn up a list of names for you to chose from. Trust me, it will be better this way. Claudine Jenkins, well . . . it's not a suitable name for a violinist of your stature."

"Yes," Hattie Mae agreed, snatching the list from old man Husch. "This is exactly what she needs, what we both need." She began to read names aloud. "Danielle Richardson, Cassandra Stanton Lewis, Mary Elizabeth Johnson, Lucinda—"

"No."

"I'm not partial to these names, either. They sound too white, Mr. Husch. Nobody in their right mind is going to believe her name is Mary Elizabeth anything. We'll think of something. How about—"

"No," Claudine reiterated, her back to Hattie Mae.

"Now, Claudine," Mr. Husch interrupted.

"I'm perfectly capable of choosing my own name."

"*Cinque minuti, per favore,*" a voice yelled.

"That was the five-minute warning. Do you have a decision already?" the promoter asked, annoyed.

Claudine whispered her choice in his ear. He nodded and rushed to the announcer. She stroked her violin and prepared to walk onstage. Everyone began speaking at once.

"Well, what is it, Claudine?"

"Yes, Claudine, come on now, we're out of time."

She ignored them all, especially Hattie Mae, and listened for her cue. She hadn't anticipated asserting her independence so soon and didn't understand the long Italian introduction, but she glided into the spotlight when the announcer extended his hand and called her name.

"*Introdurre il violinista di prima Signora Francesca Valentine.*"

Now he would know that she would remember him always.

CHAPTER 49

"*My*Lil, why come you look so much like Mommy?"

"It's 'how come,' girl, and I told you before to stop asking me that question. Sometimes people just look alike for no reason at all, you hear?"

"But why?"

"Francesca! Francesca! Come on in here and get your nosey child."

Lillian zipped up the back of her granddaughter's dress and swatted her on the behind. She thanked God every day that Jessica and Jon didn't take after their bug-eyed daddy, a private sentiment she kept to herself. She sighed heavily. They had everything, and yet Francesca still wasn't happy. She was world renowned and had graced the covers of countless magazines, dined with princes and diplomats. She'd even played for a U.S. president and one monarch. They'd succeeded in reinventing themselves after that debut concert in Siena some fifteen years ago. When they'd left Italy that night, Hattie Mae, Claudine, Willy Earl Junior, and Lula Mae didn't exist anymore. A new family was born as they traveled by train to France, and they'd never looked back. Jon and Jessica were happy and well adjusted, remembering only small bits and pieces of that time, believing Lillian was merely their nanny. Redefining their public relationship had been Lillian's idea. Better to have two different backgrounds to unearth dirt on than one. It was best they take their biological connection to one another to the grave. Lillian thought she'd done the right thing all those years ago, coming between the teacher and the student. Francesca hadn't been the same since. On rare occasions, she entertained a gentleman friend, but for the most part she was a workaholic, touring constantly, giving interviews, avoiding life. Lillian stared out of the window of the Waldorf Astoria in New York. Perhaps she didn't understand what Francesca had had with him. She herself had never experienced any emotion with a man that wasn't deceitful and perverse. Her heart had been closed since Nathan Lee broke it all those years ago, but that was her burden to bear and not Francesca's. She understood that now. Her daughter had discovered something sweet and pure with Francesco Romano, and she'd destroyed it because she didn't know what it was. How could she recognize what she'd never seen? Appreciate what she'd never had? Respect what in her mind did not exist? Things had changed between them after that, and Lillian was grateful that Francesca never mentioned her interference. She would make it up to her somehow. One of them dying alone was enough.

CHAPTER 50

MAY 2002

rancesca couldn't look at them when she'd finished. Her mind was a million miles away, lost somewhere in the duplex on Norfolk and in the halls of the Colborne, wandering through the governor's mansion, and being carried from the shack underneath the bridge on the other side of the railroad tracks. All this time had passed, and the telling was just as painful as the memories she'd kept buried for years. She'd changed her name and created her background, but she was still the same girl who longed to play the violin and depended on her mama to push her when she thought she had no more to give. She'd now broken her promise to Hattie Mae and mouthed a silent apology for weakening under the pressure.

She hoped Hattie Mae knew there was no way she could have gone on pretending while the world uncovered bits and pieces of their lives. She remembered what it felt like to be lied to, misled, believe you were someone else. She remembered how devastated she had been at learning the truth all those years ago, when she was young and naïve. Three generations of women in her family had lied to their children about who they were, all because they had to, but at what cost? Gracian had lied to Hattie Mae, Hattie Mae had lied to protect her, and ultimately she had fabricated four life stories to protect her own children. Same lie, different reasons. All three of them had surely believed they were doing the right thing, but they should have realized that lies never stay in the ground where you bury them. And now she'd overwhelmed her children with reality, just as she had been overwhelmed. How could she face them again? How would they ever forgive her?

A plethora of explanations ran through her mind. She contemplated how and to whom to apologize first. Perhaps in time Jon and Jessica would grow to love her again. Maybe they wouldn't despise her like she'd despised her own mother. But before she turned around and attempted to speak again, she sensed a warmth engulfing her. She was being held by some invisible love, and she exhaled loudly from the joy of the gift. She heard a voice whisper softly. *I forgave Gracian, you forgave me, they'll forgive you.* And so she faced her children knowing she was finally free, knowing that Hattie Mae had always cherished her, knowing that they both had done the very best they could do.

She was surprised to see Samuel. She hadn't seen him come in, never realized he was there, listening to her life story. Their eyes met, and he didn't look away. She sat down and waited for Jon or Jessica to say something. She would not move until they felt what she felt, knew what she knew. Perhaps that was an unrealistic expectation, but she needed for them to see that she wasn't running anymore. No one spoke for a long time. Jon walked around the room, avoiding her gaze, while Jessica wept quietly. She could only guess what they were thinking. Her lies had been so complete, so thorough. All of the stories she'd told them about their father, what a wonderful man he was, how he died in a plane crash off the coast of Cape Verde. How he used to send to Jessica dolls from every country he visited. How he was an orphan with no family, and how he perished with their photographs in his pocket, next to his heart. She'd even shown them a picture of an ordinary-looking man and her, taken in

Paris. Up until this moment, they'd believed he was their father. They'd trusted her, and she'd fooled them; she'd fooled everyone. She ached to comfort them but respected their distance. They would come to her when they were ready. Samuel reached for her hand.

"I should have known she was your mother."

Jon asked the first question. "Who is the man in the photograph?"

"A fan, I think."

Francesca expected him to yell and scream and tell her she was a fraud, but he didn't. She expected him to leave, but he stayed until he could meet her eyes.

"Please don't hate me," she said quietly, trying not to reach for him.

"I could never hate you, Mama," he responded, drawing her close.

She held him until he pulled away, and she wondered how long it would take for Jessica to want to be in her arms again. She knew the girl would have a million questions. She prepared herself to be honest, something she hadn't done before. She suspected her daughter wouldn't be as forgiving.

"So that was our grandmother we just buried?" Jessica asked, her back to them as she looked out over the Golden Gate Bridge.

"Yes."

"What happened after you and Hattie Mae left the mansion?" she continued, her voice strained.

"Well, your grandmother had a lot of money put away, hidden around. Like I said, we moved to New York. You were born shortly thereafter. Jon was about two then."

"And?" Jessica pressed.

"Jessica, please," Jon interrupted.

"No. It's fine. She has a right to know, Jon, and so do you. Lillian and Adell took care of both of you while I attended Juilliard."

"I don't remember her. I don't remember Adell," Jon said quietly.

"She died shortly after Jess was born. She lived a long life. I wouldn't be here without her, and neither would Jess."

"And what about Bone, Luther Mack, and our biologicial father, Willy Earl?" Jessica demanded. "What ever became of them? Did Bone ever know he wasn't your brother? And Harlan, what became of Harlan?"

"Slow down, Jess. Maybe Mother needs to lie down now. We understand if you don't want to answer any more questions."

"Speak for yourself, Jon."

"What is the matter with you, Jessica? Didn't you hear everything she just told us? Do you need for her to hurt some more just so you can feel better?"

Francesca shook her head. "I said it's all right, Jon. Everything is out in the open now. I'm tired of hiding from my past, our past. Bone was killed in Vietnam. He never knew. He died believing I was his twin sister. In hindsight, I'm glad I never told him. Lillian, your grandmother, told me Luther Mack passed away in the asylum back in 1988. Willy Earl died sometime later."

"Good," Jon said, eyeing Jessica. Jon continued, "And Harlan?"

"You know, Lillian forbade me and Adell from ever speaking his name again once we were on that train, so we never did; or I haven't until now. I found his obituary among Lillian's things when we returned from Europe. He died right after we left for Siena. The papers said it was a massive heart attack, but who knows. I never cared enough about him to find out the details."

"I loved MyLil so much," Jessica cried. "I thought we were close. She never said a word. She never let on that she was your mother, my grandmother. How could she look at me and not say anything all these years? I thought I knew her; and you, Mother, it appears I never knew you at all."

Jessica grabbed her purse and started toward the door. Jon and Samuel called after her. Francesca kept explaining, hoping she would stop and want to hear the rest.

"She was protecting me, Jessica. She spent her whole life protecting me. That's all she knew how to do. She didn't want you or Jon to be hurt by our past, our mistakes. She loved you, never forget that. She killed for me just like I would kill for you. Up until the day she died, she made me promise not to ever tell you. She didn't want any of us to suffer anymore. So yes, we made ourselves up, changed our names, created a past that didn't exist. All we ever had was each other. Do you understand, Jess? All we had was each other."

As Jessica walked out the door, Francesca implored aloud, "Mama, please help me."

"MOM," JON SAID nervously, "I think we should cancel your performance; what with all this publicity, I don't think it's a good idea. You know the venue is sold out. There are reporters everywhere. Mom, they want you to make a statement. They want to know about Lillian. And Mom, they have a statement from some woman in Georgia who says she can prove who your father is."

It had been only twenty-four hours since those photographs had shown up in the tabloids, twenty-four hours since Francesca had admitted her true identity, twenty-four hours since she'd told her children their whole lives were lies. Still, even while she was getting ready, Samuel and Jon tried to persuade her to postpone. They thought they could convince her to continue running from her past. They asked her to reconsider one last time before she took the stage, let all the hoopla die down before she made another appearance. Couldn't they tell she'd been up all night? Didn't they know she had something to do? Something that would free them all, from the papers, from the lies, from whoever sold those dreadful pictures.

She'd called the conductor in the middle of the night to change her selection. He had been irritated but agreed to accommodate her; after all, she was Francesca Valentine. She strode onto the stage when her name was announced. She would play the Sibelius Violin Concerto in D Minor, opus forty-seven. A virtuoso piece, the piece she was supposed to have performed on her birthday some thirty years ago, a day that changed her life forever.

"I would like to dedicate this performance to my mother, Lillian SaintClaire. She bought my first violin over forty years ago in Atlanta, Georgia. She sacrificed her entire life so that I could stand here now and perform for you. This was always her favorite concerto."

Francesca didn't notice the flash of the cameras or hear the gasps from the audience at her unexpected opening remarks. She noticed Samuel and Jon smiling at her, and that was enough. So she played. She played until the sweat poured down her back. She played as if Adell was sitting in the front row, listening with her eyes closed, like she used to. She played for Jessica, who was now backstage waiting for her. And when she finished the Allegro ma non tanto, with tears filling her eyes, she could have sworn she saw Hattie Mae Jones standing next to Francesco Giovanni Romano yelling, "Brava, Claudine, Brava."

ACKNOWLEDGMENTS

irst and foremost I want to thank the Creator for sustaining me through this journey. I want to thank my agent, Sasha Goodman, for falling in love with *Bliss,* feeling the characters from the moment she read it. A special thank-you to Melody Guy, my fabulous editor at Strivers Row, who took my frantic phone calls, answered countless questions, and widened my comfort zone as a writer.

Thank you ever so much to Hubert Selby, Jr., for encouraging me to find my own voice and not accepting anything less. To Dr. James Ragan at the University of Southern California for urging me to go to graduate school. You were relentless. Thank you.

To my beloved grandmother Marjorie Richardson for continuing to inspire me for the rest of my life. I miss you so much. To my mom, Diane Richardson, for her impromptu music history lessons and her unwavering support of my work. Big thanks to my aunts Denise and Delores Richardson for listening to me prattle off pages at all hours of the night. Thank you to Catherine Buford for poring over my rough drafts when I needed a second eye, my father, Ronald Buford, and my little sister Christine for bragging about me to all their friends.

Special thanks to Gina Cooper, Tracy Irving, and Julie Seibert for formatting manuscripts, rereading chapters, and urging me on when I was too tired to string any more sentences together. Special thanks to the Imani Book Club in Los Angeles for their love and support whenever I needed it.

Finally, a thousand heartfelt thanks to Richard, Julian, and Maia Pina for giving me more inspiration and material than they will ever know.

A CONVERSATION WITH GABRIELLE PINA, AUTHOR OF <u>BLISS</u>

How did you get the idea for Bliss?

I was and am still intrigued with the idea of powerful women, women who are fearless, women who can almost bend steel with their minds. And I wondered how our grandmothers and great-grandmothers survived so gracefully without battered women's shelters, high-powered divorce attorneys, and weight-loss programs. I'm also interested in the way one moment, one event, can alter the course of your life.

What would have happened if you took a left instead of a right? What if everything you believed in was a lie? What if the person you thought you were didn't exist? These questions haunted me, and *Bliss* was born out of my quest to answer them.

You open the book with the line "Sometimes a lie is the best thing." What do you mean by that?

Well, what would have happened if Hattie Mae had told Harlan she was pregnant? Would Bone have even survived without Hattie Mae? Some of the characters in *Bliss* felt their deceptions were necessary for survival. One lie affected the lives of so many people.

Why did you pick the violin?

I thought the violin was a romantic instrument, an instrument quite difficult to master. Also, I think as a society we're accustomed to seeing women of color singing and playing the piano but not necessarily mastering an instrument at that level.

How much of you is in your characters?

I can't say exactly. I think a little bit of me is sprinkled around here and there. I love food, hence the consistent macaroni-and-cheese references throughout the novel.

What writers have influenced you?

Toni Morrison, Anita Diamant, Octavia Butler, and Alice Walker. I could go on and on, as there are so many.

What do you want the reader to take away from your novel?

Feelings of hope, determination, and perseverance. I want the reader to feel the pain, the struggle, and the joy of the journey. I also want the reader to laugh. Laughter is good.

Are you working on anything else?

Yes, my second novel, tentatively titled *Anything but a Simple Woman*. Imagine that.

READING GROUP GUIDE

The questions and discussion topics that follow are intended to enhance your group's reading of *Bliss* by Gabrielle Pina. We hope that they provide new insights and ways of looking at this wonderful novel of love, hate, and betrayal.

1. Pina opens *Bliss* with the epigraph "Sometimes a lie is the best thing." What does she mean? In the end, was lying the best policy? Was there a time when lies no longer served to better Hattie Mae's or Claudine's lives?

2. In her struggle to survive, Hattie Mae's determination to succeed leaves no room for idleness or pleasure. When she finally escapes Georgia, she does not relinquish her steely resolve, and the single-mindedness she developed there never really fades. Why can't she leave her past behind and start anew?

3. Claudine's life is never wholly her own. Hattie Mae orchestrates many of the most important moments and, in some ways, lives her own life through Claudine. Was Hattie Mae using Claudine? Was she selfish?

4. In some ways, Hattie Mae has saved *and* destroyed Claudine's life. How is this?

To print out copies of this or other Strivers Row reading group guides, visit us at www.atrandom.com/rgg.

5. As much as *Bliss* is about love between mother and daughter, it is equally about the enduring power of hate. The hate Hattie Mae feels for the governor motivates many of her actions. How important is hatred in creating Hattie Mae's strength? In his own way, does the governor hate Hattie Mae?

6. Claudine's childhood was full of harsh words from those in and outside her family. When Willy Earl shows interest in her, Claudine is willing to forgive almost anything. How important is Willy Earl in saving Claudine? Would she have been better off without him?

7. Hattie Mae never experiences a loving relationship and is unable to understand the value of Claudine and Francesco's love. Was their relationship appropriate? If Claudine had not given up Francesco, would she have achieved the same success?

8. Claudine and Hattie Mae reinvent themselves in Italy in order to leave their past behind. Do they succeed? Can you ever truly escape your past?

9. As governor, Harlan has the power to manipulate those around him, and this is very much a part of what he loves about his relationship with Hattie Mae. Does he ever truly love her? Is it possible for him to ever understand her? Does he have any redeeming qualities?

10. Claudine's weight provides her with a sense of security—a cushion between her and the rest of her world. How else does she survive her childhood? Could Hattie Mae have imagined the level of emotional abuse Claudine would suffer as a child?

11. *Bliss* is a story of triumph over adversity; Claudine becomes a renowned violinist despite Hattie Mae's virtual imprisonment by the governor and the economic hardships of her family. What is the price of this success? How many people are destroyed by her climb to the top?

ABOUT THE AUTHOR

GABRIELLE PINA received her M.A. from the University of Southern California. She is a member of the adjunct faculty at Pasadena Community College and lives in Southern California with her two children, Julian and Maia. *Bliss* is her first novel.